I took out my picture of Mr Br[...]
night kiss. But kissing the [...]
disappointing somehow and [...]
real. Like, well . . . like Josh had kissed me tonight.

I had to laugh at myself. A gay guy or an inanimate photograph. Some choice.

I turned out the light and settled down to dream about Mr Brown but annoyingly I kept thinking about Josh. I'd been wrong about him. He wasn't arrogant at all. In fact he seemed really nice, just like Peter had said. I don't know why he's still so friendly to me after all the things I said to him. He mustn't be the type to hold grudges. Yeah, Josh is a really nice guy. And so gorgeous as well. It was such a shame he was gay.

Also by Liz Rettig

MY Desperate LOVE DIARY
MY Now or NEVER DIARY

Jumping to Confusions

LIZ RETTIG

CORGI BOOKS

JUMPING TO CONFUSIONS
A CORGI BOOK 978 0 552 55757 3

Published in Great Britain by Corgi Books,
an imprint of Random House Children's Books
A Random House Group Company

This edition published 2008

1 3 5 7 9 10 8 6 4 2

Set in 11/16pt Palatino by
Falcon Oast Graphic Art Ltd.

Corgi Books are published by Random House Children's Books,
61–63 Uxbridge Road, London W5 5SA

www.**kids**at**randomhouse**.co.uk
www.**rbooks**.co.uk

Addresses for companies within The Random House Group Limited can be
found at: www.randomhouse.co.uk/offices.htm

THE RANDOM HOUSE GROUP Limited Reg. No. 954009

A CIP catalogue record for this book is available from the British Library.

Printed and bound in Great Britain by
CPI Bookmarque, Croydon, CR0 4TD

*This book is dedicated to anyone who has ever wished they
were slimmer, blonder or prettier.
That's all of us then.*

*With special thanks to Kelly Hurst and Guy Rose whose
support and advice have been invaluable.*

*Also to Eileen Clarke, Claire and Josh Mize, my daughter
Carol and my long-suffering husband, Paul.*

*And finally a huge thank you to all my readers because, let's
face it, I'd look pretty silly writing books without you.*

1

It wouldn't be so bad being a size fourteen if your mother and sister weren't size sixes. And yes, you heard right, my mother is a size six. Not only that but she is blonde and, although she's nearly as old as my dad (who's forty-five), people still fancy her. And I'm not just talking old people. Some boys at my school think my mum is, 'bloody hell', not bad for her age.

Mind you, it's really my (very) non-identical twin sister Tessa who absolutely everyone at school slavers over. Like Mum she's blonde, model-slim and extremely pretty, so nearly all the boys at my school would give their World Cup season ticket, if they had one, for a single date with her.

Now don't get me wrong – I do love my sister really, even if we don't have much in common, but being the not-so-good-looking twin isn't much fun. Guys' attitudes don't help. It's so annoying. I've lost count of the number of times boys have tried to get friendly with me just to get an introduction to my sister. Mostly they're wasting their time. Unless they're really good looking, have a car and are prepared to spend a fortune on buying her stuff and taking her places, they can forget it. She's been out a few times with most of the boys who fit these requirements but now has moved on to older guys who work and have more money.

I suppose it must sound like I'm jealous. Well, it's kind of hard not to be. It's not that I'm ugly exactly. I quite like my face, which is OK, although I hate it when my mum's friends say I've got 'such a beautiful face too', which really means 'shame about the figure'. Sometimes they'll add the, *ugh*, hateful phrase, 'Puppy fat but she'll grow out of it'. I do have nice eyes though. They're deep blue, fringed with thick dark lashes and tilt up at the sides like a cat. My friends call me Cat, not because of my eyes – it's short for my real name, Catriona – but I think it suits me. Mum and Dad, of course, continue to insist on Catriona. My hair, like my lashes, is thick and dark but also curly and totally uncontrollable. Mum has tried to help me 'do something with it' and sent me to expensive hairdressers, but even they gave up eventually and finally just suggested I wear it *au sauvage* (i.e. wild). Now I just tie it back and hope for the best.

Mum is driving us all mad as we've got Americans coming to our house tonight. The company my dad works for in Glasgow has had a new chief executive foisted on them from New York headquarters. Everyone's dead scared the new boss is going to be a hatchet man who'll fire everybody or sell off the company to the Chinese or something but Dad says we have to reserve judgement and just wait and see. As he's one of the managers, Dad has had to invite the American plus his wife over and my mum is going mental with the stress of it all.

My sister and I had been planning to make ourselves scarce rather than endure the boredom of a dinner party, but now we've heard they've got a sixteen-year-old son called Josh who's coming too so we've got to be involved as well. Tessa is furious as she was supposed to be going on a date with a new eighteen-year-old boyfriend who's got his own car. She told Mum, 'I can't be bothered babysitting some stupid American geek.'

'He's sixteen, Tessa. The same age as you. In fact I think he might be a few months older.'

'Yeah, right. You just don't get it, do you? Sixteen-year-old boys are just so immature. And boring. I bet he's a dumb, spotty little dork. I've got better things to do than spend a Saturday night in my summer holidays childminding.'

But Mum wasn't taking no for an answer and for once didn't give in to Tessa's demands. 'You'll stay in this evening, young lady, and help entertain our guests, and that's that.'

Tessa was in a foul mood after that, and Mum even

more stressed, so I was grateful when my friend Lindsay came round in the afternoon – at least I'd be able to talk to someone who wouldn't snap at me as soon as I opened my mouth. We went into the sitting room, which was empty, and talked about what the Americans might be like.

Lindsay said, 'Hmm, I bet Josh will be tall. All Americans are tall – unlike Glasgow guys, who are mostly midgets.' She sighed. 'Honestly, it's practically impossible for someone like me to find a decent-sized boyfriend here. Bloody Lilliput land.'

'That's rubbish, Lindsay. You're only five foot eleven. Hardly a giantess.'

'Five feet ten and three quarters, not five foot eleven,' Lindsay corrected me. 'I measured myself just last night and I'm definitely still under five eleven.'

This was typical of Lindsay. She measures herself almost as often as I used to weigh myself because she hates being tall and is terrified of reaching six feet, but there's been no change for the last six months. For her, anyway; not me unfortunately. I looked at her now, sitting on the sofa opposite me. Her long fashion-model legs were tucked underneath slim hips and she was examining her straight, swingy chestnut hair for non-existent split ends. It's difficult to believe that someone so nice looking could have such a hang-up about her looks.

'Honestly, Lindsay,' I said, exasperated, 'if you didn't

have this stupid idea that boyfriends have to be taller than you in high heels you'd have hundreds of guys to pick from. Peter, for a start, is mad about you. And anyway, you never wear heels.'

'Yeah, I know I never wear heels but I would if I could find a guy tall enough, which your cousin Peter definitely isn't so stop going on about him. It's no good trying your matchmaking with me.'

I flushed. 'I'm not trying to matchmake.'

'Yeah, you are. C'mon, admit it. You do it with everyone. Well, except for your sister, who's never without at least two possible dates for every night of the week.'

'I so do not,' I lied. Lindsay *looked* at me. 'Well, OK, maybe sometimes. But I'm just trying to make people happy. What's wrong with that?'

'Hmm, put like that, nothing, I suppose – apart from the fact that you're crap at it. But anyway, why not start with yourself? You've never even so much as been on a date with anyone.'

'So? I'm just not interested in boys right now. I'm quite happy being single.'

It was true in a way. I've never had a proper boyfriend (which, at sixteen, makes me something of a freak), but unlike Lindsay I don't care because I'm in love with someone very special. However, unfortunately, due to my age and his occupation, we've had to keep our feelings secret. His name is Mr Brown, or David, as I sometimes like to call him privately, and he's my English teacher. One thing my sister and I have in common is that we like more mature males, but compared to Mr Brown, who's twenty-five, Tessa's dates are still just stupid boys.

Mr Brown isn't swayed by surface stuff like blonde hair and a slim figure. He is intelligent, sensitive and thoughtful. I know he has feelings for me, although of course he can't be open about them yet. He spends ages talking to me about my essays and saying how interesting and insightful they are. He also talks about books we've both read even though they aren't on the curriculum. Once he even lent me one of his own personal books when I said I liked a particular author but couldn't find the novel in the library and couldn't afford to buy it.

Of course, Mr Brown is kind and thoughtful to nearly all his pupils – well, except for people like Andy McKenna, who tippexed an obscene drawing on a copy of *Pride and Prejudice* on the last day of term (Elizabeth Bennet with very exaggerated boobs and Mr Darcy with a massive . . . well, you don't need to ask). Mr Brown doesn't put up with that kind of rubbish from idiots like Andy but he's nice to most people. However, his attitude to me I know is special.

I've known it for sure since the day last January when I was standing by his desk discussing my critical essay, which he'd just graded. As he reached over to get a red pen to add another comment, a folder fell onto the floor at my feet and some of the contents spilled out.

I knelt down to gather up the papers and stash them back in the folder, and that's when I saw it. Just fleetingly. But definitely there. It was a poem written in Mr Brown's small, neat handwriting. And it was all about me. Actually named after me. It mentioned how much he enjoyed being with me and said something about my beautiful blue eyes. I only got a second to look at it before Mr Brown took it from my trembling fingers and hid it inside the folder.

He looked a little embarrassed but admitted, 'I like writing poetry. I've had some pieces published in fact, but only in obscure journals so far.' He gave me a sheepish smile. 'I won't be trying to get this published though. A bit too sentimental. I think it's best kept private.'

At first I just nodded dumbly, too overcome to speak. But as he turned back to my work I said, 'I promise I'll never tell anyone about it. Not unless you want me to.'

He smiled. 'Thanks, Cat. I'd appreciate that. It's not a piece I'd want to share with everyone.'

Afterwards he just went on talking as though nothing had happened. Yet everything had changed because now I knew for sure that Mr Brown must feel the same about me as I did for him.

Fortunately no one else seems to have guessed our feelings. Sometimes people wind me up about being teacher's pet but they think Mr Brown likes me because I'm good at English rather than anything deeper. I'm relieved about that, but it's so hard not being able to be open about our emotions, never mind actually go out together. At least I'm sixteen now, so it's legal, but I suppose we'll have to wait until I leave school before we can finally be boyfriend and girlfriend. I wouldn't want to do anything that would get him into trouble as he's such a talented teacher and I know he wouldn't want me to be the subject of nasty, uninformed gossip.

It's so hard to wait though. For both of us. We've now been on summer holidays for four weeks and I've hardly seen him at all. I just spotted him once in town and then in Tesco. He said 'Hi' in Tesco but didn't see me in town. But those two all-too-brief encounters are all I've had to keep me going all summer. Still, in just three weeks' time we'll be back at school, thank God, and I'll get to see him and talk to him every day. Mmmm.

I must have drifted into a sort of daydream thinking about Mr Brown as Lindsay now interrupted to say, 'Hello, Earth calling Cat. Anybody there?'

'Sorry, Lindsay. I was, erm, just thinking about something.'

'I said, of course you're interested in boys. It's just that for you no one measures up to guys like Mr Darcy or Dr Who.'

I shrugged. 'Lots of people have crushes on actors.'

'Yeah, they do. But you didn't have a crush on the actors. You were in love with the characters. A nineteenth-century landowner and a Time Lord. You're never going to meet them at the school dance.'

I smiled. 'Well, I'm over them now. I've grown up. Honestly.'

'Hmm,' Lindsay said suspiciously. 'I bet you've just fallen for some other totally unobtainable male, only this time you're keeping quiet about it. C'mon, fess up. Who is it?' She giggled. 'I know: it's Spider-Man, isn't it? But not the actor in the film, who's admittedly quite hot, but the *real* Spider-Man. You want a boyfriend who can actually spin webs and use them to swing from skyscrapers.'

I laughed too, but a bit uncomfortably. It's hard keeping such a big secret from my best friend. Normally we tell each other everything, but my relationship with Mr Brown is too important to share even with Lindsay and I don't think she'd really understand anyway. When he first started at our school last year I did mention to her that I thought he was gorgeous but she'd just shrugged and said, 'Hmm, not quite tall enough. Anyway he's an English teacher. Bound to be boring.'

I didn't mention him after that and now I'm glad because the only sure way to keep a secret like that is to tell absolutely no one.

I was almost relieved when Tessa walked in on us and interrupted Lindsay's talk of secret loves, even though her face was as sour as a llama that had just swallowed a lemon. She snapped, 'Mum says you've to go now, Lindsay. Cat and I have to start getting things ready for the guests. Whether we want to or not, apparently.'

Tessa went out again, banging the door behind her. I rolled my eyes at Lindsay. 'Sorry.'

'Don't worry, I'm used to her.'

'Lindsay!' I warned.

'Yeah, yeah. All right, I know. She's your sister. She's still a pain though.'

Rather than carry on arguing about Tessa, I steered the conversation back to our American visitors as I saw her to the door.

'Don't know if I'm going to like them, Lindsay. Remember the foreign exchange student who stayed at Marianne's last summer? He was a total pain. Always boasting about how much bigger and better America was. And he had the nerve to tell us that he thought Scottish people ate too much candy and drank too much alcohol and that our weather was crap.'

'Well,' Lindsay laughed, 'he had a point, didn't he? Anyway, I'm sure not all Americans are like him. I bet there are millions of really nice ones. Mmmm . . . and really fit, tall ones too.'

Before she left Lindsay made me promise to find out *exactly* how tall Josh was and let her know. We giggled a bit about me greeting the chief executive's son with a tape measure in hand: 'Hi, I'm Cat. Now, before you sit down just let me measure you. It's an old Scottish tradition.'

She left, still giggling, then I went to peel the vegetables and set the table.

Normally when people come round for dinner Mum

gets stuff from Marks and Spencer's like beef stroganoff, duck à l'orange or chicken Kiev. Delicious – though Mum usually just moves the food around her plate for a bit before saying she's full up. However, the Americans have said they're dead keen to try traditional Scottish home cooking and Mum was freaking out. She never cooks anything. She tells everyone her slim figure is because of her metabolism, but unless she's playing hostess, she only eats stuff like lettuce and shredded celery, and her idea of pigging out is two crisp breads with half a spoonful of cottage cheese, along with tea made with skimmed milk and a saccharine tablet. She just orders carry-out pizzas and Chinese for the rest of us. I've never seen Mum cook a proper meal in my life.

I don't really mind the fact that she doesn't like cooking – lots of people don't – but I do wish she'd eat normally so I wouldn't feel so guilty every time I have anything. Sometimes she'll say things like, 'Do you really need that bar of chocolate, Catriona?' Or a bright and cheerful, 'Remember, a moment on the lips, for ever on the hips.' But it's her pained expression that says it all: I'm a greedy pig with absolutely no self discipline and it's no wonder I'm fat.

Anyway, eventually my Aunt Susan came to our rescue and made a steak pie, and a trifle for dessert, which she brought over this morning. For starters we're having smoked salmon with cream cheese. I've volunteered to prepare that.

The whole time we were getting things ready Tessa was being a pain – constantly moaning, banging pots and pans and slamming doors. I was relieved when she went off to change and do her make-up. This usually takes her ages so I wouldn't have to listen to her ranting for a while. However, this time she stomped back down after only fifteen minutes, still complaining.

'Don't know why I bother getting dressed up for some boring couple and their geeky, spotty son.'

Totally fed up with her bad mood, I snapped, 'OK, I know you're annoyed about your date tonight, but for God's sake, you can always see him tomorrow. It's hardly likely he's going to go off you by then.'

'Of course he isn't,' Tessa said, shocked at the idea of any guy dumping her. 'That's not the point. Oh, you just don't understand, Cat. It doesn't matter to you if you spend Saturday night bored senseless at home. You hardly go out anyway but some of us have a life.'

'Thanks a bunch, Tessa. I do have friends, you know. It's not like I'm a sad loner or anything.'

'Oh, I didn't mean it like that. Don't go all sulky on me.'

Tessa is my sister and I love her. I really do. But there are times when I find it very hard to like her. Tonight for instance.

Finally we were ready and at last the door buzzed. We all piled into the hall to greet them – even Tessa, who had mutinously decided not to bother but had been told by Dad she should get her arse into the hall or else.

Our three guests were tall, tanned and healthy-looking, but, oh my God, the son! He had sun-bleached fair hair, clear grey eyes and an athlete's strong, lithe physique. His smile was dazzling and his voice respectful but confident and friendly in that American way as he extended a tanned hand for my dad to shake, then turned to greet my mum, my sister and me. Honest to God, he looked like a young Hollywood film star, and for the first time ever I saw my sister blush and her normally super-confident manner evaporate as she squeaked some unintelligible reply to his friendly 'Hi, great to meet you.'

This was going to be interesting. I never thought I'd see Tessa coming over all tongue-tied and awkward because she's smitten by a guy. Glancing at her now, I smiled broadly but Josh must have thought it was at him because after a puzzled frown at Tessa he smiled warmly at me and walked beside me into the living room. Tessa quickly recovered though, and soon she was acting with almost her usual self-assurance so I was surprised when Josh didn't start drooling over her the way most guys did. I guess she'd met her match looks-wise and so he wasn't overawed by her. Still, I'd no doubt he'd give in to her charms soon enough – I could tell she was going to make very sure he did. It was strange to see my sister making such an effort with a guy. All during dinner she was smiling constantly, her head tilted to the side towards him. She pretended to be fascinated by his every word and laughed enthusiastically at even the mildest of funny remarks. I didn't know whether to laugh or squirm at Tessa's behaviour but I was more concerned about Mum.

Mum was nervous. She drank quite a lot of wine, which isn't like her (too many calories in alcohol), and talked almost non-stop. She seemed embarrassingly eager to please our guests, maybe because she thought it was important for Dad's job, but I was beginning to resent the impression she gave that they were somehow superior to us.

However, when she tried a different tack and started to boast about how good-looking Tessa was, I cringed even more. Oh yes, Tessa was beautiful, wasn't she? She'd already broken some hearts, she could tell them. The number of young admirers she'd had around this year! But, you know, Tessa was so fussy – well, she could afford to be.

The chief executive's wife said politely, 'Oh yes, *both* your daughters are lovely.'

Mum took another swig of her wine and said, 'Um, well, Catriona has a good personality.'

Thanks, Mum. She might as well have said 'not the nice-looking one then'. Everyone was embarrassed except for Mum, who just prattled on.

I know Mum is disappointed by my failure to be slim and super-attractive like her and my sister. I've tried to diet or at least 'be careful', but it's really hard. I don't have Mum's will power when it comes to food, and my sister seems to be naturally slim. At one time I'd have been hurt and humiliated by Mum's comments but not any more. Now I had David, thank God, or I would do one day, so I could laugh at Mum's attitude. Just as well.

After dinner Tessa and I cleared up while everyone else sat around the table chatting. Once in the kitchen Tessa asked if I would finish up while she 'rescued' Josh – i.e. took him off into the sitting room to chat away from adults. 'Go on, Cat. Do me this favour. You can borrow my MP3 player all day tomorrow if you like.'

I looked around the kitchen. There wasn't a square centimetre not covered with piles of dishes, pots, pans or glasses.

Tessa followed my gaze. 'OK, all week then. Mmmm, he is gorgeous, isn't he?'

Yes, I suppose he was really hot – the sort of boy who was totally out of my league. But not out of Tessa's, of course. At one time I might have felt jealous, even though I'm used to my sister getting all the attention from boys, but not any more. Now I had someone fantastic of my own. And David was so mature, intelligent and sensitive. Far better than any schoolboy. No matter how good looking.

After Tessa left I set about washing up but was interrupted by a call on my mobile from Lindsay.

'So, what height is the American?'

'Hmm, maybe just tall enough to pass the high-heel test, Lindsay, but Tessa has probably beaten you to it. I think she's really keen on him.'

Lindsay groaned. 'Tessa doesn't need someone tall, she's only five foot three, same as you. It's so unfair. Honestly, there should be a law against it.' She paused for a moment, then, seeming to accept inevitable defeat, continued, 'God, he must be something to interest Tessa. Tell me all!'

Phone in one hand, I moved to the sink and turned on the tap to soak the pots as I filled her in. 'God, yeah, Josh is gorgeous. So hot he sizzles. Total sex on legs. But don't feel too jealous. He's probably got some horrible character defect.'

'Like what?'

'Oh, I don't know. Maybe he's a mad Christian fundamentalist who believes the Earth's flat and created on Tuesday the seventeenth of March at half past four. A lot of Americans are funny that way. Or perhaps he chews gum when he snogs, wears Stars and Stripes boxers and sings "God Bless America" while shagging.'

Lindsay giggled. 'It's more likely he's gay. They say all good-looking guys are gay.'

I laughed, then turned round to finish stacking and came face to face with Josh.

I blushed furiously as he said, 'Hi, Cat. Um, Tessa's just gone upstairs to get some holiday snaps so I thought I'd come through and, uh, see if you needed any help.'

Too surprised and mortified to answer, I just hung up quickly, then stood there and gawped at him like an idiot. How long had he been there? Oh God, how much had he heard?

After what was probably a few moments but felt like a year, I still hadn't replied, so he said, 'You know, Cat, I'm not actually a religious fundamentalist or even a Christian, as it happens. I don't own any Stars and Stripes boxers, and while, OK, I admit I chew gum occasionally, I don't think I do it while snogging. What's snogging anyway? Is it the same as making out?'

He said nothing about the 'God Bless America' bit. Maybe he didn't know what shagging was either. God, I hoped not. At least he couldn't have heard Lindsay talking about him being gay. Deciding that attack was the best form of defence, I said, 'No, I don't need any help, thanks all the same, but, erm, have you never heard of knocking before entering a room?'

He smiled. 'Knock before entering a kitchen? When the door is wide open anyway? Uh, no, I hadn't thought about it. Sorry.'

He went off, still smiling. I wondered if he'd heard me saying how good looking he was. Oh God, maybe he thought I fancied him and was intending to try and get off with him. I blushed again. How embarrassing. I must make it clear that there is no way I'm competing with my sister for his attention.

By the time I'd finished in the kitchen I felt quite tired

and just wanted to go to bed with my new paperback but Mum had warned me I had to be 'sociable'. I wasn't a kid any more who could just ignore the fact we had guests; I had to do my bit to entertain. I was pretty sure Tessa – and Josh, come to that – wanted my company right then about as much as people welcome a verruca at the swimming pool but I'd have to join them.

I took my book with me and, after knocking (in case they'd already got to the snogging stage), walked in to find Tessa and Josh sitting on the sofa looking at an album of holiday snaps she had unearthed from last year's trip to Spain. Oh God, I hoped she wouldn't be showing him any of me in my bikini with an arse the size of Argentina.

I said, 'Hi,' and then curled up in the vacant armchair with my book, ignoring them. Or tried to anyway, but Josh kept looking up from the album to talk to me. What was the book I was reading? Oh yeah, he liked that author too. Had I read any of his other stuff?

At first I answered politely – he was a guest, after all – but (unfairly perhaps), annoyed by the scene in the kitchen and also sensing my sister's impatience at his failure to drool over her photos, I told him abruptly, 'Yeah, it is a good book actually, which I'm *trying* to read.'

He immediately apologized for interrupting me, which of course made me feel guilty. The truth was, I was the one being rude and his apology just seemed to underline that. I found myself unable to concentrate on my book after all. Unlike my sister I wasn't widely popular with boys, but I'd always been able to better them in any arguments and few took me on any more. Yet somehow this American had put me in the wrong without even having openly criticized or confronted me at all.

I was relieved when Mum eventually came to tell Josh his parents were leaving.

After she had left the room Tessa said, 'So, Josh, this has been fun tonight. Maybe we could meet up sometime without parents around to check up on us. Do you like tennis?'

Josh smiled. 'Sure, very much.'

'What about tomorrow then? I'm a member of a club just ten minutes from here and I know a couple of people have cancelled bookings. I'm pretty sure we'll get a court.'

God, Tessa wasn't wasting any time. I had to admire her choice of activity too. She looks fantastic in her short white tennis skirt and has always said it was probably her favourite pulling outfit.

However, instead of agreeing straight away Josh turned to me. 'Do you play, Cat?'

'No. Not my thing.'

'OK, well, maybe we should do something that we could all enjoy.'

Oh God, he was going to be one of those

well-mannered types that Tessa attracts sometimes. The ones who feel they ought to pay some attention to the plain sister too. Personally I prefer the straight-forward ones who ignore me. It's more honest and doesn't waste everyone's time.

I said, 'Look, it's cool. You and Tessa just go ahead without me.'

But Josh was adamant I be included and nothing would shift him.

Eventually Tessa suggested I come along to the tennis club just to watch. I wouldn't have to play. The thought of acting like a chaperone on my sister's date had about as much appeal as having a tooth drilled without anaesthetic but Tessa pleaded with me. 'C'mon, Cat. You *know* how you enjoy the atmosphere at the club – you often come along to watch people play.'

Yeah, right. Like as often as Scotland wins the World Cup. I can think of a million better ways to spend an afternoon – it wasn't exactly Wimbledon. Still, Tessa *was* my sister and I hadn't seen her this keen on anyone. Maybe I could get Lindsay to come along too so I wouldn't feel in the way. One afternoon wouldn't hurt, I suppose. Reluctantly I said, 'OK.'

Before the visitors left we all piled into the hall again to say goodbye. Mum was carefully trying to conceal her relief that her ordeal was over without any major mishap. Josh's mum and dad appeared to have enjoyed themselves and said they must have us over to their place sometime soon. Josh thanked us for the evening too and everything was fine until he said, 'Oh, by the way, Cat, before I forget – what does shagging mean?'

I squirmed, but worse followed: Josh's mum answered for him, 'Don't be silly, Josh, you know what shagging is. Your aunt and uncle used to do it at one time. Do you shag, Catriona? Back home it's usually older people who enjoy shagging. Grant and I used to know a couple who were very keen on it and won several competitions. But I've never known any young enthusiasts.'

I just stared at her, red-faced and horrified. She'd seemed quite normal and nice at dinner but this woman was seriously weird. Maybe all Americans are weirder than I thought. What on earth could I say?

Dad frowned at me, then said slowly, 'It's a type of dance, Catriona, which is especially popular in the south-east of America.' He turned to Josh's mum. 'No, Catriona doesn't enjoy, erm, shagging as such. She's more into modern dance. Josh must have misheard.'

Tessa put her hands over her mouth to stop herself laughing but Mum was glaring at me. I just stayed completely still and tried to look normal. Then I saw Josh grinning at me and realized immediately that he knew exactly what shagging meant here. He'd deliberately wound me up. Hmm. Decided right there and then that after tomorrow I'd have as little to do with Josh as possible.

After they'd gone I expected my parents, especially Mum, to have a go at me about the shagging thing but thankfully they said nothing. I overheard them arguing about it later though. Mum was saying that obviously I'd used disgusting, common language in front of one of our guests – it was completely unacceptable and they should have words with me about it.

But Dad just said, 'Leave it alone, for God's sake, Fiona. Let's face it, with two teenage daughters there's no point in going looking for trouble. This incident's not that important. And besides, I'm too shagged out to be arsed talking to Catriona about her bad language.'

Thank God Dad's a bit more laid back about how we speak than Mum.

Once Tessa and I had cleared up the coffee cups and wine glasses I wanted to go straight to bed but had to listen to Tessa going on about Josh. Wasn't he gorgeous! And she just loved his accent. What did I think?

I nodded my agreement and finally managed to escape to my room. I took the photograph of David and me from the drawer of my bedside table and gazed at it. When I say David and me, it's actually David and the rest of our English class taken at a book festival outing, but he's standing right next to me and, I swear, looking at me rather than the camera. I gazed at it for a moment, then kissed his head. I wish I had a bigger photo of him to kiss as my lips being larger than his whole head doesn't seem right somehow, but I didn't see how I could ask for one without people getting suspicious. Oh, David, it's such a long time until we can be together, but I'll wait for ever if I have to.

2

Lindsay couldn't come to the tennis club as she had to go shopping with her mum. Her mum was in a good mood and Lindsay was sure she could persuade her to buy the Ted Baker skirt she'd had her eye on and not just the school stuff they were supposed to be getting. You had to strike while the iron was hot.

I called some other girlfriends but everyone was busy. Luckily Aunt Susan came over to find out how the dinner had gone and Peter came with her. As well as being my cousin, Peter is also one of my closest friends so I managed to persuade him to go with me.

Peter is seventeen and in the year above me at school. Although he'd just got back from a two-week camping holiday in Greece his broad freckled face wasn't tanned. His fairish red hair looked a bit blonder though, and he'd had it cut in a new spiky style that suited him. I wondered if Lindsay would like it. Peter wasn't really what you'd call fantastic looking but he'd a good body –

very fit and muscular – and he was smart too (he was going to do medicine next year) so quite a lot of girls fancied him. However, he wasn't tall enough for Lindsay so the new hairstyle probably wasn't going to change anything. A pity because he's dead keen on her.

Mum asked me to make her and Aunt Susan some tea. Peter came to help me while Tessa went upstairs to get ready for her tennis date. As soon as we were alone Peter said, 'Next time you see Lindsay, tell her I've grown over the summer. Quarter of an inch. That makes me five foot ten and three quarters now. Exactly the same height as her.'

I studied him sceptically. 'You look just the same to me.'

He challenged me to measure him, so I did.

'Five foot ten and a half,' I said, putting the tape measure away. 'Exactly the same as last time I measured you. The extra quarter of an inch is your spiky haircut.'

'You could tell Lindsay anyway, Cat. It would just be a little white lie.'

'It won't work.' I sighed. 'Even if you'd grown a quarter of an inch you still wouldn't pass the high-heel test and you know it.'

Peter groaned. 'What is it with some girls? They're so picky and difficult to please! Can't she just wear flat shoes? And what does it matter anyway if she's a couple of inches taller than me when she wears heels. Everyone would know it was because of the heels.

People aren't daft . . . unlike some girls I could mention.'

'Watch it. That's my friend you're talking about.'

'But, OK, if she really wants to wear heels,' Peter continued as though I hadn't said anything, 'and the height thing bothers her, she could just wear them when sitting or, um . . . lying down.' He seemed to go off into a little dream of his own.

I couldn't help wishing Lindsay wasn't so obsessed with the height thing. Peter has fancied her for years and I knew he'd treat her really nicely if she was his girlfriend – unlike most of the tossers Lindsay chases after just because they happen to be tall.

Dad, who'd been working on his laptop all day, came in to get a coffee so I made one for him.

'Thanks, love, I needed this,' he said, taking the mug from me.

'It's Sunday, Dad,' I said, looking at his tired face. 'You need a rest. Do you really have to work every weekend?'

'Just another half-hour or so to do. I'm fine. Honestly.' He turned to Peter. 'So, I hear you're going along with my girls to meet this young American lad?'

'Yeah, Cat asked me.'

'He seems nice enough but you never know,' Dad said, his voice mock serious. 'Some of these Yanks can be smooth-talking charmers when they want to be. You'll take care of my girls for me, won't you? Especially Catriona. I think he might have taken a bit of a shine to her.'

Peter made a sweeping bow. 'I'll defend our country-women's honour with my life, sire.'

'You idiot, Peter.' I laughed, then smiled at Dad. 'Honestly, I'll be perfectly safe. Josh was just being polite last night.'

My dad is really nice. Unlike Mum, he seems to think that I'm just as pretty as Tessa. Mental, I know, but I suppose, like people say, 'Love is blind,' and I must admit it's nice to have one parent who doesn't see me as the plain daughter.

Aunt Susan let Peter borrow her car so he could drive us to the tennis courts – she would get a lift home from Mum. Since Peter passed his driving test six months ago, his mum lets him have the car nearly all the time pro-vided he also chauffeurs her about as she hates driving. This means that it's almost like Peter owns a car. I've mentioned this to Lindsay several times but she wasn't impressed. Or not enough to go out with him anyway.

It was past time to go so Peter was getting annoyed by the time Tessa came down the stairs looking at her watch to time our departure.

Tessa's policy is to be at least ten minutes late for a date, often more. She looked particularly good today in her white tennis gear, her hair up in a neat swingy pony-tail and wearing just a hint of make-up. I sighed. It was hard not to be jealous of her but I was oddly proud too. Yes, the best-looking girl in the whole year, probably the whole school in fact, was my sister. I was sure Josh couldn't have dated anyone prettier than her in America. She would be a credit to Scotland.

Peter and I hurried out to the car while Tessa strolled along behind us. When he ushered me into the front seat, however, Tessa jogged up to complain about being relegated to the back.

'I get car sick in the back. You know I do.'

'Quit moaning,' Peter said. 'It's only a ten-minute drive. You'll be fine.'

Tessa got in the back, scowling.

Like Lindsay, Peter isn't keen on Tessa. In fact I don't think he actually likes her at all. We had a fight over it once when he said she was a selfish cow and so up her-self it wasn't true. We fell out for six weeks over that until eventually he apologized and promised never to insult her again. At least to my face. I wasn't happy with the last bit but put up with it. After all, Tessa can't be bothered with Peter either and usually ignores him.

Josh was waiting outside the clubhouse when we arrived. He was also wearing tennis gear and looked tanned and relaxed. I couldn't help thinking what a good-looking couple he and my sister would make. Maybe this would be the guy who succeeded in dating her for longer than the six weeks that had been her record up till now. He spotted us as we got out the car and waved.

I introduced Peter and they shook hands. The court

Tessa had booked wouldn't be ready for another fifteen minutes so we ordered Cokes from the club café and, as it was a warm sunny day, sat at a table outside where we could watch the tennis and chat. To Tessa's annoyance Josh and Peter were soon engrossed in a conversation about baseball and largely ignored us. I tried to divert Tessa by talking about her plans for next week but she wasn't interested so I just tuned everyone out, sat back and sipped my Coke while enjoying the sunshine on my face.

Eventually, fed up with being ignored, Tessa interrupted Josh and Peter. 'So, Josh, is there anything other than baseball you miss about America? Did you have a girlfriend there maybe?'

'No one special.'

'Me neither. I'm not seeing anyone at the moment.'

Peter said, 'I thought you were seeing that guy from—'

'Not any more,' Tessa snapped. 'That finished a while ago.'

Peter raised an eyebrow sceptically. 'Don't suppose you've bothered to tell *him* about it.'

Tessa scowled and was about to have a go at him but then changed her mind. Instead, looking at Josh, she said, 'We just kind of drifted apart.'

Yeah, right. As soon as she set eyes on Josh. More like an avalanche than a drift. I smiled at the thought.

Josh smiled back at me. 'What about you, Cat? Do you have a boyfriend?'

Before I could answer Peter butted in. 'Nah, Cat is still single. No one's been brave enough yet to get past all the "Keep off", "Don't touch", "You haven't a chance" signals she posts up loud and clear.' He looked at me. 'Isn't that right, Cat? You don't date.'

I laughed. 'With all the idiot guys around, you can hardly blame me.'

Peter looked at Josh and shrugged. 'See what I mean? Pricklier than a porcupine with PMT. And that's when she likes you.'

Josh smiled. 'Is that true, Cat? Aren't you interested in dating? Or maybe you're just waiting for the right person?'

I thought of David and smiled dreamily. 'Mmm, yeah, maybe I'm just waiting for the right guy.'

'Oh, for God's sake,' Tessa interrupted. 'Are we going to sit around here talking rubbish all day?' She looked at Josh. 'Our court has been available for over five minutes now. Are you playing or not?'

I was a bit taken aback by Tessa's rudeness but I expect she was put out by Josh not paying her much attention. She's not used to being ignored by guys.

Josh frowned and I thought for a moment he was going to tell her to shove it, which really would have been a shock, but he just said pleasantly enough, 'Sure. Ready when you are.'

Tessa is quite a good tennis player but it was soon obvious that she was totally outclassed by Josh. Except on TV I'd never seen anyone play tennis like him. For the entire game he just seemed to stand casually in the middle of the court, lobbing balls easily over the net, sending Tessa running all over the place after shots she was almost never able to return.

After just twenty minutes it was game, set and match, with Josh winning each set by a crushing six–love, so they returned to our table. Tessa's face was scarlet and dripping with sweat. That and her grumpy expression made her look as close to ugly as I'd ever seen her. She threw down her racket and gasped that she was going off to the changing room to freshen up.

By contrast Josh was cool and relaxed: he looked as though he'd done nothing more strenuous than stroll in the park. He remained standing at the table, twirling his tennis racket. 'Anyone else for a game? The court's still ours for another half-hour at least. What about you, Peter?'

'No, sorry, not my game. Cat used to play though.'

Josh turned to me. 'Really? That's great. You up for a game, Cat?'

It was true I used to play when I was younger and I wasn't that bad at it. However, the summer I turned twelve I broke my ankle and was unable to do anything but sit at home, watch TV and eat chocolate. That was also the summer my periods started and my once-slim hips started to morph into the fat arse I've got today. By the following summer I knew I wouldn't be doing anything that involved wearing shorts or a white skirt in public and I packed it in. I was wearing black combats today and wouldn't look a complete sight, I thought, but I decided that I wasn't going to be humiliated on court like my sister by a show-off American. Aloud I just said politely, 'No thanks, it was too long ago – I think I'll just pass.'

But Josh had taken me by the hand and, none too gently actually, hauled me up from my chair. He passed me my sister's racket and said, 'C'mon, Cat, no sense in letting the court go to waste. I'll give you a refresher lesson. I coach tennis back home in fact so you're in good hands.'

I found myself reluctantly agreeing to play. I hadn't much choice really as he'd kept hold of my hand and walked me onto the court. As it turned out though, I had a great time. Josh, knowing I hadn't played in ages, was really nice to me. We didn't play a proper game at first. Instead he just lobbed very easy shots to me until I was consistently returning them, then he made them gradually harder. Later on he taught me how to serve properly, first demonstrating a few times, then guiding my arm and racket, showing me how to aim and swing. Afterwards I just practised serves, which Josh stopped dead then lobbed over for me to try again. Eventually I managed to smash one into the far corner of the court so that he missed it. Yes, result! I threw my racket in the air in triumph and Josh came to the net to high-five me.

Finally we played a set, which I lost six–love, but at least I managed to make it last a while. When our time was up on court I was actually really disappointed. As we walked back Josh said, 'You know, Cat, I think you've got a real flair for tennis. With practice you could be very good.'

'Do you really think so?' I said, flattered that someone as good at tennis as Josh thought I had talent.

'Sure. But you'd need to work on your technique – and of course . . . fitness.'

He might as well have said 'fatness' and be done with it. I was mortified and furious. He'd no right to make comments like that to me; no one had asked for his opinion. Josh had made a fool of me. I should have known better than to let my guard down with someone like him and I silently vowed it wouldn't happen again.

Josh's mum was supposed to be picking him up but Peter offered him a lift so we all piled into the car, Josh sitting in front. Tessa and I were both in bad moods but, typical guys, Peter and Josh didn't seem to notice and just chatted about sport, then cars and driving. I wasn't paying much attention until Josh mentioned that he missed his car and that in the States you can drive at sixteen and are taught in school. Now he'd have to wait another three months at least then learn to drive on the left.

I nudged Tessa. 'Imagine being taught to drive at school. And at sixteen. How cool is that?'

'So what? I can always get some guy to drive me whenever I want. Why bother learning? It's just a hassle.'

Since it was obvious Tessa was too annoyed to attempt any kind of conversation with me I amused myself by daydreaming, as usual about Mr Brown. In this particular fantasy he was confessing the love that he'd tried too long to suppress and telling me he couldn't wait any longer. We'd just elope today and face the consequences together tomorrow. As long as we loved one another nothing could come between us.

I was interrupted in this, mmm, very nice dream by Josh, who had twisted round in his seat. 'You look happy, Cat. What are you smiling about?'

I frowned at the interruption and was about to tell him, 'Nothing really,' and hope he'd go back to minding his own business when suddenly, Oh My God, I spotted *him* going into W H Smith. I shouted, 'Stop the car!'

I think I must have given Peter a fright because suddenly he pulled in, jerking us all forward, before saying, 'Christ, what's wrong?'

Quickly unbuckling my seatbelt, I said, 'Erm, nothing, I just need to, er, buy a book. Right now.' I opened the car door and slid out. 'See you all later. I'll make my own way home. Bye.' Then I slammed the door shut and hurried off.

It was a big branch but fortunately Mr Brown is quite tall and I spotted him easily over by a magazine stand. Taking a deep breath to steady myself, I positioned myself close to him, picked up a magazine and pretended to be engrossed in it. To my joy he noticed me nearly right away and said, 'Hi, Cat.'

I flushed with the pleasure of just hearing his voice again. It was a lovely voice; not like some teachers, harsh and strident, but rich and soft like molten chocolate. And he always called me Cat rather than Catriona the way most other teachers did. I turned to look at him and his warm brown eyes gazed into mine. I said, 'Hi, Mr Brown.'

He smiled at me then glanced at my magazine. 'I didn't know you were interested in fly fishing.'

I blushed. 'Erm, no, just, er, browsing.' I put the magazine back on the shelf and grabbed one from the stand opposite, which had a picture of a woman on the front. 'This is more my thing,' I told him.

I'd thought it was *Cosmo* or something but, oh God, flicking it open I could see that the photographs inside were much more explicit than the one on the front – it was in fact a men's magazine. I put it back, my face by now probably as red as Tessa's after the tennis game earlier. But Mr Brown just smiled at me again and said, 'Your taste in reading material is a bit more eclectic than I'd thought, Cat.'

His eyes crinkled at the sides when he smiled and I found myself smiling back, not embarrassed any more but sharing the joke with him. He chatted with me for a while about mundane stuff like the weather and if I'd gone away on holiday, but even ordinary social conversation seemed so intimate and exciting when it was Mr Brown talking to me. All too soon though, he excused himself, saying he was going downstairs to look at the book section. I thought it might look too obvious to follow him down right away – we had to be wary of gossip after all – so I just said I'd finish looking around up here and check out the book department later.

I gave it exactly ten minutes, then followed him down. He was browsing in the poetry section. I know he's an English teacher, but still, a guy who reads poetry! And, of course, as I now remembered with a happy glow, *writes* poetry too. In fact we are really very similar. Like me, Mr Brown may seem a sensible no-nonsense type on the surface but underneath he's romantic and passionate.

After pretending to browse in other sections I casually moved over to stand near him. He didn't notice me right away this time as he was engrossed in a book, but I was happy just to be close to him and watch him undetected for a while. I'd missed him so much.

He closed the book, saw me and smiled. 'Oh, hi, Cat. Still browsing? Not found anything you like yet?'

I gazed at him and reddened. Yeah, I definitely had. Only it wasn't a book. Oh, David, if only we could talk openly about how we felt, but of course this was impossible right now so instead, just like at school, we talked about books.

'That's what I love about holidays,' Mr Brown said.

'Finally I get the chance to read just for pleasure instead of work.'

'Yeah, me too.' But then I added meaningfully, 'But in some ways, you know, I'm actually missing school.'

I hoped he understood what I really meant but he just replied carefully, 'Yes, I suppose the long summer holidays might get boring after a while.'

Oh, Mr Brown. It will be so amazing when we don't have to talk in code like this any more. But maybe I hadn't made myself plain enough. Perhaps he wasn't quite sure that his feelings for me were returned. I went on even more boldly, 'Actually, it's the *people* I miss most.'

He paused for a moment before replying, 'Yes, that's what I used to miss, but I went to a boarding school so everyone scattered to different bits of the country over the holidays. Surely you're still able to keep in contact with friends?'

This was so exciting. Was he really suggesting what I thought he was? That he wanted to keep in touch with me over the holidays? Oh My God. How to answer this? Of course, I'd have to be careful in my response. I must make it clear to him that I knew our meetings would have to be strictly platonic for a while since he was still my teacher – and totally secret because of the nasty minds of people who wouldn't understand our relationship. What to say?

I was still thinking about the wording of my reply

when my mobile rang. I ignored it but Mr Brown, probably assuming I wanted to answer the call, said, 'See you later, Cat,' then took his book to the cash desk.

Damn. I opened my phone and looked at the caller ID, which I didn't recognize. Whoever it was had probably just ruined the most important moment of the year, maybe of my whole life. I punched the answer button and said crossly, 'Yeah, what is it?'

Josh said, 'Hi, Cat. Hope you don't mind but you left in such a rush I didn't have time to ask for your number – Peter gave it to me.' I was too annoyed even to bother to reply to this so after a pause Josh went on, 'I'll take your silence to mean that it's OK then. The thing is, I really enjoyed this afternoon and wondered if you'd like another tennis lesson soon. Or maybe we could just take in a movie or something.'

I was stunned into silence. What was he saying? Was he asking me out or what? Asking me instead of Tessa? Could he be serious?

When I didn't reply he started talking again. 'Look, it's cool. I'm not asking for a date or anything.' He laughed. 'Apparently you don't date, right? So, OK, sure, we could just meet up to, uh, get to know each other a bit better. See how things go and take it from there. What do you say?'

I said suspiciously, 'So, you want to teach me tennis or go to a movie but it's not a date? Just you and me?'

'Well, yeah. But, you know, if you don't feel

comfortable with that you could ask some friends along. Or your sister maybe. Whatever. It's cool.'

Ah ha! So that was it. He wasn't confident enough to ask Tessa outright so he was using the 'pretend friendliness with the not-so-hot sister' technique. Yeah, right. It might not have been quite so bad if the activities he'd suggested were a bit more appealing. Like I really wanted another lesson about how I should work on my fatness . . . oh, sorry, fitness. And I wondered what the movie would be about. Probably some stupid story featuring brave American heroes who save the entire planet from destruction watched by a grateful but pathetically useless world. I didn't say any of this of course – my mum would have a fit if she heard I'd been this rude to my dad's boss's son, so instead I just had to content myself by replying, 'Sorry, I'm busy this week and I'll probably be busy for quite a while actually.'

Then I hung up.

I hoped that was the last I'd be hearing from Josh.

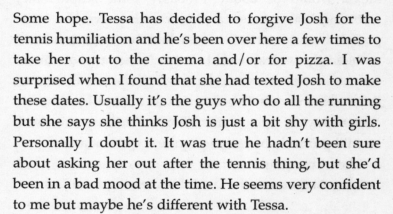

3

Some hope. Tessa has decided to forgive Josh for the tennis humiliation and he's been over here a few times to take her out to the cinema and/or for pizza. I was surprised when I found that she had texted Josh to make these dates. Usually it's the guys who do all the running but she says she thinks Josh is just a bit shy with girls. Personally I doubt it. It was true he hadn't been sure about asking her out after the tennis thing, but she'd been in a bad mood at the time. He seems very confident to me but maybe he's different with Tessa.

Peter has also taken a liking to Josh so I've bumped into him a few times at Peter's house. I've never actually been rude to Josh on these occasions but I don't go out of my way to be nice either. He seems puzzled by my unfriendliness and has asked me if he's offended me in any way.

Peter has told me privately that he thinks Josh is actually a nice guy and not up himself at all. 'He's OK,

Cat. He wasn't trying to insult you with the fitness remark. Fitness is important in all sports. Only a weight-obsessed female like you would read anything more into it. You should really give up this stupid notion you're fat anyway. You're just curvy, that's all. Lots of guys like that.'

'Don't call me curvy. It's just another word for fat.'

'Shit. You're not fat. OK? In fact, well, some of my friends have said you're actually not that bad at all. Just a bit odd.'

'Thanks a lot.'

'Not mental odd,' Peter explained quickly. 'Just a little defensive sometimes and sort of spacey at others. I don't mean druggy, but you know, one minute you're talking and laughing with some guy, the next you've gone off to the planet Zorg and he may as well be talking to himself. You must admit you daydream a lot.'

And this was Peter's attempt to pay me a compliment! Honestly, some guys!

I laughed. 'Well, Peter, I don't know what to say. I'm just totally, erm, overwhelmed by this flattery but I'll try not to let it go to my head.'

However, afterwards I did think over what he'd said. (About Josh, that is, not his friends' comments on my attractiveness.) Perhaps I've been unfair. After all, it's not Josh's fault that he's rich, good looking and talented. He doesn't know what it's like to be a total disappointment to a parent; he's never experienced the humiliation of trying (but failing miserably) to squeeze into a size-twelve skirt when your sister can slip into a six with room to spare. I've probably been over-sensitive about his fitness remark. It wouldn't be the first time I've taken offence about something like this when none had really been intended.

I resolved to be nicer to Josh, especially as it looked like he was going to be important to Tessa and, according to Dad, around for some time. Josh's parents are thinking about sending him to our school. This is good news for us, apparently, because it must mean that his dad intends to stay in Glasgow for at least a couple of years so isn't just a hatchet man, here to wind up the company then run.

So when Josh called round unexpectedly today I was quite pleasant to him. I told him Tessa had gone out shopping and wouldn't be back for at least another hour but he asked to come in anyway as he'd something he wanted to talk to me about.

I ushered him into the living room, where he told me that his dad had definitely decided to send him to our school since it offered the international baccalaureate, which he could use back home. Then he said, 'I'd really like to meet some more students before the start of term, Cat. You know, as I'm a kinda new kid on the block, the more people I get to know the better. I was thinking of throwing a party at my place next Saturday and hoping you might help me with invites and arrangements. Peter too of course. I've OK'd everything with my parents.'

I thought about it. Yeah, a party would be great. The long holidays were getting boring and it would help take my mind off Mr Brown. Also Iona and Marianne, my two best friends after Lindsay, have been moaning about never meeting any decent-looking guys. Maybe I could set them up with someone at the party. Peter had told me Josh's place was huge so we'd be able to invite loads of people.

'Are your parents going to be there?' I asked.

'Nope. They'll be at a neighbour's house. Another American family on secondment to Scotland. They've promised not to come home until around two in the morning unless needed. And, erm' – he smiled – 'I definitely don't think we're gonna need them.'

'Cool.' I grinned back at him. 'I'm pretty sure we can cope without them too. Of course I'd be happy to help you organize the party, and I'm sure Tessa will too.'

Soon I was happily texting and phoning people to spread the news and making lists of stuff we'd need. Josh suggested a barbecue but I told him this was Glasgow, not New York, and you couldn't plan a week ahead for that. We'd have to take a rain check. Literally.

He seemed pleased by my enthusiasm and let me make decisions about music, numbers, start time, etc. It was so exciting getting to organize things. I prattled on about who I planned to invite: there was Lindsay of course, plus Iona and Marianne. I wanted to ask Helen, but if I did I'd have to invite her boyfriend Mark too, who was a total pain. Also Mark wouldn't be able to come if I asked Beth since they split during the holidays and she's still upset. Maybe I would invite Steve since he's always fancied Beth, but perhaps it wouldn't be a good idea just getting her on the rebound . . .

Josh had been listening patiently but now interrupted to ask, 'What about you, Cat? Are you planning to bring someone to the party? Peter says you're still not dating at the moment. Well, no one special anyway.'

Not dating at the moment! God, Peter had been diplomatic for once. The nearest thing I'd had to a date was a snog with Billy Cameron when I got drunk at the school Christmas party last year. Billy isn't bad looking but I find him pretty boring – all he talks about is his pet python which, as far as I can make out, sleeps all the time. He's nice though and we're still friends but he's not special. Not like Mr Brown.

Oh yes, David was special all right. As always, I smiled at the thought of him. At last I had someone wonderful in my life even if we couldn't be together quite yet. Aloud I said dreamily, 'As a matter of fact there *is* someone special. But, erm, he won't be able to make the party.'

Josh said politely, 'Lucky guy, but yeah, pity he can't be there.' Then he got up suddenly and said, 'Look, I gotta go now.'

'Don't go yet. Tessa will be here soon.'

'No. I really gotta go. I've got stuff to do.'

After he'd left I started to worry about what I'd told him. Of course, I hadn't given any clue as to who my 'someone special' was; still, it was dangerous to mention him at all. I mustn't be so indiscreet again. It was so hard though, keeping my feelings secret. I can't wait for the day when I'll be able to tell everyone that Mr Brown, or David I should say, is my boyfriend.

When Tessa got back she was annoyed at missing Josh but excited about the party and looking forward to seeing inside Josh's place.

'I've only seen the outside of his house so far, Cat, but it's enormous. Must cost a fortune to rent, but then his family are rich. Are you sure his parents won't be there?'

'Yeah, they're not due back till two in the morning.'

'Great. Maybe I'll be able to tempt Josh away from his party host duties for a while and spend some private time alone with him.'

She giggled, then leaned close to me. 'You know, Josh is different from most guys I've been out with. Can you believe he hasn't even snogged me yet?'

'No, really?'

'He's been such a gentleman. Makes a change from the usual crass idiots I meet, who always start trying to paw me on the first date. Still, I've decided he's been a gentleman long enough. It's time he got his reward.'

Hmm, she did sound keen, and I wondered how far

she intended to go with Josh at the party. Unlike me, my sister isn't a virgin, but she isn't a slapper either and has only had sex with a few of the hundreds of guys she'd dated. Lindsay says only the ones with money but she's being unfair. Tessa just likes guys who are a bit classy, that's all. I supposed Josh would be one of the ones she'd sleep with so I just hoped she wouldn't dump him soon afterwards, which she'd done before. Not with Josh's dad being our dad's boss. Still, what could Josh do about it? He could hardly tell his dad to sack ours because Tessa wouldn't shag him any more. I hoped not anyway.

The next few days I was busy with arrangements. Lots of girls I invited were keen to know about Josh so were disappointed when I told them he'd already been taken by Tessa. However, it didn't put them off the party, and by the time Peter and I had finished sixty people were definitely coming.

On the afternoon of the party Tessa asked me to come and help her choose which outfit she should wear. She often does this – she's told me I've got good taste and she doesn't trust anyone else to give her unbiased advice. She tried on loads of different things and looked fantastic in all of them. Honestly, if you're thin, dressing is just so easy. You don't have to think about what colour, fabric or cut is going to be slimming, or in my case less fattening; you can just throw on almost anything and it will look at the very least OK.

She said she wanted to go for a sexy rather than subtle look tonight so I suggested she wore her tight low-cut white jeans with her off-the-shoulder red silky top, then I went downstairs to let Lindsay in – she was coming to the party with us.

Lindsay was excited about it too, especially as Scott would be there. Scott is six foot one but, to Lindsay's fury, had been going out all last term with Tracy, who is barely five feet tall. However, they've split up over the summer and it's rumoured Scott has grown another inch.

Lindsay said, 'Six foot two, Cat. Imagine it. Six foot two and free!'

I didn't want to put a damper on Lindsay's plans but I was a bit concerned. I don't know Scott very well but it's rumoured he's not all that nice sometimes and that Tracy finished with him because he constantly hit on other girls while they were dating. I tried to warn Lindsay but she wouldn't listen.

Later we went upstairs to my room to put on some music and get ready. Lindsay had decided on a short denim skirt that showed off her long, model-slim legs and a summery pink top. As usual I wore all black. Lindsay says looking into my wardrobe is like peering into a black hole as almost every garment I possess is black (barring underwear and night stuff that no one sees). My dad says I'd be all right if we got a spate of funerals to attend but it would be nice to see me in something more cheerful for a change. However, the fact is there is no other colour as slimming as black so it's a no-brainer for me. Sometimes I get fed up with it myself and long to go mad and wear shocking pink or scarlet, but when you're a size fourteen colour is not an option.

And so tonight it was my trusty black velvet trousers with black lacy top. The top had very thin straps so I toyed with going braless. My breasts are nice. Not too big that I have to wear a bra for support nor so small that I needed to squash them together to make a cleavage. Lindsay always says I should show them off more and tried to persuade me to go braless tonight, but the last time I did that some idiot said, 'Christ, look at the tits on that,' which embarrassed me.

'But,' Lindsay argued, 'that happened two years ago. The boys we know will be a lot more sophisticated now.'

'Sophisticated? You've got to be kidding me. Remember last winter when a whole crowd of them tried to write their names in the snow with pee for a laugh? And most of them still think whoopee cushions are totally hilarious.'

'Yeah, you're right. Still some idiots around. Wear your plunge bra with the thin straps.'

When I'd finished getting ready I inspected my image in the mirror. Not bad. The trousers minimized my bum and my top half is a bit slimmer anyway. My arms and calves aren't fat at all actually, just my torso – especially my arse. And yes, I really do have a nice face, I think.

Lindsay helped me with my hair tonight so though it was still wavy it wasn't frizzy, and cascaded down past my shoulders in shiny ripples. Yep, not bad at all.

Just then my sister came into the room, stood beside me at the mirror and said, 'You look nice, Cat.'

I know she meant to be kind, but comparing our two reflections, I instantly felt like elephant girl.

Lindsay frowned at Tessa and asked in a none-too-friendly voice what she wanted now. I do wish my friends would be a bit nicer to her but I've had to settle for frosty politeness.

Tessa just smiled at Lindsay and said, 'Oh nothing, just came through to see what you two were up to. You look nice too, Lindsay. So tall and elegant.' Lindsay scowled at the word 'tall' and looked like she was about to start an argument but Tessa just made for the door and, still smiling, said, 'See you later.'

Lindsay was furious. 'She does it deliberately, Cat. She knows I hate being too tall and that's why she said that.'

I tried to calm her. 'No, Lindsay, I think you're wrong about Tessa. You've got model proportions and Tessa's really impressed. She really did mean it as a compliment.'

'Yeah, right. You know that's crap. Why are you always defending her?'

'She's my—'

'Yeah, I know she's your sister, but for God's sake,

there are limits. She's also a spoiled, selfish c—'

'Shut up, Lindsay. That's enough. I don't want to hear any more.'

We were quiet for a while, both of us annoyed. Lindsay was the first to break the silence.

'Look, I'm sorry, forget it. But bloody hell, you've got to admit Tessa can be really infuriating. I don't know how you put up with her.'

'You don't understand, Lindsay. I know Tessa can be difficult sometimes but things haven't always been easy for her, you know. She's had some really tough times too.'

'Yeah, I know. You already told me. So she was picked on at primary years ago – that's no excuse for being a pain now. But like I said, forget it. She's your sister; I don't want us to fall out about her. Let's just drop it. OK?'

I nodded and Lindsay chatted on about the party but I wasn't really paying much attention – I couldn't help thinking about Tessa and that awful time when we had to leave our school because Dad lost his job and couldn't afford the fees any more.

We went to a local state primary, where some of the kids used to slag us off for being snobs because we'd gone to private school before. I tried to ignore them and soon made friends with some nice kids there but Tessa found it a lot more difficult to fit in. While people stopped calling me names they never let up on Tessa and even some of the OK kids used to talk about her behind her back, saying she was 'up herself'.

One day, instead of walking back home with Tessa after school, I went to a friend's house. That was the day a crowd of neds surrounded Tessa. First they called her horrible names, then they kicked, punched and even spat on her. They were awful.

My parents were furious and complained to the school. Of course the neds lied that Tessa had called them 'dirty council estate rats' so she'd had it coming. Mum and Dad didn't blame me for what happened, but I did. I knew I should have been there to stand up for her. I vowed then that I'd look after her and never let anyone hurt her or slag her off ever again. I've kept my promise too, even if sometimes it's been difficult. Like when she's so bloody tactless with my friends.

Lindsay interrupted my thoughts. 'C'mon, Cat, it's a party we're going to, not a funeral. Look, I've got just the thing to cheer us up.' She rummaged in the rucksack she'd brought with her and pulled out a half-bottle of vodka. 'This will get us in party mood. Can you go down and sneak us two glasses and a bottle of Coke from the kitchen?'

She turned on some dance music and I hurried downstairs to fetch the glasses and Coke. On my way back I bumped into Mum just as I was coming out of the kitchen.

'What's that?' she said in a disapproving tone while eyeing the Coke bottle.

Oh God, don't tell me she'd sussed I was sneaking this

upstairs to mix with alcohol. 'Nothing, Mum. I mean, erm, Coke.'

'Wouldn't you be better with Diet Coke, Catriona? There are almost no calories in Diet Coke. Whereas this' – she looked at my normal Coke bottle as though it was a giant turd or something – 'is loaded with them. I'm sure you'll find there's a diet bottle in the fridge. Just a suggestion of course. Don't let me pressure you. I mean, if you're absolutely certain that the calorie-loaded sort is what you'd prefer, well, that's your—'

'No, Mum, you're right, good point,' I interrupted, relieved, then hurried back to fetch the Diet Coke. Honestly, sometimes I wonder whether Mum would really care if I downed a whole bottle of vodka provided it was calorie free.

Lindsay's suggestion worked and by the time we'd drunk two vodkas and Cokes while dancing around like lunatics, we were giggling and in a great mood.

Peter came to pick us up. He'd already been at Josh's, helping to set things up. Rain had been forecast so the barbecue option was dropped. Instead Josh's parents had paid a catering firm to provide all the food and soft drinks so we just had to get the booze – not that this last was mentioned by Josh's parents of course.

Tessa didn't come with us, saying she'd stuff to do first, but I knew, because she'd told me, that she wanted to make Josh keener by keeping him waiting for her to arrive. These were little techniques I should learn from her for when I finally started dating. However, she did ask me to make sure no one else got their talons into him before she got there. I agreed, although how I was going to do this I wasn't quite sure. I'd never been anyone's chaperone before.

Just before we left, Tessa took me aside and reminded me of my promise. 'Look after Josh for me, Cat. There are bound to be lots of girls there who will try to hit on him. Make sure they don't get anywhere.'

'If you're that worried, I think you'd best come and look after him yourself.'

'I'm not that worried. Just being careful. Anyway, I already told you it's best to keep guys waiting for a while. Makes them keener. Please, Cat.'

'Well, OK, I'll do my best,' I agreed reluctantly. 'But there are limits. What am I supposed to do? Tie him up with duct tape and lock him in a cupboard? It *is* his party after all. He's supposed to talk to people. Circulate.'

'He can circulate all he likes. With guys. If you see any nice-looking girls around him, warn them off.' She smiled at me. 'You can be the duct tape. Stick to him all evening until I get there.'

'What if he doesn't want me sticking to him?'

'He will. He likes you. He's told me so.'

Peter and Lindsay were already at the door and getting impatient. 'Hmm, well, all right then,' I told Tessa.

'Thanks, Cat. Now don't let him out of your sight.

Promise?'

'I promise.'

I had a feeling that, before the night was over, it was a
promise I was going to regret.

4

Peter suggested Lindsay sit in front so she'd have more room for her legs.

Lindsay said, 'OK, but this time don't fondle my thighs pretending that your hand slipped when changing gear.' As she got into the car she warned him, 'If you try that again I'll slap you whether you're driving or not. Hard.'

Peter grumbled, 'Right, fantastic. You'd be quite prepared to hit a driver, thus possibly causing a multiple pile-up and untold carnage, just because I accidentally brushed your knee with my hand? Call that proportionate?'

Lindsay said, 'Thigh, not knee, and accidentally my arse.'

It took around five minutes to get to Josh's. The house was huge, especially for just three people, and it had a long driveway plus a walled back garden. Quite a lot of people were already there but the place didn't look crowded because of the large high-ceilinged rooms. Lindsay spotted Scott right away (being the tallest guy there, he was easy to spot) and made a bee-line for him, which depressed Peter.

'What does she see in that tosser, Cat? No, OK, don't bother to tell me. He's over six foot, right? He could be the Boston strangler or Bluebeard, but if he's over six foot she'd still go chasing after him.'

'Hmm, I don't think she likes beards,' I said.

'Yeah, very funny, Cat. It's OK for you. You never seem to fall for anyone. You don't know what it's like to want someone so much you can't think about anything else.'

God, to listen to Peter you'd think I was the Ice Queen and he's known me all my life. Still, I suppose since I can't speak to anyone about my feelings for Mr Brown and I'm not attracted to anyone else, it must look like I'm just not interested in romance at all. How wrong can people be?

I said, 'You may be surprised at just how romantic I really am.' Then I tried to cheer him up. 'Maybe Lindsay will get over (ha ha) the height thing or high heels will go out of fashion one day. Or you could wear stilettos and tower over her . . .'

Peter grinned, put an arm around my shoulders and steered me into the kitchen to get me a drink. 'So what do you think of the house? Great place for a party, isn't it?'

I nodded. 'Yeah, cool. Especially the floors.'

'What?'

'Well, they're nearly all wooden or tiled, and the rugs have been taken up. Fantastic surfaces for people to spill drinks or be sick on – they'll clean up, no problem, and Josh's parents will be none the wiser!'

Peter laughed. 'Yeah, I see now I've been wrong about you, Cat. A born romantic.'

The kitchen was crowded but I spotted Josh, who was drinking beer and talking to two really attractive girls I'd never seen before. Damn. Who invited them anyway? It must have been Peter or one of his pals. Josh saw us too and waved us over, offering me a glass of wine and Peter a Coke (since he was going to drive back tonight). Peter took the Coke and eyed the girls appreciatively but was called over by two guys who wanted him to drive some more people to the party.

I accepted the wine, then, ignoring the girls, said pointedly, 'Tessa's asked me to tell you she'll be along soon. So how did you both enjoy the movie on Wednesday? I heard it was good.'

I prattled on about him and Tessa, making it absolutely clear that he and my sister were dating, but the girls didn't take the hint and stayed where they were. Fortunately Josh had to go and help carry in another load of beer so I took the opportunity for a bit of straight talking with his admirers. 'You're too late. Josh is dating my sister, so hands off.'

The tall blonde one with the big boobs wasn't fazed.

'He's only been here a few weeks. Your sister doesn't own him, does she? I don't see her name branded on his forehead. Or has she tattooed it on his bum? Maybe I'll just check and see later tonight.'

The other one just giggled. Chaperoning Josh was going to be more difficult than I thought and I hoped my sister would get here soon. When Josh came back I grabbed his arm, saying I fancied a dance, and started to pull him away from the girls into the next room.

He said, 'Sure, Cat, but, uh, wouldn't it be better to put some music on first?'

I blushed but he just asked me to pick out some good dance songs. Other people started dancing as soon as we put the music on so I was able to join in and enjoy myself without that awful feeling of being watched. While we were dancing Josh chatted to me about the people I'd invited, which was OK until he started asking nosy questions about my 'boyfriend'.

'So, how come your boyfriend couldn't make it tonight?'

'Oh, erm, busy,' I mumbled.

'What was his name again? Does he go to the same school as you?'

Oh God. He'd been talking to Peter, who'd have said he didn't know anything about my boyfriend. Josh probably thinks I'm a sad person who makes up stories about having a boyfriend because I can't get one. What to say? If only I could tell the truth. *My boyfriend's name is*

David, and yes, he does go to the same school as me but he's not a pupil. He's a member of staff. He can't come to the party tonight because of the stupid prejudices and petty rules of people who can't understand that unimportant stuff like age and occupation should be no barriers for people who love one another.

Of course, I couldn't say anything like this, so instead, with a silent apology to David for my betrayal, I said, 'Oh, actually it was just a short relationship and, erm, we've split now. I don't really want to talk about it.'

I felt guilty as Josh was so nice to me. 'I'm sorry, Cat. I shouldn't have brought it up. Pretty crass, right? I hope I didn't upset you. It's always difficult ending a relationship. Just forget I said anything, OK? We don't have to talk about anything you don't want to.'

Somehow his being so nice unsettled me even more than his nosy questions and I felt an urgent need to get away from him. Looking around, I spotted Billy at the edge of the dance floor. I stopped dancing and, taking Josh by the hand, moved towards Billy, saying there was someone I'd like him to meet.

I introduced them and said, 'Billy has got a pet python and I think it's just about to shed its skin.' I looked at Billy. 'Isn't that right?'

He nodded. 'Yeah.'

I said, 'Josh doesn't know about your python yet, Billy. I'm sure he'll want to hear all about such an interesting and unusual pet.'

I fled to the kitchen, where I found Lindsay talking to Scott. It looked like she was making headway with him as he was smiling and nodding at her, but I couldn't help noticing he was also surreptitiously scanning the room and eyeing up other girls too. I knew it would be no use mentioning my doubts to Lindsay so I just chatted with them for a while before going to talk to some friends I hadn't seen since school broke up. Later we moved next door to dance when, bollocks, I spotted Josh with the blonde again, plus two other girls. Honestly, this promise to my sister was proving hard work. Chaperoning a good-looking American was obviously a full time job.

I strode over and interrupted the conversation. 'So, Josh, this is a lovely house. Would you mind showing me round? What's upstairs?'

Josh smiled. 'Yeah, I heard you particularly liked the flooring. It's just bedrooms upstairs. Do you want to see my bedroom, Cat?'

I made a mental note to tell Peter to keep his mouth shut and stop passing on stuff I say to everyone. I also decided I wasn't going to be embarrassed by this deliberate wind-up. I was determined to prise him away from his relentless admirers, so even though I probably sounded like a slapper, I just hooked my arm through his and said, 'Yeah, why not? Let's go.'

Josh's room was large and, as I'd expected, stuffed with thousands of pounds worth of things. The first thing I noticed was a plasma TV with a screen the size of a small cinema connected to a DVD player and PlayStation. A computer, printer *and* laptop sat atop a solid wooden desk, plus there was a lot of sports equipment scattered about the room. Everything looked top-of-the-range expensive and (except for the sports stuff, which showed signs of use) shiny new. The room also had an ensuite bathroom, which I envied Josh more than anything else. It would be great not to have to share – Tessa always spent ages there in the morning and sometimes made me late for school.

Josh sat on the double bed and looked at me. 'So, Cat, what do you think of my room?'

'It's kinda what I thought an American teenager's room would be like.'

Josh smiled. 'So what's the difference?' He looked around. 'Seems normal to me. Just a room with a bed. We don't sleep in coffins or anything.'

I moved over to the window and looked out, scanning the street for any sign of Tessa, who was coming by taxi. Nothing yet. I didn't reply to his question. Instead, noticing a baseball glove on the shelf, I asked him if he played. He went on about the game enthusiastically while I continued to keep a look out for Tessa. I found the topic about as interesting as Billy's python but I just nodded occasionally as though paying attention and that was good enough. However, when he mentioned that he and his dad had actually got tickets for the final of the World Series (which NY Yankees had won), I thought I'd better show some interest so I asked what other countries the NY Yankees had beaten to win.

He looked puzzled. 'Well, not any other countries. All the teams were American.'

'You can*not* be serious. In a *World* Series? You don't compete against other countries in a *World* Series?'

Josh frowned. 'Well, put like that, um, well, there is one Canadian team, but otherwise, I suppose . . .'

I laughed. 'God, you Americans.' Then I turned to window again and – yes, at last – Tessa! I made for the door. 'C'mon. Tessa's here.'

Josh said, 'Wait a minute, there's no hurry. I've something I want to show you.'

He pointed to a photo on his bedside table of a large house surrounded by trees; you could just make out a swimming pool and tennis court in the grounds. I guessed correctly. 'Home? Bloody hell, you're practically slumming it here. But I thought you lived in New York? This looks nothing like it.'

'I live in New York State, not the city. We're about an hour's drive from New York city.'

He handed me the photo and I examined it more closely. A beautiful mansion drenched in sunlight. 'Your house is fantastic. Don't you miss it?'

'Yeah – not the house so much but, well, my life. Everything. I was supposed to stay with my cousins while my parents were here but I got into trouble at school so they decided I'd better come with them. Make a new start.'

'What sort of trouble?'

'Oh, the usual stuff. Cutting classes, grades slipping, getting involved with the "wrong" crowd. According to my parents anyway. I called it having fun.'

I smiled and handed him back the photograph. 'Why did you want to show me this?'

Josh shrugged. 'Thought you might be interested, plus you'll notice the tennis courts on the grounds. My folks were keen on the game and I've been playing since I was three so I can really kick ass on the tennis court when I want to. I coached back home so I could teach you if you like. You've got potential, Cat.'

To be honest I was starting to feel a bit sorry for this American. Despite all he had going for him, like rich parents and nice looks, he seemed oddly lonely. Like a glossy-coated Labrador puppy surrounded by terriers, he didn't fit in. Still, I was sure Tessa could cheer him up, particularly as she seemed to have definite plans for him tonight. I told him 'Maybe' and shooed him out to meet her.

Downstairs I spotted Tessa and waved to her. To my fury, she waved lazily back, then continued to flirt with the two guys she was talking to, presumably to appear totally cool about seeing Josh again and probably make him a bit jealous. This was too much. I took Josh's hand and guided him firmly over to Tessa, then, despite her embarrassed frown and his amused smile, I said, 'Here he is,' then left the pair of them to it.

Tessa got me on my own a bit later and had a go at me for being obvious and crass, but I refused to feel guilty. Looking after Josh for her had been hard work. Now I was free to enjoy myself at last.

I spotted Iona standing in a corner by herself and looking a bit nervous, so I went over. Iona has long, wavy blonde hair and is really pretty but she's very shy and about as timid as her beloved pet gerbil, Twinkle. However, I managed to get her chatting to some boys who play football with Peter. I was a bit worried when she accepted a Bacardi Breezer as I know she can't handle alcohol. Still, I didn't say anything. I'm not her mum after all – it's up to her what she does. Instead I decided to just chill out.

Everyone seemed to be having a great time and there was enough food and drink to feed an army. The music was good; people were dancing and chatting. Yes. I'd organized a successful party. Everything looked set for a perfect night.

Well, not quite perfect. David wasn't here. It would be so wonderful if he could have been with me tonight. I amused myself for a while imagining what it would be like. Everyone would be amazed of course, and things might be a bit awkward at first, but David's wit and charm would soon put people at their ease; most of the girls were sure to be jealous of me.

David and I would dance, laugh and chat to everyone. Maybe even steal a quick kiss in a secluded corner as he'd be much too mature to snog in public. Of course, as he is an adult with his own flat, after the party we could go back to his place and snog as much as we liked in total privacy. Mmmm.

As it turned out though, I didn't get much chance to dream of David as I had to spend most of the time trying, and failing, to stop Iona making a complete idiot of herself. She'd only had three Bacardi Breezers and a Bailey's Irish Cream all night but that was enough to get her totally plastered. When will she ever learn that she just *cannot* handle her drink?

I tried my best to calm her down and talk her out of the worst of her drunken antics but she wouldn't listen to anyone and only stopped when she eventually threw up over a pile of jackets in the hall.

I helped her clean up the mess. It wasn't easy, or pleasant, trying to mop up vomit from clothes with paper towels and a damp cloth, but eventually we managed to remove all visible traces – although the jackets still smelled so we sprayed them with a bottle of perfume Iona had in her bag. It was cheap flowery stuff she'd got free with a magazine so some of the boys later complained they'd have preferred their jackets to smell of puke but I'm sure they didn't mean it. Almost sure anyway.

By the time we'd finished cleaning up, Iona had

sobered up a lot and was mortified. Not just about being sick over people's belongings but also her pole-dance on the banister, lap-dance on Terry's knee (he's the head boy and she doesn't even like him) and the thankfully incomplete strip on the kitchen table (she'd been too drunk to manage buttons and zips). I called her a taxi, which we waited for in the toilet, partly because she was scared she might be sick again but mostly because she couldn't face seeing anyone.

I tried to comfort her. 'Honestly, Iona, nobody noticed you. Well, OK, maybe Terry, but he's a tosser anyway and, erm, will probably be so drunk by the end of the party he won't remember.'

Iona stared desperately into my eyes. 'Do you really think so, Cat?'

I forced myself to stare right back at her. 'Of course,' I lied.

Once I'd bundled her safely into a taxi I had a great time – until, that is, Lindsay and Peter fell out. Peter had taken over responsibility for the music and she said he'd deliberately changed a nice slow song to a fast hip-hop one the moment Scott asked her to dance. Peter denied the accusation, saying he'd just decided it was too early in the night for slow numbers. I tried to defend him, but Lindsay was probably right about his motivation and she knew it. When Scott left later with another girl, 'five feet two and no earthly need for someone that tall', Lindsay consoled herself by getting drunk, then passing out. So much for her promise to help clear up.

As usual at parties I ended up in the kitchen washing up. I think it's because I'm not interested in getting off with anyone now, and if you're not snogging some guy people assume you've got nothing better to do. I suppose I haven't. Josh's parents had hired cleaners to come in the morning but that was a waste of money and time – there was no way we could let anyone find all the empty beer, wine and spirit bottles or clear up spilled drinks and worse. I'd have to be extra thorough too: I've heard American parents get more freaked about under eighteens drinking since the legal age there is twenty-one.

Josh came to help for a while and took bags of empties out to the boot of Peter's car for disposal at the dump. I asked Tessa to help but she said she couldn't because of the white jeans, which might get dirty, and I had picked them after all. I handed her a striped apron that was hanging on the kitchen door but she looked at it like I'd just passed her a rotting carcass and said, 'Ugh, no way.' On Josh's return she spirited him off, so in the end me and Peter were left to clean up.

At least Josh's parents had locked all the bedrooms so I wouldn't have to send Peter upstairs to search for used condoms. There are some clean-up jobs I just *won't* do. Nevertheless Peter checked out the cupboard under the stairs and the two downstairs toilets but found nothing incriminating.

At twenty past one I did a final quick search of each room for party debris. Found two discarded beer cans that had been used as ashtrays and one half-empty Bacardi Breezer bottle (also with a cigarette butt floating inside) but that was it. I was satisfied that unless Josh's parents had hired a team of forensic scientists they'd never know what had really gone on at the party.

Hmm – or would they? The place still smelled of alcohol, cigarettes and sick. I got a can of air freshener from the bathroom and sprayed it as liberally as I dared throughout the whole house. I didn't go totally mad like Lindsay had at her last party – her mum had an asthma attack when she got home and had to be rushed to hospital. I wasn't sure whether either of Josh's parents was asthmatic or not but I wasn't prepared to risk it.

At last I was finished and ready to go home. Everyone had gone except Peter and Lindsay (who was fast asleep on the sofa). Also, of course, Josh and my sister, who had gone upstairs a while ago. Peter woke Lindsay up but she was still fairly out of it and he had to half carry and half drag her out to the car. I wanted to wait for Tessa to come down but Peter was tired and told me to go up and offer her a lift home now – otherwise she'd have to make her own arrangements.

I was a bit embarrassed about disturbing them but Josh's parents would be back soon so I'd have to warn them. I made my way upstairs, meaning to knock gently on the door of Josh's bedroom. However, before I got there Tessa came hurtling down the stairs, sobbing.

Oh My God. Tessa almost never cries. What had happened? What had he done to her? For a moment I thought he must have hit on her, but she'd wanted that, hadn't she? I know because she'd even put two condoms in her bag tonight 'just in case' and giggled about it. I'd been a bit shocked actually as she hardly knew him. Still, it wasn't my business what she got up to. Not everyone was prepared to wait for love like David and me.

She wouldn't speak to me at first; just rushed past me through the hall and out the front door. Josh appeared at the top of the stairs. I glared at him and shouted, 'You better not have hurt my sister.'

Josh said, 'I didn't do anything to her, Cat. She's just a bit upset, that's all. Maybe had a little too much to drink tonight.' He was walking down the stairs, probably intending to tell me a load of lies and excuses, but I decided I'd get the real story from Tessa first. I told him I needed to talk to my sister and not to bother seeing me out, then stomped off, banging the door behind me.

Tessa said nothing in the car, but as soon as Peter dropped us off and I'd manoeuvred a still drunk Lindsay into bed, she filled me in on what had happened. Turned out it was much worse than Josh making an unwanted pass. Tessa had tried to snog him and he'd turned her down. She explained to me between sobs that he'd told her he didn't think of her in 'that way' and just wanted to be friends.

I couldn't believe it. He'd knocked back my beautiful sister. Why would any guy do that? And how would Tessa ever get over the humiliation?

5

Next morning Tessa was still upset: she couldn't face breakfast and stayed in her room. Lindsay was too hung over to eat anything and my mum had her usual half-grapefruit sprinkled with low-calorie fake sugar so I made bacon, scrambled egg and toast for Dad and me.

Delicious. But sometimes I wish I lost my appetite when I got upset like my sister does. At least then there would be the consolation of losing a few pounds and having people fuss over me concernedly – 'C'mon, Cat. You really should eat something, you'll waste away.' Instead I tend to comfort myself with food. A minor upset might be treated with a packet of Maltesers or a couple of chocolate digestive biscuits but for more serious stuff, like Tessa was experiencing now, it would have to be intensive therapy: several chunky bars of Cadbury's followed by a packet of Jaffa Cakes and a carton of ice cream.

I sighed. In this, as in most other things, I wasn't like

my sister, but she was really miserable this morning and I wished I could do something to cheer her up. After breakfast I took some tea up to her, but after a few sips she pushed the mug away and flopped down on her bed again.

'I'm so humiliated, Cat. Nothing like this has ever happened to me before. I must be ugly.'

'Don't, Tessa. Of course you're not ugly. You're beautiful. The best-looking girl in the whole school. You know you are.'

Tessa gave me a weak smile but then put her hands over her face and said, 'Not nice enough looking for Josh though.'

'Of course you are. You're way too good for him. Don't let that up-himself tosser upset you. He's not worth it.'

But nothing I said or did seem to help, and as I left her to go downstairs again I heard her sobbing. I haven't seen her like this since that terrible day she was attacked by those thugs at primary. The memory, even after all this time, made me flush with guilt. Lindsay always tells me I shouldn't feel responsible for what happened to Tessa and I wasn't to blame for any of it but she's wrong. The thing is, I've been too ashamed even to tell my best friend the whole story: that Tessa had said she didn't want to go home by herself and begged to come with me to my friend's house but I wouldn't let her. I knew my friend wasn't that keen on her, but that's no excuse. If I hadn't been so selfish then Tessa wouldn't have got beaten up. It was all my fault.

Miserably I chewed on some cold toast left over from breakfast while thinking about what had happened last night. Somehow I couldn't help feeling that I'd let Tessa down again but this time I really wasn't responsible. There was no way I could have known that any guy would mess Tessa around like that. It was Josh who had caused all this. He'd pretended to like her, then insulted and humiliated her. I hated him.

Later on, when Lindsay had recovered a bit from her hangover, I talked to her about what had happened.

'Josh turned her down? Oh My God. Bet that didn't go down well with Tessa.'

'No, she's gutted. Look, Lindsay, I know you don't like her much, but she's my sister and I won't let anyone get away with humiliating her.'

'I didn't say anything—'

'Yeah, but I know you think Tessa's selfish, and she can be sometimes, but she's not that bad, and anyway she's much too good for him. I mean, who does Josh think he is?' I continued, getting madder the more I thought about him. 'Well, I suppose I know who he thinks he is. A superior American rich kid who looks down on us just because our dad isn't as well off as his. If you ask me this is just typical of the shallow materialistic values of his whole nation. Well, he doesn't make me feel inferior. Our country might not have money, power and influence but we've got loads of other more important things.'

'Jeez, this thing with Tessa has really got to you, hasn't it? I've never seen you so mad.'

'She's my sister.'

'Right. But c'mon, it's not as though Josh has actually done anything to her. He's just, well, erm, *not* done things to her. You can't blame him for that.'

'Not done anything? He's only led her on then totally insulted her!'

'OK, OK. Calm down,' Lindsay said, hurriedly backing off. 'So, erm, what other things?'

'What?'

'You know, other more important things that our country has that America doesn't?'

'Oh, er, well, loads of things like, yeah, thousands of years of culture for a start and, erm, lots of other things like, er, yeah, Black Pudding suppers, and world sporting events where we compete against other countries. Who needs America anyway.'

'Oh, right. Well, that's good. But it's still OK to shop at Gap though? And we *are* going to TGI Fridays next week?' Lindsay asked anxiously.

'Well, yeah, I suppose so.'

'Good.' Lindsay paused for a moment, her expression thoughtful. Then a new worry seemed to grip her and she looked at me in panic. 'Oh God, I know Josh has upset your sister but we *can* still buy Levi's, right?

And Nike trainers. I mean, we won't have to wear crap?'

'Yeah, well, the Americans are good at some stuff. Obviously,' I conceded. 'I'm not suggesting a total boycott.'

Lindsay sighed with relief. 'Great, let's drink to that. Ugh, not alcohol though. Coke or Irn Bru?'

'Irn Bru,' I said firmly.

In the afternoon I was surprised and annoyed when I got several texts and calls from Josh, which of course I didn't respond to. What a nerve. As far as I knew he hadn't contacted Tessa at all, which was just as well. She was still in her room and so depressed she wouldn't speak to anyone, even me, and only had a half-slice of toast to eat all day. I was really worried about her.

Meanwhile Lindsay hung around, mostly moaning to me about how Peter had ruined her chances with Scott and what was she going to do to him when she next saw him. I'm so lucky to have someone who truly loves me so I don't have to suffer all the hassle of relationships with boys that Tessa and Lindsay have to put up with.

It was nearly four o'clock and I was having a mug of tea with Lindsay in the kitchen. She was still on about how perfect Scott was and how awful Peter had been, but I was only half listening as I was thinking about Mr Brown and how great it would be when the school holidays were over and I'd see him every day again.

I was having a nice daydream where Mr Brown asked

me to stay behind at lunch to help clear out some cup-boards, but instead he'd taken me in his arms and kissed me, telling me that he couldn't wait a moment longer to be together properly, when the doorbell rang. Bollocks. I hoped it wasn't Peter as Lindsay really had it in for him, but he always phones before coming round. Mum was upstairs hoovering and Dad had gone to the office to catch up with some paperwork, even though it was Sunday, so I went to answer the door.

Josh! Bloody nerve. He was carrying a bunch of pink roses, which I supposed was for Tessa, but if he imagined for a second she'd accept them, or that this pathetic gesture was enough to make up for what he'd done, he was even more of an idiot than I'd thought. I tried to slam the door on him but he was ready for this and jammed it open with his foot.

He said, 'There seems to be something the matter with your phone, Cat, so I just came round to check things were OK and thank you personally for all your help with the party.' He held the flowers out towards me. 'These are for you.'

I glared at him. 'There's nothing the matter with my phone. I just got some nuisance calls, which I ignored. Now piss off and take those with you.'

Just then I heard my mum's voice behind me. 'Oh, Josh, it's you. Catriona, why are you keeping Josh on the doorstep like that? Where are your manners? Come on in, Josh, for goodness' sake. I'll tell Tessa you're here.'

Despite my scowls Josh came in – and, I must say, charmed Mum with his respectful but sociable manners. He gave her a dazzling smile and thanked her, then asked her not to mention his arrival to Tessa just yet, he wanted to surprise her. Also he'd like to have a few words in private with me first.

Mum smiled indulgently. She ushered us into the sitting room before giggling girlishly and backing out, saying, 'Your secret's safe with me.'

For God's sake, Mum could be so embarrassing at times!

Josh put the flowers on the coffee table, then, dropping the charm like a snake shedding its skin, turned to me and asked, 'Just what is your problem?'

'My problem!'

'Yeah. I haven't done anything wrong except refuse to make out with your sister. Like America, Scotland's a free country, isn't it? Nobody has to date anyone if they don't want to, right? When you get right down to it, it's a question of free choice. An individual's inalienable right to say thanks but no thanks. Why are you so pissed at me?'

'Nothing wrong? Yeah, right. You only led my sister on then insulted her. Tosser.'

Josh looked puzzled. 'What's a tosser? Is it the same as a jerk? Jeez, you're difficult to understand sometimes, and not just because of language problems.' He paused, then continued more calmly. 'Look, I didn't mean to insult your sister. She's a very attractive girl. Obviously. She's just not my type, as it happens. That's all. No offence.'

I hesitated. Maybe he was right and I was making too much of this. But then again, Tessa was every guy's type. He must have some other reason for refusing to go out with her. He probably thought his family was too good for ours. I turned away from him and headed for the door. 'I think you should leave now. Tessa doesn't want to see you and neither do I.'

Before I got to the door, however, he grabbed my arm, pulling me back. 'Wait. I'm not done yet.'

I looked at his hand, which was still clutching my arm tightly, then glared up at him, astonished. He seemed surprised at himself too and let go of me. He held his arms out, palms open towards me in a conciliatory gesture, and muttered, 'Sorry.'

Huh, so he should be. Even more furious now, I told him never to touch me again, then added, 'Just because your dad is my dad's boss doesn't mean *you* can tell us what to do. Honestly, you think you're so superior just because your dad is rich and important, but it means nothing to me. Absolutely nothing. You're still a tosser as far as—'

'Thanks, Cat, I get the picture,' Josh interrupted. 'If it's any consolation to you or your sister, my dad thinks I'm a loser too. I'm pretty sure I'm a huge and continuing disappointment to him so, no, I don't think I'm superior to anyone because of my dad.'

He paused, then continued in a more apologetic tone. 'I didn't mean to offend your sister last night and the last thing I wanted to do was upset you. I'm sorry.'

'Well, so you should be.'

But I wasn't really quite as mad any more. He sounded sincere. Lindsay and Peter are always saying that I jump to conclusions about things too quickly and end up being totally wrong. Maybe he was telling the truth.

And what he'd just told me about his dad had definitely struck a chord with me. I knew what it was like to be a disappointment to a parent after all. But I couldn't see how on earth Josh could be a disappointment to his dad. OK, I know he said he'd got into a bit of trouble at school but, though I hated to admit it, he was very nice looking, smart and good at sport. I couldn't see how any-one could think of him as a loser, especially his own dad. But the way Josh had said it – the kind of sad, bitter tone in his voice – I just knew he'd been telling the truth about that at least.

I asked him curiously now, 'Why does your dad think you're a loser?'

He was silent for a while, then he said slowly, 'Because I'm not like him, I guess. He wants a son to follow in his footsteps and it just isn't going to happen. He still won't accept it though. He's not a guy used to failure.'

I thought about Mum and me. It was the same problem really, but at least Mum has Tessa, who takes after her looks-wise, and is everything she would have wanted in a daughter, so I suppose that takes the pressure off me.

Tessa. I just couldn't understand why any guy would knock my sister back. I asked him now, 'So why don't you want to go out with Tessa?'

Josh swept a hand over his hair. 'It's, uh, complicated, Cat. Well, not so much complicated as, well, difficult to explain right now. Maybe later, when we know each other a bit better. This isn't the right time.' He paused again, then continued, 'Look, I probably didn't put things quite right last night with your sister. I was tense; Tessa was a bit smashed. Maybe I came across all wrong. Give me a chance to talk to her now. I'm sure I can make her see there was no insult intended. Just give me a chance to fix things.'

I didn't think there was any way he could do this and said so but Josh continued to plead with me, saying he really believed he might be able to smooth things over with Tessa. Also he seemed genuinely unaware that he'd led Tessa on and sorry that he'd upset her.

Eventually I agreed to let him try and he smiled at me. A dazzlingly American smile that had me smiling back at him despite all the trouble he'd caused. He was a charmer all right. Maybe he could manage to charm Tessa out of her bad mood even though he was still knocking her back. I found myself hoping that he could.

It took a while but eventually I persuaded Tessa just to listen to what Josh had to say. She said she'd give him five minutes max and his explanation had better be good. Then she made him wait for half an hour as she'd 'some things to do first'. Of course this really meant washing her hair, changing and putting on her make-up. I helped her blow dry her hair and select an outfit. Personally I couldn't see the point of going to all this bother for a guy who'd knocked her back. Maybe she hoped he'd change his mind and then she could tell him to get lost but I didn't see that happening. She'd looked fantastic at the party but he'd still turned her down.

Finally she was ready and we joined Josh, who'd been waiting in the kitchen with Lindsay. He stood up when we came in, smiled a little sheepishly and said, 'Hi, Tessa.'

Tessa put on a brave, dignified expression. 'Hello, Josh.' Then she turned to Lindsay and me. 'You can leave us now.'

Bloody hell. I felt like domestic staff who'd just been dismissed. Lindsay looked furious. She remained sitting and crossed her arms mutinously in front of her.

I pleaded with her. 'C'mon, Lindsay. Let's go watch TV in the sitting room. Josh and Tessa want a bit of privacy.'

Muttering darkly, Lindsay finally agreed.

About five minutes later we heard Josh leave, with Tessa showing him to the door and sounding quite friendly. We were both curious to find out what had happened so we were pleased when Tessa came into the room right after.

I don't know what I expected but I was surprised when she laughed, sounding embarrassed. 'I don't know how I could have been *so* stupid. I mean, I should have *known*. It was just so *obvious*.'

I said, 'Known what? What was obvious?'

'Well, about Josh. Of course he's gay. That's why he's never made a pass on dates. Oh God, how could I have been so stupid?'

Lindsay said triumphantly, 'Told you, Cat! Guys that good looking are always gay. Didn't I tell you!'

But I was still sceptical. 'Doesn't seem gay to me.' I looked at Tessa. 'Did he actually tell you he was gay? What did he say?'

'Oh, he didn't actually say so. Obviously he hasn't "come out" yet and probably doesn't want everyone to know. But he as good as admitted it. He said that I was very attractive, stunning in fact' – here she smiled contentedly – 'and that he could see why most guys would want to date me. Then he told me that his tastes were maybe a bit "different", that was all, so I shouldn't be offended. The fault was his in not appreciating me.'

I thought about this. It made sense. What guy wouldn't want to date my sister? Answer: a gay guy.

Maybe that's the problem with Josh and his dad too. What had Josh said? His dad just couldn't accept that Josh wasn't like him. Poor Josh. It was so unfair. At least with Mum and me it was really my fault we didn't get on. If I didn't eat so much I could be slimmer, then she'd be happy, I suppose. But what could Josh do about being gay? Nothing.

I wondered again about the trouble he'd got into at school in the States. Maybe it wasn't all his fault. If people had found out that he was gay they might have made life difficult for him. Perhaps that was why he'd started dogging school in the first place. It was going to be hard for him to fit in here too. Some idiots were sure to take the piss out of him just for being American. What if they found out he was gay? I know some gay guys have been bullied horribly at our school. Even some who people mistakenly thought were gay.

I said to Tessa and Lindsay, 'We can't tell anyone about Josh.'

Lindsay just nodded. Tessa laughed. 'Why should I want to tell anyone I fancied a gay guy? God, I was such an idiot.'

But I needed to be sure. I could rely on Lindsay but Tessa was the world's worst keeper of secrets. She'd betrayed every single confidence I'd trusted her with when we were kids so now I don't tell her anything. I said, 'You'd better keep it a secret, Tessa, or I might tell one or two of yours.' I dropped my voice and whispered out of earshot of Lindsay, 'Your hair is looking nice today. Very blonde.'

Tessa's face reddened. 'I won't tell anyone.'

I nodded, reassured. My sister was blonde up until she was about ten years old, when her hair gradually darkened, so she started to bleach it. However, she tells everyone that she's a natural blonde and is always boasting about how she doesn't need to use any products on her hair. Only Mum and I know that she has to touch up her roots every three weeks.

Just then Tessa spotted the flowers, which were still sitting on the coffee table. 'Oh, aren't these lovely! They're from Josh, I suppose. He must have forgotten to give them to me before he left.' She picked them up. 'Beautiful pink roses. My favourite. One thing about gay guys, they've got fabulous taste.' She giggled. 'Except in girlfriends of course.'

Tessa went off to put the roses in a vase and take them to her room. I didn't want to spoil her good mood by claiming them for myself so I just let her. I was glad she was happy again but I was starting to feel bad about how nasty I'd been to Josh. I called him and suggested we meet up to talk over what had happened.

He asked me to come round to his house, and when I got there he was outside in the garden practising shooting a basketball into a net that was attached to the wall of the house. When he saw me he stopped, smiled and invited me inside but I shook my head.

We might as well talk out here, away from his parents.

'Look, Josh, I'm really sorry about slagging you off today. I hadn't realized that when you said Tessa wasn't your type you meant she *really* wasn't your type.'

He said, 'No problem. Forget it.'

'I won't tell anyone,' I assured him.

Josh, probably being careful just in case, pretended to be puzzled. 'Won't tell anyone about what?'

'About Tessa, you know, not being *your type*.'

Josh affected a careless shrug. 'Not anyone else's business, is it?'

'No, you're right, and you can rely on me. I'll never tell another soul. Nor will Tessa.'

'Um, good. Right, uh, that's cool.'

'So, Josh, I'd, er, really like to be friends. If you still want to?'

'Sure. Yeah, I'd like that.'

A bit embarrassed now, I waved goodbye to him and turned to leave. But he caught my left hand so I turned back and offered him my right hand to shake, which is what I supposed he'd meant. Instead, to my surprise, he took my other hand in his and kissed me lightly on the mouth. He said, 'Thanks, Cat.'

I blushed, totally confused. This couldn't be a pass, not from a gay guy. Maybe Americans are just more friendly and laid back about kissing. Like the French, for example. Hmm, but French people kiss you on the cheeks, not the mouth. And I don't remember the exchange student kissing anyone like that. Perhaps gay guys were just a bit more demonstrative than straight ones then. Yeah, it's probably quite normal for American gay people to kiss you on the mouth.

I said, 'Fine, yeah, don't mention it. See ya.'

He released my hands then and I hurried off.

All that evening I felt restless for some reason and couldn't concentrate on the DVD I'd planned to watch with Tessa. Despite my late night I wasn't tired but eventually I went to bed anyway. I took out my picture of Mr Brown and gave him a goodnight kiss. But kissing the flat glass frame seemed disappointing somehow and I longed to be kissed for real. Like, well . . . like Josh had kissed me tonight.

I had to laugh at myself. A gay guy or an inanimate photograph. Some choice.

I turned out the light and settled down to dream about Mr Brown but annoyingly I kept thinking about Josh. I'd been wrong about him. He wasn't arrogant at all. In fact he seemed really nice, just like Peter had said. I don't know why he's still so friendly to me after all the things I said to him. He mustn't be the type to hold grudges. Yeah, Josh is a really nice guy. And so gorgeous as well. It was such a shame he was gay.

6

I almost didn't recognize Iona when she turned up at TGI
Fridays to meet Lindsay and me for lunch because she
was wearing wraparound dark glasses and her blonde
hair was tucked under a large floppy hat that covered
most of her face.

She sat at our table and pulled her specs down her
nose a bit so she could see the menu, then glanced
furtively from side to side. 'I feel like everyone in the
restaurant is staring at me. Do you think they've heard
about what I did at the party?'

'Hmm, no, I don't think so, Iona,' I said. 'I think
maybe they're wondering why you're wearing dark
glasses and a sun hat when it's been raining all day.
You'll have to stop trying to hide away like this. You
weren't that bad at the party anyway. It's not as though
you really did take all your clothes off.'

'Yeah.' Lindsay giggled. 'You were way too drunk to
manage a strip.'

Iona blushed then groaned. 'But it's not just that. It's what I did with Terry.'

Lindsay said, 'The lap-dance with the head boy? Don't worry about it. Just a bit of fun. At least you didn't pass out at the party like me.'

Iona seemed to relax a little. 'So you haven't heard then? Maybe he won't mention it. God, I hope not.'

'Mention what?' I said.

'Oh, nothing.'

At first Iona refused to say anything more but we knew she'd confess sooner or later as she is hopeless at keeping secrets – from her friends at least. Instead she concentrated on choosing something to eat, which took ages as she is very fussy about food. She never eats meat, only fruit, nuts and vegetables. Also these have to be completely natural with no artificial additives. Eventually she settled on salad and chips, but not before asking me, 'You're sure the salad's organic? And they definitely haven't used animal fat to fry the chips?'

'I'm sure,' I lied. 'Now, c'mon, Iona, you know you're going to tell us sometime so it might as well be now. What happened with Terry?'

'Oh, all right then.' She paused, looked around to make sure no one was near enough to listen in on our conversation, then whispered rapidly, 'I asked him to have sex with me in the cupboard under the stairs but changed my mind when it turned out he didn't have organic condoms.'

'You asked him for sex in the cupboard?' I said, shocked.

'Shhh, keep your voice down,' Iona begged.

'What are organic condoms?' asked Lindsay. 'Are they made of recycled paper or something? Not too safe, if you ask me.'

'Very funny,' Iona huffed.

'Or maybe,' I said, 'they're made from sheep gut like they used to be in the olden days.'

'Ugh,' Iona said. 'That's gross. I'm a vegetarian, remember.'

'So?' I giggled. 'I don't think they ate them afterwards.'

'Stop being stupid, you two,' Iona complained. 'Organic condoms are biodegradable, that's all. Much better for the environment.'

'Well,' I said, 'at least you were *environmentally* responsible at the party.'

Iona smiled weakly but it was obvious she was still mortified so we stopped winding her up about it and just let her talk. Apparently it wasn't just the embarrassment that was upsetting her.

'It's Billy,' she told us. 'I suppose there will be no chance of my getting off with him now.'

'Billy Cameron?' I said. 'The one with the python?'

'Yeah, well, I know you think he's a bore but you always find fault with any boy who's ever shown an interest in you. I think he's gorgeous and a really nice guy too. Don't suppose he'll want anything to do with me now that everyone believes I'm a slapper. Especially if Terry tells people about the cupboard thing. Do you think he will?'

'Of course not,' I said in what I hoped was a convincing tone. 'A head boy will be way too mature for that.'

Trying to take Iona's mind off the party, I decided a change of subject would help.

'Guess what? Tessa's got a new boyfriend.'

'Already?' Lindsay said. 'Who's the unlucky victim this time?'

I ignored Lindsay's jibe. 'A guy called Sean. I haven't seen him yet but Tessa says he's nineteen and drives a sports car. A new one, not second hand.'

'Sports cars aren't good for the environment,' Iona said, but then asked eagerly, 'What kind?'

'Don't know. I just caught a glimpse. It was red anyway. No, wait a minute, I think Tessa said a BMW Z something or other.'

'Oh my God. A BMW Z4,' Lindsay said, impressed. 'He must be loaded. Or his parents anyway.'

'Yeah, he must be,' Iona agreed. 'And I suppose if he uses unleaded fuel it might be OK. Wonder what he looks like.'

'Hardly matters, does it?' Lindsay laughed. 'I mean, with a BMW Z4 he's bound to be hot. Bet Tessa hangs onto this one.'

After the meal Iona didn't come back to Lindsay's but scurried off home with a hunted look. I told Lindsay, 'It's a real shame about Iona. You know, I do think Billy could be ideal for her. I mean, they both love animals, so his going on about Monty all the time wouldn't annoy her, plus he's not bad looking and quite nice. Maybe I should talk to him. We've stayed quite friendly despite the snogging thing. What do you think?'

'I think,' Lindsay said firmly, 'you should stop trying to matchmake. I've told you before, you're hopeless at it. Remember the last time you tried to find a boyfriend for Iona?'

'Yeah, but—'

'Iona, Cat. A vegan who eats stuffed cabbage for Christmas dinner and never even touches dairy products as it "deprives young mammals of their natural sustenance". You set her up with Kevin, whose dad is a butcher and whose uncle owns a pig farm. For her birthday, instead of flowers or chocolates he gave her a haunch of veal from his dad's shop.'

'Oh God, I know I shouldn't have. I just thought he was so right in every other way.'

'*Veal*, Cat,' Lindsay said. 'Meat from baby calves slaughtered before they grow up. Iona cried for weeks.'

I flushed guiltily at the memory. Iona really had been so upset. 'I was sure I'd told Kevin that Iona didn't like meat but I must have forgotten. I won't make that mistake again.'

'And then there was Marianne,' Lindsay continued relentlessly, 'who asked you to find her a guy who was good looking, intelligent and non-sleazy. She was sick of sleazers like her last two boyfriends. You introduced her to Michael.'

'Well, c'mon, be fair. Michael was everything she'd asked for.'

'Yeah, I suppose he was,' Lindsay agreed. 'Good looking, intelligent and definitely, definitely not sleazy . . . Just a pity he was also a trainee priest.'

'I didn't know about the priest thing. Honestly. They don't wear special clothes or anything when they're training. But OK,' I conceded, 'maybe not my most successful matchmaking attempt. They didn't all end in failure though. What about Susan and Mark? That was love at first sight and they're still mad about each other.'

'Hmm, yeah, you're right. From the first moment they met they couldn't keep their hands off each other. When is the baby due? November, is it? I suppose that will dampen their ardour a bit. Babies are very demanding, I'm told.'

'I'm sure Iona will be more careful,' I said.

'Don't do it, Cat. You know it'll only end in disaster.'

But I'd already made up my mind. I was sure Billy and Iona would work out well. However, there was no point in arguing with Lindsay so I just nodded non-committally and changed the subject.

'Imagine Josh turning out to be gay – he's just so gorgeous, it's a shame.'

'Yeah, I suppose,' Lindsay said. 'But you know, Cat, I'm not so sure any more that he really is gay. I mean, he doesn't act gay. Not like my cousin Alistair, for example.'

I thought about this. Lindsay's cousin Alistair is nearly as good looking as Josh but is totally open about being gay. He's also very camp. 'Not all gay guys are like Alistair. Some of them act straight most of the time. Especially if they're keeping it a secret.'

'Hmm, I guess you're right, but really, what evidence do we have? Just that he doesn't fancy your sister. Not everyone fancies Tessa, you know.'

'Yeah they do. Name me one guy that doesn't.'

Lindsay was silent for a long time. 'Well, erm, I can't think of anyone offhand. But I'm sure there must be.'

'Yeah, there is. Your cousin Alistair.'

'OK, point taken. But really, how do we know for sure? We've only got Tessa's opinion to go on.'

'Josh is definitely gay,' I said. 'I went to see him after you left on Sunday and he sort of admitted it.'

'He did?'

'Well, not right away. At first he pretended not to know what I was talking about. But then I think he was actually glad I knew and still liked him as long as I'd keep it a secret. He says he'd like us to be friends.'

This finally convinced Lindsay, who just moaned about the waste of a reasonably tall person being out of her reach. 'But you're right, Cat. If he wasn't gay I guess Tessa would have snapped him up.'

We talked for while about what Alistair was doing (working in a clothes shop while trying to break into acting), gays in general and all the annoyingly good-looking gay actors there were. Then I told her that Josh had rung me this morning and suggested we play tennis next week and go do something else afterwards. 'But what should we do, Lindsay? What would an American gay guy like to do in Glasgow?'

'Shopping,' said Lindsay confidently. 'All gay guys love to shop and have fabulous taste. It's a known fact.'

Hmm.

The day with Josh turned out to be really good, although the shopping trip wasn't quite as successful as I'd hoped.

I enjoyed the tennis. Josh really is a fabulous coach. However, when I suggested shopping afterwards, although he agreed right away, he didn't look as keen as Lindsay had said he would be.

As we tramped along the high street he was patient but didn't seem that interested in the clothes shops and much preferred browsing in HMV, where he bought around a dozen DVDs, paying from a wallet which, I couldn't help noticing, was stuffed with £20 notes. Must be nice to have so much money you can be totally casual about the cost of things like that. He even told me he'd have bought more in the States as it was much cheaper 'back home'.

Finally I'd got everything I needed except for underwear, so when we got to La Senza, which had a sale on, I suggested to Josh that he go home and I'd finish shopping on my own, but he was reluctant.

'Sure, if you want, but it's early yet and I've got no plans for the day. I was hoping we could go for a burger or something when you're done.'

'I don't know, I don't think—'

'I'll just hang around and wait for you outside the store if you like. I won't get in the way.'

'Well, OK then. If you don't mind waiting.'

In the end, however, I decided it was a bit stupid to make him stand outside as there was no reason to be embarrassed in the circumstances, so he came in with me.

He seemed totally cool about being surrounded by bras and knickers and told me he'd been underwear shopping with girls before so I soon relaxed and in fact he was quite helpful. The shop was very busy because of the sale, and there weren't enough assistants that day, so when I was trying on bras and hadn't got the fit quite right, it was Josh who brought different sizes to my cubicle. Then, when I thought I'd got the perfect one but wasn't quite sure if I bulged a little at the side, I asked Josh to adjust the straps for me. Well, why not? He was gay, after all, so really it was just like shopping with a girlfriend.

Unfortunately this was spotted by, of all people, Naomi, the assistant head's daughter and the nosiest person in the whole school who, I realized too late, had been trying on things in the next cubicle.

'Oh God, Josh,' I apologized. 'She's bound to tell everyone about this. People will probably think we're going out together instead of just being friends.'

Josh shrugged. 'So what? Let them think what they like. It's cool.'

He really didn't seem bothered at all. Hmm, maybe it was good cover for him.

Once I'd bought my stuff we went for a burger, then afterwards he invited me back to his house to watch a DVD but I said no. I wanted to get home to dump my shopping. I'd arranged to go over to Billy's, saying I wanted to see him feed his snake as I knew this was the day Monty got his fortnightly feast. Yuck. My real reason of course was to talk to him about Iona.

Billy defrosted the tiny mouse in the microwave and placed it in front of Monty's mouth. Monty's tongue darted out and sort of sniffed the air around the soft grey creature but he didn't eat it. I suppose he just wasn't hungry enough. Thank God for that. Watching Monty swallow the wee thing whole would have been gross.

Billy put the python back in his cage and said affectionately, 'Not hungry today, Monty?' He dropped the rejected mouse in the bin. 'We'll try you with a freshly defrosted one tomorrow.'

For a moment I wondered whether Iona would approve of Monty's diet. But no, surely even Iona wouldn't expect a snake to live on lentils.

I said, 'It's a shame I didn't get to see Monty having his dinner today. I'm afraid I'll be too busy tomorrow.'

'Maybe some other time then, Cat. By the way, thanks for inviting me to Josh's party. Cool place. I had a good time.'

'Yeah. Everyone enjoyed themselves. Some people maybe a bit too much. Iona, for instance. But she's not usually like that.'

Billy laughed. 'I noticed. Loved the pole-dance.'

'And she's very pretty.'

'Yeah, great bum.'

I frowned but decided to let it pass. 'So you find her attractive then?'

Billy looked at me suspiciously. 'Are you trying to set me up with Iona?'

'No, of course—'

'Because if you are that would be great. I think she's gorgeous.'

I smiled happily. 'You do?'

'Totally.'

'You know she doesn't like meat? And, erm, can't drink very much.'

'Yeah, I know.'

'Great.'

We chatted for a bit, but I was keen to leave so I could call Iona with the good news. Billy saw me to the door and waved goodbye but as I walked along the path he suddenly called, 'Cat!'

I turned round. 'Yeah?'

'Just one last thing. Where can you buy organic condoms?'

Then he laughed and closed the door.

Damn Terry.

7

School today. Thank God. Finally I'd get to see Mr Brown.

It was weird to put on my uniform again. It's a dark-blue skirt and blazer with a white blouse and looks OK, but I wish we could wear what we want as Mr Brown always sees me in the same clothes. I know he is too mature to be influenced by looks, but still, I'd prefer to be in my favourite black when I see him. There's no chance of that though. Mr Fitzgerald, our headteacher, is really strict about uniform, and even wearing a slightly different shade of blue can get you into serious trouble.

I left earlier than Tessa as I'd arranged to meet Josh at the school gates and take him to meet Mr Fitzgerald before the start of school. Sure enough, he was already there waiting for me, leaning against the railing and looking relaxed and confident, as though the first day at a new school was no big deal. I can't say I shared his confidence: I was gobsmacked to see that he was wearing loose low-cut jeans, a baggy New York Yankees T-shirt and a baseball cap.

'Where's your uniform?' I asked. 'You'd better go home and change. Fitzgerald will have a fit.'

But Josh just assured me calmly that, yeah, his parents had bought him the school uniform but he wasn't really into the whole 'uniform idea' so he'd decided not to bother with it. 'No one wears school uniforms back home, Cat. People need to express their individuality. It's the American way.'

'But you're not in America now, Josh. Fitzgerald will go nuts.'

It was no use. Despite my warnings he insisted on going to see Fitzgerald as he was. He would just explain his views on uniform to our principal and he was sure to understand. I wasn't to stress myself. It was cool.

He just so didn't get it. Not wearing uniform at this school was like, well, turning up naked. It was that serious. Mr Fitzgerald had nearly expelled a girl last term for wearing a pink shirt two days in a row even though she'd pleaded her white blouses had got dyed because she'd accidentally washed them with her red knickers. She was warned that next time was it. It would be three strikes and she was out. I tried to explain all this to Josh but he wouldn't listen; just said he would deal with it and I wasn't to worry, although eventually he agreed to take off his cap.

When we got to Mr Fitzgerald's office I knocked and a brusque voice loudly told us, 'Enter.'

Mr Fitzgerald was seated at his desk reading some document. He looked up as we came in, peered at Josh over his reading glasses and scowled.

Seemingly oblivious to the headteacher's expression, Josh sauntered over to stand in front of the desk, extended his hand and said, 'Hi, I'm Josh. Great to meet you.'

Mr Fitzgerald looked at Josh's hand as though a large turd had been offered to him. Without moving he said slowly, 'What are you wearing?'

Josh looked down at his clothes, pretending to examine them, then held his arms out. 'Uh, jeans, a T-shirt and, um, sneakers.' When Mr Fitzgerald remained silent Josh continued, 'And, oh, yeah, boxers.' He winked at me. 'Plain blue boxers; not Stars and Stripes.'

'Josh, is it? Ah, yes, the American boy. It's good of you, Josh, to wear at least one garment that conforms to school uniform, but unfortunately that's not quite enough. Have you and your parents not been informed of our policy on school uniform?'

'Oh, yeah, but, uh, I'm not really into the whole uniform concept. I mean, yeah, it looks cute on Cat' – he smiled at me – 'but it's not really my thing.' As Mr Fitzgerald continued to glare at him, Josh went on a bit less certainly, 'I mean, this isn't the military. Right? And, um, Scotland is a democracy like the States. Freedom of choice, self-expression and all that.'

Mr Fitzgerald stood up, then he said very, very slowly, 'Scotland is indeed a democracy. So you and your parents are free to exercise your right to select another educational establishment if this one isn't to your taste. Otherwise you will report to my office tomorrow morning wearing full school uniform or you will not enter these premises ever again. Have I made myself clear?'

I thought Josh was going to argue some more so I stood on his foot and cast him a warning look.

Josh said, 'Very clear.'

Mr Fitzgerald sat down again, gave me instructions to look after Josh for the day, making sure he knew where he was to go and how to 'comport himself' when he got there, then dismissed us.

Josh gave him a sarcastic military salute before leaving but fortunately Mr Fitzgerald had started reading his document again and didn't see it.

'Why did you do that?' I hissed once we'd got out.

Josh shrugged. 'He was being a pain in the butt, Cat. I wasn't disrespecting him earlier, just trying to put my view across, but he wouldn't listen. I don't care for people pushing me around.'

Oh God, looking after Josh today wasn't going to be easy.

* * *

We got our timetables at registration. I was disappointed at first to see that English wasn't until last period, but then it would give me something to look forward to all day and I might catch a glimpse of Mr Brown in the corridor at break or lunch time.

As usual Tessa wouldn't be in any of my classes except for PE, partly because the school seems to think it a good idea to separate twins, but also because last year we opted for different subjects. Fortunately though, Josh turned out to be in the same classes as me for most of the day so at least showing him how to get to places would be straightforward.

The first two periods were OK except that Josh introduced himself to the teachers without waiting to be spoken to first, chose where he wanted to sit (he prefers the window side, where he can see the sports grounds) instead of having a seat allocated to him, and generally behaved like a person who has rights and preferences instead of someone whose status is on a par with a galley slave.

All this didn't impress the teachers, who thought he was being cheeky. Actually I'm sure Josh doesn't mean to be. From what he's told me, teachers in America aren't as formal and bossy as ours so the way he behaves is normal over there. He'd better learn what ours are like soon, or he'll never be out of trouble.

While he hadn't made himself popular with the teachers so far, he certainly hadn't put the girls in the class off and they eyed me enviously. Word has got round that I'm dating Josh, partly because I've had some tennis lessons with him and we've gone to a couple of movies together (even though I'd always invited someone else along as well so Josh could get to meet more people before starting school) – though mainly, of course, because of nosy Naomi, who'd caught us underwear shopping.

By break time I still hadn't even caught a glimpse of Mr Brown. It was so frustrating to know that at last we were in the same building but probably wouldn't see or talk to each other for hours yet.

Hmm, maybe I could just quickly dash along to the English corridor and see if he was in his classroom, or perhaps catch him walking along to the staffroom. But I still had Josh to look after. 'Let's go check out the English department, Josh.'

'What for? English isn't until last period, according to the schedule.'

I took his arm and hurried him along the corridor. 'Yeah, but, erm, English is the most important department in the whole school. You really should see it now.'

I was in luck. I could see through the glass window on the door that Mr Brown was still in his classroom sorting out some jotters. I was considering knocking and trying to think up some excuse for seeing him when he got up and walked towards the door. Seeing me through the window, he smiled (he really has a gorgeous smile) and opened the door. 'Hi, Cat. What can I do for you?' He looked at Josh and smiled again. 'I take it from your outfit that you're the new American boy. Great T-shirt but I bet it didn't go down too well with Mr Fitzgerald.'

Josh shook his hand. 'Hi, I'm Josh. Great to meet you. And, uh, no, not too good.'

'Nice to meet you too, Josh. I believe you'll be in my class period six so we can have a talk then about how to integrate your studies in the States with what we do here.' Mr Brown turned his attention to me again. 'So, Cat, what was it you wanted to see me about?'

'What? Oh, erm, yeah, the reading list. Can I have the new reading list for the year?'

'Can't wait until sixth period to find out?' He looked at Josh. 'Cat's a very keen reader. And, erm' – he caught my eye again – 'enjoys a very diverse range of reading material. I don't think I've ever known a pupil with such eclectic taste, in fact.' He smiled at me, his eyes crinkling like they had in the bookshop. 'Just wait here a moment and I'll dig out the list from my files.'

He went back into the classroom, leaving Josh and me at the open door. As I watched him, all I could think of was that *he remembered* our meeting in W H Smith. Every detail. It must have been just as important to him as it was to me. I was interrupted in this lovely thought by Josh. 'Hey, Cat, I need to go to the bathroom. Is there one near here?'

'You mean toilet?' I said, frowning. Mr Brown had found the list and was coming back.

'Yeah, whatever, I need to pee.'

'Don't be vulgar,' I hissed, then I took the list from Mr Brown's hand, allowing my fingers to brush his lightly and lingering as long as I dared. 'Thanks, Mr Brown. I really appreciate all the trouble you've gone to for me. So how do you decide on the reading list each year? Is it always the same or—'

'Cat,' Josh interrupted again, 'I really need—'

'Along there.' I waved a hand distractedly in the direction of the toilets. 'On the right.'

'Thanks, I'll, uh, catch up with you later. Nice meeting you, Mr Brown.'

As Josh loped off I continued my conversation with Mr Brown but unfortunately he soon had to go. He told me he wanted to grab a coffee before the end of break but I'm sure the real reason was to avoid people getting suspicious if they saw us chatting too long. Maybe I should have suggested carrying on our talk in his class-room but then we might have been spotted through the windows. The trouble with this school is that there is almost no privacy. That and the nasty-minded gossips who wouldn't understand our relationship.

Still, at least I'd seen him and talked to him, so when he left I just stood in the corridor and replayed the whole encounter in my mind.

'Hey, thanks, Cat.' *When had Josh got here? I hadn't*

noticed him walking towards me. 'So, OK, maybe I should have, like, been more specific, but I thought you might have figured that I wanted directions to the guys' toilets and not the girls'.'

'Oops, sorry, Josh, I wasn't thinking. You didn't go in, did you?'

'Yeah. The door was open and I didn't look at the sign so now I've probably got a reputation as some retard or pervert Yank. Take your pick.' Josh smiled ruefully. 'But, hey, at least I now know where to get Tampax should I ever need them.'

I giggled and apologized again but Josh interrupted me. 'Please, Cat, just tell me where the bathroom – sorry, *guys'* toilets are.'

I told him but just then the bell for the end of break rang. 'You'd better leave it till later, Josh. It's Mr Smith next and he hates pupils who aren't punctual. If you're late first time you'll make a really bad impression.'

'If I pee my pants I'll make a really bad impression too. Yeah, I know' – here Josh imitated my voice (very poorly, I might add) – ' "Don't be vulgar, Josh," but I really gotta go. Don't want to get a reputation as an *incontinent* Yankee retard and pervert.'

Mr Smith, the history teacher, wasn't pleased, and even though Josh was only a few minutes late and was new he gave him a detention on Tuesday. I felt bad as I'd promised Josh's mum that I'd look after him at school. I've met her a few times over at Josh's and she's really nice. Very easy to talk to (as long as it's not about shagging!). I resolved to take better care of him.

At lunch time I told Josh the school cafeteria was rubbish and no one ate there since it started some stupid 'healthy eating' initiative. All salads and no chips – a menu only my mum could enjoy. Instead we met up with Lindsay and headed for the chippy.

I spotted Tessa on the way there, sitting on a wall outside the Italian café. As usual she was surrounded by a group of boys, all desperately trying to chat her up. One of them handed her a wrapped baguette that he'd no doubt been delegated to fetch for her. He refused the money she offered him for it and was rewarded with a smile. Poor guy looked delighted with himself but I seriously doubted if this meant he was getting anywhere with her. I don't think Tessa bought her own lunch at school more than a half dozen times last term and she didn't date any of the hopeful boys who treated her. I waved over to her but she didn't notice me. Since we never spend lunch time together anyway – I prefer not to get in the way of her fan club – I just hurried on.

The queue was a nightmare but Peter had got there early and kept a place for us. Scott was just in front of him, and to Peter's annoyance Lindsay chatted him up as we waited.

Scott is one of those tall, lanky guys who can eat a zillion calories without gaining an ounce and I looked on with envy as he ordered deep-fried pizza and Mars bar.

Not that I would have wanted what he'd ordered, which is quite minging – but just imagine scoffing exactly what you liked without even a twinge of guilt!

As the assistant dropped the pizza and Mars bar into the vat of boiling fat Josh looked on with horrified disbelief. 'You guys *French fry* your pizza and, Jeez, your candy?'

Josh was a bit wary of ordering anything after that, worried that everything might be cooked like Scott's lunch, so I chose for him. He enjoyed the chips with curry sauce more than he'd expected, especially as apparently he'd imagined he'd be eating soggy crisps. We ate our lunch on the way back to school, then, after we'd finished, Peter's friends suggested a game of five-a-side football and invited Josh to play.

Josh was confused at first as he thought they were talking about American football (which is more like rugby), but when he saw them start to kick the ball about he understood.

'Oh, you mean soccer. I've never played soccer – back home it's usually just chicks who are into it but, hey, yeah, I'll give it a try.'

Oh my God, he *so* should not have said that. I tried to stop him going on the pitch but he wouldn't listen to me. He was completely useless at football but that wasn't the point. Even his own team, furious about the soccer being 'just for girls' insult, continuously fouled him, tripping him up and kicking him, so that at the end of the game he limped off the field covered in mud and probably bruises. He was pretty cool about it though: afterwards he just said to his 'team mates' and me, 'I really shouldn't have made that remark about soccer being for girls. Right?'

We all chorused, 'Right.'

I was mad at Peter's friends for getting Josh in such a state though. What would I say to his mum? However, oddly enough the football disaster seems to have acted as some kind of male bonding thing as they were all really friendly afterwards. And guys say girls are illogical and difficult to understand. Go figure (as Josh would say).

Josh cleaned up as best he could, which made him very late for class again so he now has detention on Wednesday too. As first days go this wasn't working out too well, although Josh seemed to think everything was going fine – 'It's cool – relax, Cat' – and I was beginning to wonder what he'd been like at school in the States. Maybe the trouble he'd got into hadn't been anything to do with his being gay after all.

Finally it was period six and I put all worries about Josh aside as I prepared to enjoy a whole hour of Mr Brown's company – not exclusive company, but still, after the long, long summer holidays when I hardly saw him at all it was a delicious luxury and I planned to savour every moment.

We had to wait outside his door for a Third Year class to file out. They took their time about it and I felt like telling them to hurry up for God's sake, they were cutting into my time with Mr Brown, but wisely restrained myself. I was surprised to see Scott waiting with us but then I remembered he'd failed English last year so must be repeating. Lindsay will be gutted she's not in our English class, although I've often felt relieved about this. Knowing me as well as she does, she might have guessed my secret if she saw me regularly around Mr Brown.

At last we were in. Mr Brown suggested that Josh sit beside me so I could help him catch up with the course work we'd started at the end of last term. Then he added, 'But I hear you two are already friends anyway.'

Oh no. Don't tell me Mr Brown had heard this stupid rubbish about Josh and me dating. 'He's just a friend, Mr Brown. Not my boyfriend,' I told him firmly.

'Fine, Cat,' Mr Brown said.

But I still wasn't convinced that he completely believed me. 'No, really he is. I don't have a boyfriend. I wouldn't do that.' Oh God, I almost said *to you.*

Mr Brown smiled. 'I think you've made yourself clear. But you will help Josh with the work he's missed, won't you?'

His relieved smile told me I'd finally managed to convince him. Poor Mr Brown. He must have felt so upset when he heard that ridiculous rumour.

Later he set us some work, a pretty easy inter-pretation, so I was able to answer the questions while watching him do some marking at the front. Some people were chatting – Mr Brown doesn't mind us talking as long as we finish our work on time – but I was happy just to bask in the pleasure of being near him again after so long and daydream about how wonderful it would be when we were together at last.

I was rudely interrupted by Naomi, who nudged me and hissed, 'Just a friend, my arse. Not when you let him see you in your underwear and fix your bra strap for you.'

'Oh, Naomi,' I hissed right back, 'don't tell me you didn't see the bit where we had full sex in the cubicle then invited everyone to watch on CCTV. That was *so* cool. You really missed out.' The people around us laughed so I pressed home my advantage. 'It's also about as believable as all the other nasty little rumours you spread about people.'

'I saw what I saw,' Naomi huffed.

Mr Brown looked up from his marking. 'Is anything wrong, Cat?'

Honestly, he's always so protective of me. 'No, nothing I can't handle, sir.' I looked at Naomi as I said this. She scowled at me but then looked away.

I decided to get on with my work and ignore Naomi but then tosser Scott started. 'I believe you, Cat. If you say Josh is just a good friend then that's what he is. Can I be your friend too? We could be *bosom* buddies.' Here he made a gesture like cupping his hands around my boobs.

Hilarious. Peter is right: Scott is a tosser. I don't know what Lindsay sees in him. Well, I do, all six feet two inches, but really, does she have to be so, well, one-dimensional in her taste in boys?

I ignored Scott but unfortunately Josh didn't. Instead he stood up, pushed Scott's desk away from him, and said, loud enough for the whole class to hear, 'Why don't you just **** off, asshole.'

The whole class. Including Mr Brown. So now Josh has detention on Tuesday, Wednesday and Thursday. Brilliant.

I felt bad when I said goodbye to Josh at the end of school. What an awful start. Nearly expelled before school even began, black and blue after a game of football, and detentions until Friday, but Josh seemed more upbeat.

'I wasn't expelled, Cat. I learned a bit about soccer and made some friends, plus I've no detention on Friday. Sounds pretty good to me.'

You've got to hand it to Americans. They're an optimistic lot. But I had a feeling that today wasn't going to be the end of Josh's problems. Or mine.

8

On Tuesday Josh turned up in uniform. I thought he looked really good but he complained he felt like he was in a straitjacket. 'Why do they make us wear this shit?'

After reporting to Mr Fitzgerald Josh loosened his tie and unbuttoned his shirt collar. 'At least I can breathe now. Hey, Cat, if I survive the week here, how about coming over to my place on Friday? We could have some pizza and maybe watch a DVD to celebrate.'

'OK. But only if you listen to my advice: keep out of trouble, and don't get any more detentions.'

'Yes, ma'am.'

I laughed. 'I suppose that must have sounded a bit bossy.'

'No, ma'am.'

'Stop it, Josh.'

'Yes, ma—'

Josh ducked to avoid the slap aimed at his head.

When safely out of range he said, 'Not bossy at all. Don't know how I got that dumb idea.'

Whatever Josh thought of my bossiness he seemed to have listened to my warnings, as he made it through the day without getting into trouble with anyone. Although I did have to remind him about detention with Smith at four.

'Any chance he might have forgotten about it, Cat? I did.'

'Smith? No chance,' I said.

After Josh reluctantly trailed off to detention, Tessa caught up with me, saying she wanted to walk home with me. She almost never does this now so I was immediately suspicious that she had some ulterior motive and I wasn't wrong.

'It's only twenty pounds, Cat. Then I'll have enough for the shoes I need to go with the tangerine skirt I got last week.'

'You don't need tangerine shoes to go with the skirt, Tessa. Black is fine. Classy.'

'Not classy enough for Sean and his friends,' Tessa sulked. 'Honestly, they're all loaded – or their parents are anyway. I can't be seen in the same thing twice. Even shoes.'

'Look, Tessa, I'm sure Sean won't mind what you wear. You look fantastic in anything. He isn't going to dump you because you're not wearing tangerine shoes, for God's sake.'

'Please, Cat.'

'Why don't you ask Mum or Dad?'

'I have. They said no.'

We were interrupted by some idiot Sixth Years, who shouted and whistled at Tessa from an old battered Ford Escort then slowed to a halt beside us. The driver was Phil Stuart, a sleazy friend of Scott's. He leaned out of the window and said, 'Want a lift home, girls?'

Tessa eyed the car contemptuously. 'Girls who look like me don't accept lifts in cars that look like that.'

If Phil had been nice I might have felt sorry for him when his friends laughed but as it was I enjoyed Tessa's put-down. When they drove off Tessa continued her pleading. 'Sean's just so right for me, Cat. I need every-thing to be perfect. At least at first. It's a sort of investment.'

I resisted for a bit longer but Tessa can be quite persuasive when she wants to be and eventually I was somehow convinced that my sister's whole future happi-ness depended on the successful purchase of a pair of size five and a half tangerine wedges. Today.

Once we got home I gave her the money (which meant I only had a fiver to last me until the end of the month) and she dashed off to the shops. I knew I'd probably never get the cash back as Tessa's idea of a 'loan' is a bit flexible, but to be fair dating seems to cost a lot of money. Not an expense I've ever had to worry about.

After she'd gone I made myself a cup of tea and opened a packet of Maltesers I'd bought at lunch time but kept as a treat for later. Mum came into the kitchen as I was starting the packet and stared at it. Immediately I felt guilty for eating chocolate before dinner as I know she disapproves, but she surprised me by saying, 'Oh, Maltesers. They're not too high in calories, are they?'

'Erm, no, Mum, not too high.'

'About a hundred and eighty calories a pack. Am I right?'

I squinted sideways at the information on the packet. 'Yeah, well done, Mum. You're right. A hundred and eighty.'

'So how many Maltesers in the bag then?'

'I'm, erm, not sure. It doesn't say.'

Mum smiled at me. 'Don't be silly, Catriona, you can count them, can't you?'

'You want me to count them?' I asked incredulously. Mum nodded.

And she calls me silly. For God's sake. I took them out and counted them onto a plate. 'Eighteen.'

'So ten calories per Malteser then? That's not too wicked. I think I'll indulge myself. May I have one?'

I nodded towards the plate of Maltesers and she helped herself to one. One single Malteser.

'Delicious,' she said. 'I'd forgotten just how nice they are.'

'Have another, Mum.'

'No, no. One is quite enough. I don't want to get fat. Besides, I'm full.'

Then she went off into the sitting room and I watched her in wonder. I've always known Mum had a lot of willpower with food, but honestly, a person who can eat a single Malteser and stop! Everyone knows that they're mainly little bubbles of air and about as substantial as pixie dust; most normal people could eat a truck load of them and still have room for a double fish supper afterwards. To eat one Malteser then say 'No more for me thanks' – it's, well, awesome. I also now know that I will never, ever be as slim as Mum if this is the kind of discipline it requires. I ate the other seventeen Maltesers. Delicious. Then I made dinner for Dad and me.

Tessa got back from shopping just after we'd finished eating. I couldn't help noticing that she'd bought two new tops as well as the tangerine shoes. She saw me looking at them and said, 'Oh, erm, I discovered I'd a bit more money than I thought so I couldn't resist these. They're gorgeous, aren't they?'

I didn't know whether to laugh at my own idiocy or slap her. By the time I'd definitely decided on the slapping option she'd disappeared upstairs. Typical Tessa.

Josh rang before I went to bed. Although it was quite late we chatted for ages. Somehow I find him so easy to talk to and he always makes me laugh. When I'd finally said goodnight and was about to hang up he asked, 'Are we still on for Friday if I'm a good student?'

'Maybe, but only if you promise not to call me ma'am.'

'Deal. Goodnight, Cat.'

I wasn't sure whether he'd make it to the end of the week without getting into some sort of trouble but found myself really hoping that he would.

It's Friday and Josh has kept his word. He didn't have detention today so I walked back to his house with him straight after school. I'd suggested inviting Lindsay and Marianne (who lives near Josh) too as neither of them was doing anything, but he just laughed and said one chick was all he could handle tonight.

His mum wasn't in: she'd left a note in the kitchen saying she'd popped out to the stores and would be back soon. She'd also left a plateful of warm, home-baked chocolate chip cookies on the table. Josh smiled. 'She still bakes cookies for me even though I gave up cookies and milk after school about seven years ago.'

He asked if I wanted a drink, then took two Cokes from the fridge, grabbed a bag of pretzels from the cupboard and offered me some.

I shook my head. 'I've had pretzels before but I'm not really sure whether I like them or not. Can I have one of your mum's cookies? God, a mum who bakes for you. Amazing!'

He passed me the plate and popped a few pretzels

into his mouth. 'Know what, Cat? I've been eating these since I was two but I'm still not sure whether I like them or not either.' He tried some more. 'Nah, still not sure.'

When we'd finished our snack Josh asked whether I wanted to watch a DVD in the sitting room or his bedroom. I said his bedroom so that we wouldn't be in his mum's way when she got back. Picking up my school bag, I followed him upstairs, where he showed me a huge selection of DVDs.

'Why don't you look through these and see if there's anything you like,' Josh said. 'If not we can always rent something.'

'I'm sure I'll find something among this lot. God, you like movies, don't you?'

'Yeah, it's what I'd like to work in when I leave college. Not acting; I'd like to direct. My dad won't take it seriously though so I'll probably have to do law school first.'

Josh left me to browse while he sat at his computer and checked his email.

I soon found a DVD I liked but Josh was still busy reading and answering email. He offered to stop what he was doing and watch the movie with me but he was obviously catching up with news from all his friends back in the States so I suggested he finish off while I did my maths homework. It was the only homework I had for the whole weekend, so doing it now would get it out of the way.

I sat on Josh's bed, spread out my work and started on the problems while he tapped away on his computer. Normally I struggle with maths but this exercise wasn't too bad and soon I'd completed my last question and was checking over my answers. I noticed I'd made a mistake in my diagram for question three and looked in my pencil case for my rubber but it was gone. Damn – now I remembered. I'd lent it to Lindsay, who as usual had forgotten to give me it back. I put my work down and sat back. I'd just have to correct it when I got home. But then it occurred to me that Josh would probably have one.

I looked over at him. 'Have you got a rubber, Josh?'

Josh turned away from his computer screen, then said in a puzzled tone, 'Excuse me?'

'Have you got a rubber?'

'Well, um, yeah.'

But he made no move to give me it.

'Very funny, Josh,' I said. 'OK, when I said, *Have you got a rubber?* I really meant, *Have you got a rubber and if so can I borrow it please?*'

'You want to *borrow* a rubber?'

'Yeah,' I said with exaggerated patience. This was so not funny and Josh was starting to annoy me. 'It's kinda, you know, why I said *Can I borrow a rubber?*'

'Well, um, yeah, I suppose, but, uh, why do you want a rubber? I mean, uh, right now?'

Totally exasperated, I threw out my arms palms forward. 'What do you think I want a rubber for? What do most people want a rubber for? Now can you just give me one? *Please?'*

Angrily I turned away and, picking up the DVD I'd selected, pretended to read the blurb again. Out of the corner of my eye I saw Josh come towards me. I was surprised when he opened the drawer of his bedside table. Odd place to keep a rubber.

Then Josh handed me a condom.

I stared at it. And stared at it. Then I looked at Josh. 'And just how am I supposed to rub out my isosceles triangle with that?'

So anyway, now I know what the American slang for a condom is and in future if I feel the need to rub something out and am speaking to an American I will ask for an eraser.

Both of us were howling with laughter when we realized what had happened. Josh had collapsed on the bed beside me and went over our conversation.

'Jeez, Cat, when you asked to *borrow* my rubber, like you guys re-used them or something. Totally grossed me out.'

'And when,' I said, corpsing again with laughter, 'and when, Oh My God, I said, *Well, what do you think I want a condom for? What do most people want it for? . . .'*

We were both laughing so loud we didn't hear Josh's mum coming home. The first I knew she was here was when, after knocking just once, she opened the bedroom door and came in. She smiled and said, 'You guys sure sound like you're having fun.' But then her smile froze and her whole body stiffened as she spotted the condom in my hand. She said tersely, 'Josh, I'd like a word with you downstairs. Now.' Then she left.

I wasn't worried as I'm sure Josh could explain our misunderstanding to his mum. She's really nice and would probably find it funny. But it occurred to me that his mum didn't realize he was gay, which is kind of sad. The other thing that occurred to me is that Josh must not only fancy other boys but actually have sex with them, or at least plan to if he keeps condoms in his room. And I just couldn't help thinking it was a bit minging.

His mum enjoyed the story about the rubber mis-understanding but nevertheless suggested that we watch the movie in the sitting room, where we'd be 'more comfortable'. God, if she only knew how little need there was to chaperone us!

Josh's dad came home shortly after the movie was finished, while we were eating pizza in the kitchen. He said 'Hi' to me quite pleasantly but asked to speak with Josh alone in the library. He didn't sound pleased.

I heard them arguing – Josh's dad had just found out about all the detentions he'd got this week. His mum came into the kitchen while this was going on. She said, 'Don't worry about this, Catriona. It will blow over. Josh and his father are both very strong-willed so they clash quite a lot. You get used to it.' Then she sighed. 'I'll sure be happy when the teenage years are done though.'

A couple of minutes later Josh returned. He tried a bit of pizza but it was cold so he tossed it in the bin and said, 'Shit!'

'You want me to pop the other piece in the microwave for you, honey?' his mum asked.

'Thanks, yeah,' Josh said. 'After that, how about you tell Dad he's not everyone's boss once he leaves the office – or better still, just divorce him. I must be the only one of my friends whose parents aren't divorced at least once. It's embarrassing.'

'Divorce your dad? Sure, honey. I wouldn't want you shamed in front of your peers because you're the only one with an intact family. Soon as George Clooney asks me to run off with him I'll get my lawyer on to it.'

Josh laughed, his bad mood gone already. He gave his mum a hug and kissed her on the cheek. I envied how easy and affectionate they were with each other. My mum wasn't the cuddly kind. She never liked being hugged in case it messed up her make-up or creased her outfit. Dad used to be more affectionate but once I turned twelve and started wearing a bra he never really cuddled me any more. Still, at least he's not as bossy as Josh's dad. Just as well Josh has a really nice mum as his dad seems awful. It's a pity he hasn't told her he's gay. I'm sure that, unlike his dad, she'd be understanding.

We finished off the pizza, then Josh told me he'd had to change our tennis lesson from Saturday morning to Sunday as they'd accidentally double-booked us.

'Is that still OK with you, Cat?'

'Yeah, I think so, but could you give me a ring tomorrow?'

'Excuse me?'

'I said, yeah, probably, but I'd like you to give me a ring first.'

Josh looked puzzled. 'You want me to give you a ring?'

'Yes please.'

'Well, um, OK, I guess. But, uh, what kind of ring?'

'What?'

'Well, I get a pretty generous allowance but, hey, if it's diamonds you want I'd need to save up for a while.'

'You idiot, Josh.' I giggled. 'I meant a ring on the telephone.'

'Oh, yeah, right. You want me to *call* you.'

'Finally! Yeah, I want you to call me. You know, you're going to have to learn proper English now you're living here.'

'Yes, ma'am.'

'Stop it, Josh,' I warned, but I couldn't help smiling.

We sat around for ages after that, just talking and laughing, mainly about people at our school. I'm discovering that the more I get to know Josh the more I really like him. He's just a very nice guy: funny, kind, and while he is pretty confident he's not at all big-headed.

Thinking about this at home later after Josh's mum

dropped me off, I was ashamed of my disgust at what he does (or would like to do) with boys. After all, I guess it's perfectly natural if you're gay. It was just my stupid prejudice. I'd cure myself of it – and I knew the perfect way to rid myself of my homophobic tendencies. Yes. I'm going to find Josh a boyfriend.

9

'You're not seriously going to try and find Josh a boyfriend, Cat?' said Lindsay, frowning. 'You've had enough disasters with straight matchmaking, for God's sake. Please tell me you're not going to do this.'

'Why are you always so negative, Lindsay? OK, I've had a few failures in the past, it's true.'

'A few,' Lindsay snorted.

'But this time,' I continued, ignoring her, 'there shouldn't be any problem. Josh isn't vegan or even vegetarian, I'll definitely not set him up with a priest even if I have to veto any Catholic boys to make sure. And of course this time pregnancy won't be, erm, an issue.'

'Well, yeah, that's true, I suppose,' Lindsay conceded grudgingly. 'Nobody's likely to get pregnant this time. But you're bound to screw up some other way.'

'C'mon, you're being a bit unfair. I *have* had some successes. Well, one anyway. You've got to admit Iona and Billy are still really happy. They're so loved up they're even planning to adopt an orang-utan together.'

Lindsay continued to argue with me but I didn't pay much attention to her. Instead I spent much of the following week thinking about who might be suitable for Josh. The real problem was that I didn't know many gay guys. There was Martin in my form: when he was seven years old he told his parents and his teacher that he was gay. He had an awful time at primary and for most of secondary because of this admission, although people seem to have accepted him now and he doesn't get bullied any more. I remember asking him last year how he knew he was gay at seven since no one fancies anyone at seven. He told me with a weary sigh that being gay isn't just about sex. It's about identity. When I read *Cinderella* didn't I imagine myself marrying the handsome prince? Well, so did he.

Unfortunately Martin has been going out with Steve since last year's Christmas dance at school. This was a real blow to Lindsay as Steve is over six foot tall and really good looking. He'd only started at our school that year and before the Christmas dance no one knew he was gay so Lindsay had her heart set on getting off with him. Anyway, whatever, Martin and Steve are very loved up so there's no chance for Josh there.

There are quite a few boys I suspect are gay, but like Josh they're not saying and I don't want to risk embarrassment by making wrong assumptions. Anyway, perhaps it would be better if Josh dated someone out of school as there would be less chance of anyone finding out.

Like Alistair, for instance. Yes! Why hadn't I thought of this before? Lindsay's gay cousin Alistair would be ideal. He's nineteen and used to go to boarding school. Although he's really smart he chose not to go to university and is now working while he tries to break into acting, so far without much success. Although obviously camp, he's a nice guy and a great laugh. Alistair had just split up with his boyfriend Nigel and was gutted. Maybe Josh would help him get over it.

Of course, Nigel would also be free now – according to Lindsay, no one else was involved in the break-up. He has a great body since he is always working out at the gym but I don't know whether Josh would really be attracted to him or not as he always wears leather jeans (even on hot sunny days) with vests, plus stupid-looking studded collar and wrist bands.

No, Nigel is a bit brainless, but Alistair? Smart, funny Alistair? I suppose at nearly twenty he's a bit old for Josh but then I'm in love with Mr Brown, who's twenty-five. It really depends on the person and I think, like me, Josh is probably mature enough to handle the age gap. Yeah, it could work. I didn't discuss my plan with Lindsay right away in case she tried to put me off. Instead I decided to tell her about it once Josh and Alistair had been introduced.

After a bit of persuasion I managed to get Josh to agree to come shopping with me again after my tennis lesson on the following Saturday: I planned to pay a visit to the boutique where Alistair worked; then we'd all have lunch together.

Peering outside that Saturday morning, I realized it was raining. I curled up under my duvet, looking forward to a blissful, lazy, long lie-in, assuming that Josh would have cancelled our lesson, but then I found that he'd called to say he'd organized an indoor tennis court and I'd have to move fast as he'd booked it a half-hour earlier. Bloody hell, if Josh was anything to go by, Americans were a determined 'can do' lot. Unfortunately.

My tennis is definitely improving though, and I do enjoy it. Josh is so patient and encouraging. Maybe next summer I'll join the club again. After all, there's no law that says you have to wear white pleated mini-skirts or shorts. Anyway, I think I've actually lost a bit of weight recently. I can't be sure as at the end of last term I decided to give up weighing myself (it was just too depressing) but my clothes feel a little looser now. Maybe the extra exercise I'm getting is doing something. Anyway, as Tessa has told me on several occasions, 'At least your fat doesn't wobble, Cat.' I was far from overwhelmed by my sister's flattery, but I suppose she means well and it's true that firm fat is better than wobbly.

Before visiting Alistair's boutique Josh wanted to go

to a sports shop, where he looked at some tennis rackets and talked to me about the pros and cons of different types. He selected a couple and handed them to me, asking what I thought of the 'feel' of them. Finally he chose one and paid for it. Eighty pounds. Bloody hell. And there was nothing wrong with the one he had as far as I could see.

But I was even more gobsmacked when he presented the racket to me with a flourish, telling me it was my 'reward for being a good student'.

There was no way I could accept it and I told him so. We argued for a bit. He wanted to give me a present – what was wrong with that? There weren't any strings attached (ha ha). Anyway, I couldn't keep using my sister's racket. I needed one of my own. Finally I agreed to check with my parents if it was OK but warned him that I'd probably have to return it so he should keep the receipt.

We got to Alistair's shop just before his lunch break, as I'd planned. He was behind the counter at the cash desk. At first all seemed to go well. Alistair eyed Josh the way most people would look at a large helping of chocolate cheesecake with double whipped cream after they'd been on a starvation diet. He shook Josh's hand, holding it much longer than you normally would. 'Oh, hi, Josh. I'm *so* pleased to meet you.' Then he turned to me. 'Now just where did you find this gorgeous guy, Cat? You lucky, lucky girl.'

'I told you on the phone. He's my dad's boss's son and we're just friends.'

I hadn't told Alistair that Josh was gay as I couldn't go back on my promise to keep it a secret but I sort of assumed that Alistair would be able to tell. But, OK, maybe not immediately. I went on, 'So is it your lunch break now? Can we go? I'm kinda hungry.'

Alistair looked past us – someone was waiting to pay. 'I'll just serve this customer. Why don't you two go on ahead and bag a seat. Prêt à Manger is always positively hoaching at this time.'

I nodded my agreement and turned to go, only to almost walk into, Oh My God, Mr Brown. He put out his hands to steady me. Actually touched me. But unfortunately this was only fleeting, and then he just said, 'Oh, hi, Cat. Sorry, I was standing too close behind you.' He turned to Josh. 'Hi, Josh.'

Josh nodded. 'Hi.'

Flustered by the unexpected meeting, I squeaked, 'Oh hiya, Mr Brown.' I took a deep breath to calm myself and lowered my voice to a normal pitch. 'It's OK, it was my fault really. I should have looked where I was going. So, erm, what are you doing here then?'

Mr Brown raised one eyebrow and smiled. 'Er, shopping?'

'Oh, yeah, well, of course. What I meant was, erm, what kind of shopping? That is, I mean, *obviously* clothes shopping, but what kind of clothes? I mean, what are you actually buying?' Even as I said this I realized how nosy it must sound.

'Well, *actually* just these.' He held up two pairs of black boxers.

I flushed crimson and looked at my toes. No one said anything, so to fill the embarrassed silence I replied, 'They're, erm, really nice. Er, lovely.' When Mr Brown made no comment I babbled on, 'Black's my favourite colour, you know. It's very slimming and, erm, doesn't show the dirt so you don't have to wash clothes as often.' *Oh God, what was I saying?* 'Not that you'd let underwear get dirty of course. I was talking about, well, coats and jackets and things. Dry cleaning really. Not boxers, which you'd wear once then wash. Obviously.'

I looked up. Mr Brown was grinning at me. He said, 'Obviously.'

Josh rescued me. 'C'mon, Cat, let's go get some food. See ya, Mr Brown.' He checked his watch, then, looking at Alistair, said, 'It's a quarter after one. We'll grab a table and see you in, what – five, ten minutes? You want us to order for you?'

Alistair told us he'd be along in ten minutes and he'd decide what he wanted to eat when he got there.

Completely mortified by now, I mumbled 'Bye' to Mr Brown and hurried off to Prêt à Manger. What an idiot I'd made of myself. I cringed. Bumping into him (literally) like that had been so unexpected I'd no time to prepare what to say. And when he showed me his underwear! Well, not the underwear he was wearing of course, but still.

Mmmm, black boxers. They were nice. Very classy.

'Look, Cat,' Josh interrupted, 'they've got pastrami on rye. I love pastrami. What are you having?'

I had the same as Josh, and although it was good, for once I was too distracted to focus on the food.

Alistair soon joined us and proceeded to tuck into two large baguettes filled with chicken, ham, egg and mayonnaise, followed by banana cake for dessert. Why, oh, why can guys eat so much and still be slim?

I told him about Mr Brown being our English teacher. He said that he knew 'David' was a teacher as he came to the shop quite often and sometimes chatted to the staff. Everyone had wondered how he could afford to buy stuff like that on a teacher's salary as the clothes cost a fortune – 'And most of it tat of course, Cat. Don't tell anyone I said that. Although he's got good taste actually and can sift the chic from the shit.'

Alistair went on to say it was rumoured that Mr Brown's family had money and that he just taught because he wanted to.

This would be so like Mr Brown. Teaching for the love of the job rather than more mundane stuff like money. I questioned Alistair (subtly, I hope), trying out find out if there were particular days or times when he shopped there. Not that I was going to stalk him or anything. It would just be nice to meet him 'casually' in the shop when I was prepared so that I didn't come across like a complete idiot as I had today. But there didn't seem to be any set pattern to his visits. However, Alistair did mention that Mr Brown was interested in his amateur drama group and had said he might go along to watch some time. I made a mental note to ask Alistair about this in the future and perhaps accidentally-on-purpose come along at the same time, but I let it drop for now as I didn't want to appear too interested.

Instead I concentrated on trying to get Josh and Alistair together. However, over lunch, although Alistair paid a lot of attention to Josh, he didn't really flirt with him the way I'd seen him do with guys he fancied; he just gossiped waspishly about his manageress.

'She's just so definitely had Botox. She still screeches like a hyena with a hernia but can't scowl at us all any more. Of course she's denying it. And I'm thinking, why just Botox? I mean, have you seen her nose? Bigger than a pelican's bill and almost the same shape. Now, I ask you, if you're going to spend money on cosmetic enhancement why not a nose job first? I mean, *please* – Botox. With a nose like that? Why bother?'

'I don't think Josh is that interested in cosmetic surgery, Alistair,' I interrupted. 'He's more into sport and, like you, he's very interested in film and loves going to the movies.'

But Alistair didn't take the hint, and instead of suggesting he and Josh go see a film together, just chatted about film-making and what various celebrities were up to. 'Did you see the dress she had on at the opening? Teal-blue silk sheath, very simple, very chic, but of course probably cost more than the gross domestic product of Scotland. But her co-star. Ugh. Flowery tapestry. I ask you. I suppose she was going for the peasant look but she looked more like she'd dressed in her grandmother's curtains. *Quel horreur!'*

I was beginning to suspect Alistair couldn't tell that Josh was gay after all. When Josh went off to get another Coke I said to him, 'We really are just friends you know. I'm not, erm, *his type.'*

This was as much as I dared say but Alistair still didn't pick up on it. 'Just friends, Cat? You have *got* to be joking. Trust me: no guy buys anyone an eighty-quid present unless he's planning to shag them at some point. You lucky girl, Cat. He is just *so* cute. Mmmm, I'd grab that one fast before someone else gets their talons into him.'

Talking with Josh later didn't prove hopeful either.

'So what did you think of Alistair then?'

Josh shrugged. 'Seemed an interesting guy. Good sense of humour.'

'He's gay, you know.'

Josh raised his eyebrows in mock surprise and said sarcastically, 'No kidding. I'd never have guessed.'

'He's recently broken up with his boyfriend. Alistair was gutted at the time but, erm, I think he's ready to move on now.'

'Good.'

'Alistair plays tennis too. Or he did anyway. I think he was quite good at it.'

'Oh really? Well, um, OK, maybe I'll give him a game sometime.'

And that was it. Josh changed the subject and never mentioned Alistair again.

When I got home I told Mum about the tennis racket, but to my surprise she didn't tell me to return it. 'Eighty pounds, Cat? That's a lot of money. Of course, the family is wealthy. Still, Josh must be very keen on you.'

'I've told you before, Mum, we're just friends.'

Mum beamed at me. 'Oh, Catriona, you are still so naïve. No boy spends this amount of time and money on a girl unless he's interested in her. Very interested.'

'You don't understand, Mum—'

She laughed. 'Of course I don't. What would I know about boys? Oh, by the way, Catriona, I notice you've lost a bit of weight recently. Well done. Of course, love can do that to a girl—'

'Mum, stop it!'

It's so frustrating. Finally Mum approves of me but it's for reasons that are all in her imagination. No doubt when she finds out that I haven't managed to land myself a rich boyfriend after all she'll go back to thinking of me as the plain, disappointing daughter I've always been to her.

Back at school on Monday I confessed to Lindsay about my failed matchmaking plan. Luckily she didn't seem too annoyed.

'Oh, God,' she said. 'I knew you'd try something like this. There's no stopping you once you get one of these stupid ideas in your head.'

'What do you think went wrong though? I know Alistair thought Josh was gorgeous but straight. But Josh definitely knew Alistair was gay yet he didn't seem interested.'

Lindsay shrugged. 'Maybe the "chemistry" just wasn't right, Cat. You can't expect Josh to fancy someone just because the guy's gay. You don't fancy guys just because they're straight, after all, do you? Now tell me you're going to drop this mad scheme.'

Hmm, maybe. Actually I hadn't given up hope as I'd heard over the weekend that Steve and Martin had had a big argument. However, a few days later all thoughts of my matchmaking project went out of my mind because I heard rumours about Mr Brown and the new young French assistant, Mademoiselle Dupont. She has a figure to die for – very slim but with big boobs – and of course a French accent, which all guys seem to find sexy. Since she arrived lots of boys have tried to swap Spanish and German classes for French but have been told to forget it.

I couldn't care less about all the stupid boys who fancy her but she's been seen chatting to Mr Brown almost every break and lunch time, plus he's given her a lift after school twice this week already and it's only Thursday. Everyone is talking about it and it's rumoured they are dating. Naomi has even claimed they were caught snogging in the English store cupboard by Mrs Campbell, the head of English, but most people don't believe her.

I know I should trust him and that he is probably just being nice to a new member of staff but I can't help worrying. She is very attractive and, well, two years is such a long time to wait. Maybe a man like him gets frustrated. I mean, it's unlikely he's a virgin, and perhaps he misses sex: he might be tempted by someone like her pursuing him. I wished she'd just leave him alone.

On Thursday, like Monday, we have English last period. At the end of the lesson I managed to get Mr Brown involved in a discussion about our critical essay just as the bell went and he went on talking to me as everyone else filed out. Josh had asked me back to his house after school but I told him to go ahead and I'd catch up with him later, so everything was fine until *she* turned up and French-kissed Mr Brown in front of me. OK, I don't mean tongue-down-the-throat-snogging French kissing but that stupid kiss-on-each-cheek thing. It might be all right in France but this is Scotland and she shouldn't do it. Especially as they were both teachers and still in the school.

But Mr Brown did nothing to stop her – he didn't even

show disapproval. And when I tried to get back to our discussion he cut me short. 'Sorry, Cat, but we'll have to leave this for another day. I've promised Mademoiselle Dupont a lift home now.'

'But it won't take long – I'm just so interested in what you were saying about the imagery of the flowers at—'

For the first time ever Mr Brown frowned at me. 'I said not now, Catriona.' He turned to Mademoiselle Dupont. 'Sorry about that. Are you ready?'

I couldn't believe it. He'd spoken to me like I was, well, a pupil. And an annoying one at that. Totally humiliated me in front of her. I left the classroom, gutted. Too upset to go straight home, I went to the toilets and tried to calm myself, but instead I started to cry. Fortunately there was no one there to see me. After a while I forced myself to stop and washed my face to disguise the fact that I'd been blubbing, but my eyes were still red.

Reckoning that most people would have gone by now, I left the toilets and made my way out to the school grounds, only to spot Mr Brown in the car park opening his car door for *her*.

There wasn't anyone else around so he must have seen me but he didn't so much as acknowledge my existence. At least I was too far away for him to notice the tears that had sprung back to my eyes. I was grateful for that.

As I watched him drive off I broke down completely

and started to sob; then I heard a familiar voice behind me. 'Cat, what's wrong?'

Josh. I turned round. He held out his arms – I walked into them and he hugged me close. For a while I said nothing, just cried into his chest, but then at Josh's gentle prompting I told him everything. The secret I'd kept for years. The secret I hadn't shared with even my closest friends. I spilled out everything. My love for Mr Brown. My unswerving belief in his love for me – until today anyway. Everything.

Oh God, I hope I haven't made an awful mistake.

10

At first Josh didn't say much, just listened to me, but when I'd finished and calmed down a bit he said gently, 'We've all had crushes on teachers, Cat.' Annoyed, I pushed away from him but he still held me. 'Don't be mad at me. I'm not trying to belittle how you feel. Just trying to put the whole thing in perspective.'

'It's not a crush. I love him and he loves me. Or he did anyway.'

'But he's too old for you and he's your teacher. It isn't right. Anyway, you don't really know the guy.'

'I *do* know him. I've known him for over two years now and seen him practically every day. And we've talked about everything. Really deep stuff like love and death and sex.'

'You've talked about sex with him?'

'Well, only in a literary sense. You know, *Romeo and Juliet, A Street Car Named Desire* and, erm, *Sons and Lovers.* That kind of thing.'

'But, Cat—'

'OK, I know what you think. Talking about books and plays isn't the same as real life, but I'd much rather talk like this with Mr Brown than snog some stupid drunk boy at a party.'

I couldn't tell Josh about the poem as I'd made a solemn promise to keep that private, though I could see from Josh's face that he didn't believe Mr Brown had ever been interested in me.

'Look,' Josh said, 'please don't take this the wrong way but nothing you've told me so far proves that Mr Brown thinks of you as anything more than one of his students. Yeah, he likes you, but what makes you so sure he isn't just being friendly?'

'I just know, OK,' I said, impatient now. 'I can't tell you any more. What's the matter? Do you think I'm too ugly for any guy to fancy me?'

'No. Jeez. Of course not. It's just . . . Look, never mind, forget it.'

We were silent for a while, then finally Josh said, 'So this guy, Mr Brown, he's the real reason you don't date? You're putting your life on hold for him? Does he know this? Have you talked about it with him?'

'Yeah, he knows, but, erm, we haven't talked about it directly. It's too dangerous, given our situation, and anyway we understand each other perfectly. Well, we *did*, but now I don't know.' My eyes teared up again. 'Maybe he's got tired of waiting for me.'

'I guess if this guy really loves you then he'll wait for you,' Josh said. He still sounded very sceptical but he hugged me close again anyway and I didn't argue with him – just enjoyed being held and comforted when I was feeling so miserable. Then Josh said, 'Maybe you need to talk to him about all of this.'

He was probably right. Perhaps I should speak to David. But what if he said he didn't love me any more – or at least not enough to wait for me? What would I do? Thinking about my life without the belief that we'd be together one day was unbearable.

I told Josh I didn't want to talk about it any more – could we still go back to his house and just 'hang out' like we'd planned?

We went straight up to his bedroom, and when his mum came up and suggested we might be more comfortable downstairs he told her we wouldn't be. 'No, Mom, we're planning to have a lot of hot sex this evening so we'd probably prefer some privacy.' His mum laughed, but a bit uneasily. Josh smiled at her. 'Trust me. I'll leave Cat unmolested. We're just gonna watch some movies and chill. OK? And do me a favour. Keep Dad off my case tonight as well.'

Josh deliberately chose some completely unromantic horror movies to take my mind off things, but even so I couldn't help feeling a bit tearful. The first film was about a woman terrorized by a deranged stalker. Not that I'd want some psychopath to stalk me or anything, but at least he was committed to her – unlike Mr Brown, I was beginning to suspect, was to me. In the second film the vampire's intended victim had to hammer a wooden stake through his heart. It was quite sad really. He'd been so in love with her and wanted them to spend eternity together. He wouldn't have left her for a French assistant with big boobs.

When I shared this last thought with Josh he told me I was 'one weird chick', but then laughed and said, 'Come to me, Catriona, then you will be mine for ever and ever and ever.' He spread his arms out like bat's wings and curled his lips back, at the same time sticking out his top teeth to give a fair imitation of a vampire ready to pounce. I laughed, then squealed theatrically and managed to avoid him by slipping off the bed, but ended up on the floor, where Josh pinned me down and pretended to take a bite out of my neck.

Not the best time for his mum to come in and ask what all the noise was about. She thought she'd heard someone falling. I was embarrassed but she didn't seem too annoyed – probably because she thought this was just a bit of energetic snogging – we'd all our clothes on after all.

We went downstairs and Josh made sandwiches from the cold meats and salad his mum had left out for us. While we were eating them his dad came to get a beer from the fridge. He smiled at us and said, 'Hi.'

He was about to go out again but then turned to Josh.

'By the way, I called the principal at your school today to see how you were doing and he's very pleased with your progress. You know, if you put in the effort over these next two years there's still a good chance you could get to go to Harvard.'

Instead of being pleased Josh frowned and said, 'Checking up on me again? I already told you I'm not interested in going to Harvard.'

Josh's dad's smile vanished. 'We'll discuss this later.'

'Nothing to discuss. I've no intention of working my butt off at college so I can spend the next thirty years bored out of my mind in an office. It's not gonna happen.'

'I said, we'll discuss it later.'

Josh didn't reply and his dad left the kitchen.

I said, 'Why are you so cheeky to your dad, Josh? He's just interested in how you're getting on at school. All dads are like that.'

Josh smiled. 'What's cheeky mean? Sounds funny. Is it disrespectful?'

'Yeah, sort of.'

'But I do respect him. He's a very smart guy. I just don't want to be him, is all. I'm different but he just can't accept that.'

Maybe Josh was right. Perhaps the real problem was that his dad suspected or knew that Josh was gay and refused to acknowledge it. I suppose most dads would find this difficult, especially an ambitious, bossy man like Josh's dad.

Whatever his dad suspects, Josh's mum still has no idea he's gay. After we'd finished eating she gave me a lift home. On the drive back she said, 'Josh seems to like you a lot, Catriona. I don't think I've ever seen him this keen on a girl.'

I'll bet. I looked at her smiling profile and wondered sadly when, if ever, she would discover the truth about her son: that he could be locked in his bedroom with me stark naked and begging for sex for a week and absolutely nothing would happen between us.

Before going to bed I took out my photograph of Mr Brown as usual, but I didn't kiss it. Instead I examined his expression closely. Was he really looking at me? Or had I just imagined it?

Depressed, I returned it to my drawer. After lying wide awake for most of the night I eventually drifted off to sleep.

And dreamed of Josh. I was lying on the floor of his room and he was sucking on my neck vampire-fashion, but then his mouth moved up to my lips and we were kissing passionately as he caressed me. Mmmm. I wrapped my arms around him and he whispered, 'You're beautiful, Cat. Beautiful.'

I said, 'Oh God, you too. It's such a pity you're gay.'

Then I woke up. My sister was shaking me and saying I was going to be late for school and had I seen her cherry crush lipstick? I hadn't borrowed it, had I? It was her favourite shade and she'd looked everywhere for it.

I murmured groggily, 'Leavemealoneangoway.' But she wouldn't stop going on about it and, glancing at the clock blearily, I could see she was right. If I didn't get up now, I'd be late. I dragged myself out of bed and rummaged for my clothes, saying, 'I don't wear lipstick, Tessa. The stuff never stays on me so what's the point? I think you dropped a lipstick on the bathroom floor last night and I put it in the cabinet. Don't know whether it's cherry crush though.'

Tessa retrieved her lipstick, then I dashed into the bathroom for a quick shower but didn't wash my hair as I'd no time. I just scraped it back with a hairband, then hastily brushed my teeth, pulled on my clothes and grabbed my school bag.

By this time Tessa was back in the bathroom, carefully applying her mascara. 'You ready? We're going to be late,' I said.

Tessa paused but didn't put away the mascara brush. 'Not yet. I've another two coats to do once this has dried. Sean is giving me a lift to school so I don't need to hurry.' She looked at me critically. 'Christ, you look awful. I mean, have you bothered to even brush your hair, never mind wash it? And your skirt is crumpled. You really should make more of an effort, you know, or you'll never get a boyfriend. Especially now you're hanging around with that gay boy all the time.'

'His name is Josh, Tessa, not the "gay boy". I wish

you'd stop calling him that. Anyway, maybe I don't care about getting a boyfriend. Maybe it's my choice. Has that ever occurred to you?'

'Don't be stupid. You're not a les, are you? Of course you want a boyfriend. As for Josh, well, he *is* gay, isn't he? Even though no one else realizes it. Even Mum. Imagine her thinking he's your boyfriend. I mean, really. As if he'd be dating you if he were straight.' Seeing my expression, she put her hand over her mouth. 'Oh, Cat, I'm sorry. I didn't mean that. Really.' She tried to hug me but I shook her off. 'Honestly, I mean, you're fantastic. Such a nice person and you've a great p—'

'Personality,' I finished for her.

I was annoyed by Tessa's tactless remarks but, thinking it over, I realized she was right. I *did* want a boyfriend. I wanted David. But right now it didn't look like he was going to wait for me. She was probably right about Josh as well. If he wasn't gay he'd be spending his time with her or someone like her. No, I was glad Josh was gay or I'd never have got to know him. Especially now he was the only person I could talk to about Mr Brown's betrayal.

However, then I remembered my dream. It had been really weird imagining Josh like that. The last thing I needed after Mr Brown was to fall for a gay guy; maybe Tessa was right and I was spending too much time with him. Lindsay and other friends have been complaining they don't see much of me these days. Perhaps I should give Josh the chance to socialize with other gay people outside of school. There must be clubs where people like him could meet. I trudged off to school, feeling miserable. My only consolation was that I didn't have English today so I wouldn't have to deal with seeing Mr Brown just yet.

I spent the whole of break time with Lindsay, who was also depressed. She'd been talking to Scott quite a lot this week and they'd exchanged phone numbers, but last night she'd texted him suggesting they meet up after school. He'd knocked her back, said he was busy all this week and next. 'But he said, "Maybe the week after that." Do you think he means it, Cat, or is he just trying to let me down gently?'

I said truthfully, 'I don't know.' I didn't add that in some ways it might be best if he didn't mean it. I really didn't like Scott. But still, if that was what Lindsay really wanted, I suppose I'd try to be happy for her.

At lunch time Lindsay wanted to watch the guys play five-a-side football since Scott was involved. He was in the team playing against Peter and Josh. Josh was still useless, but to be honest Scott wasn't much better. However, Lindsay cheered him on as though he was a top Brazilian striker. But it didn't do her any good: after the game he ignored her. Instead, to my surprise, he came up to me and asked to speak to me privately. I hesitated but, thinking he might want to ask me about Lindsay, I agreed, despite frowns from Peter and Josh.

I don't know exactly what I expected but was gob-smacked when, after asking me about his game – and failing to notice my sarcasm when I told him, 'Yeah, you were great, honestly' – he said, 'So, Cat, you know, if things don't work out with you and this American guy, and you, like, well, split, I might be interested in going out with you.'

I was speechless for a moment. Astonished. Then I said slowly, 'Well, erm, thanks for that, Scott. It's good to know that I've got something to fall back on.'

Again Scott seemed unaware that I was joking because he added, 'I'd have asked you before but I thought you were a les until you started dating.'

What a nerve. Honestly! Just because I don't fancy stupid boys like him, that makes me a lesbian? Some people were so quick to jump to ludicrous conclusions on the basis of almost no evidence whatsoever. I didn't know whether to laugh at Scott or slap him. While I was deciding he continued, 'You know, *obviously* you're not as good looking as your sister but I've always thought you weren't bad. And you've got better boobs. Definitely.'

I studied his smiling face. Yeah, he really thought this was a compliment. I tried but failed to suppress a giggle. Scott kept smiling but looked a bit uncertain. 'So what's so funny, Cat?'

'Nothing.' I forced myself to stop laughing and put on a serious expression. 'I'm just, well, totally overwhelmed. No – really. I mean, thanks. Thanks a lot.'

The idiot smiled and said, 'No problem. I really mean it, you know. Definitely.' He waved magnanimously, then strolled off.

Still giggling, I made my way back to Lindsay, who was waiting for me on her own as Peter and Josh had gone off to clean themselves up before class. I was dying to tell her what a tosser Scott was but changed my mind when she said anxiously, 'So what did Scott say? Did he ask about me?'

Oh God. 'Erm, yeah,' I lied. 'But just, erm, what you thought of the game.'

'What did you say? Did you tell him I said he was ace? He's got real talent, you know. Of course, it helps to be tall.'

'It's football, not basketball,' I said tersely. 'Peter is much better than Scott.'

'Mmmm, Scott would be fantastic playing basketball. He could just pop the balls in without having to stretch, never mind jump. Anyway, what were you laughing about?'

'Oh, nothing,' I said vaguely. 'Just some stupid joke.' I paused, took a deep breath and continued, 'Please don't be mad at me, Lindsay, but I really think Scott isn't right—'

'Don't say it, Cat. I know you don't like him but that's because you don't really know him like I do. It's not just his height. It's everything else as well.'

'Such as?'

'Oh, erm, just everything. He's so t—'

'Tall?'

'Talented.'

Yeah, right, but there was no use arguing with her any more. Why, oh, why can't she see that Peter is so much nicer than Scott, plus better looking and dead keen on her too? Honestly, sometimes I think if Prince Charming were right there in front of her, Lindsay would say, 'Sorry, I'd rather snog this enormous toad thanks. It's taller than you.'

Lindsay asked me over to her house on Saturday, along with Marianne. I wasn't keen at first as I was depressed about Mr Brown and worried that people would notice. That's the problem with a secret romance. When it's over no one understands how you feel. However, Lindsay was adamant. 'C'mon, Cat, it'll be fun. We'll put on face packs, then eat chocolate and watch romantic movies all night. Oh, and slag off boys of course. A real girly night in. We haven't done that in ages.'

In the end I agreed. I hadn't seen Marianne outside of school in a while and she's usually a good laugh. Although she has flaming red hair, she doesn't have the temper that's supposed to go with it, and is usually completely laid back and good fun. Yeah, maybe an evening with Lindsay and Marianne was just what I needed.

I went over at seven with a box of Dairy Milk, two

DVDs and a face pack. Lindsay's mum was out but Marianne was already there, and she and Lindsay had started on a bottle of wine smuggled from the kitchen. I wondered if Lindsay's mum ever noticed the disappearing bottles. I suppose she didn't mind so long as Lindsay doesn't steal too many.

Marianne poured me a glass. I settled down on the sofa, determined not to look too depressed in case my friends wondered what the matter was and started asking awkward questions. I needn't have worried though: Marianne and Lindsay were too busy moaning to notice.

Marianne sighed. 'A Saturday night and here we are. Not a boyfriend between us. It's pathetic.'

'It's not our fault,' Lindsay said. 'I mean, look at the rubbish we've got to choose from. Most Glasgow guys are midgets or tossers or both.'

'Yeah,' Marianne agreed. 'Sad losers or sleazers, the lot of them. Well, nearly the lot of them anyway. Finding anything decent among the dross is almost impossible. I'm so desperate I'm even thinking of asking Cat to set me up with someone again. But then I remember Michael and think, erm, maybe not.' She turned to look at me. 'I'm still heartbroken about him, you know.'

'I'm sorry, Marianne. I'd no idea he was a priest. He didn't look like one.' Actually this wasn't strictly true. I *had* heard a rumour he was thinking of being a priest but didn't think he was serious about it, never mind actually definitely decided. I thought it wiser not to mention this to Marianne afterwards.

'Hmm, I suppose,' Marianne said. 'But didn't the fact that he was going to study at a college in Rome, spoke Latin and always carried rosary beads tell you anything? Never mind,' she continued without giving me the chance to answer. 'At least we've stayed friends. He emails me from Rome sometimes, you know, and tells me he prays for me.'

'That's nice, Marianne.'

'Yeah. I pray for him too.'

'You do?' I said, surprised. I'd never imagined Marianne was religious.

'Definitely. I pray, *Please God, give me Michael back. You don't need such a good-looking priest. Amen.*'

We laughed, then Lindsay poured another glass of wine and said, 'You seem to have done a good job with Iona this time though, Cat. She and Billy are still all loved up.'

'Yeah.' I smiled. 'He's over at her house tonight – her parents and her sister are out and I've seen her searching the Internet for organic condoms. I think this could be The Night.'

We talked about them for a while, then I opened the Dairy Milk and Lindsay got the first DVD ready to play. We were just ready to settle down and watch the film when my mobile rang. It was Iona. I looked at my watch. Seven thirty. Billy was meant to go over to Iona's house at seven so he can't have been there very long. Surely they hadn't had sex already? She couldn't be calling to tell me about it, could she? Puzzled, I took the call.

'Bastard's eaten my Twinkle,' Iona screeched.

'Billy's eaten your gerbil?' I said, horrified.

'No, you idiot, his sodding python. He brought that evil reptile with him.' Iona started to sob. 'I hate him, Cat. Hate him!'

'You hate Monty? But—'

'No. Billy, you imbecile. But actually, yeah, both of them. Billy and his murdering snake.'

I was shocked. Not just at what had happened but at Iona. I'd never heard her speak like this. She's usually as quiet as a mouse. I suppose this trauma must have brought out an aggression no one has ever heard before.

However, after this outburst she just sobbed un-controllably over the phone, too upset to speak, while I tried to calm her. Eventually she just said, 'It's over, Cat. I'll never forgive Billy or Monty for this.'

I tried to reason with her. 'Look, Iona, this is a terrible tragedy but it's not really Billy or Monty's fault. After all, it's sort of natural for a python to eat a rodent. You could say it's, well, kind of organic really.'

Iona hung up on me.

Oh God, maybe Lindsay is right and I'm no good at matchmaking.

11

All day, instead of looking forward to English last period I was dreading it. As well as feeling miserable and upset I was afraid I might do something really stupid and embarrassing like bursting into tears in class. In the end I coped by avoiding looking at Mr Brown. Instead I just kept my head down and got on with my work like, well, like a pupil, which is probably all I meant to him now. I didn't answer any of his questions all lesson, which isn't like me (in English class anyway) and prompted him to say, 'You're very quiet today, Cat. Is something wrong?'

As if he didn't know what was wrong! Almost said as much but stopped myself in time and just muttered, 'No, I'm all right.'

At last the lesson was over and Josh and I filed out with the rest of the class, but as I got to the door Mr Brown said, 'Just a minute, Cat. I almost forgot. You wanted to talk to me about your critical essay.'

'It's OK, I'm sure you're very busy,' I said coldly. 'I don't want to take up too much of your time. It's not important anyway. Not any more.'

'Nonsense, I'm not in a hurry today – and, yes, I think your idea of the rhododendrons at Manderley being a metaphor for Rebecca's beauty is valid and very insightful. I really think you should explore this idea further. May I see what you've written so far?'

I couldn't really refuse – he is my teacher after all. As I rummaged in my bag for the essay I told Josh, who hadn't left with the rest of the class but was standing protectively beside me, to wait for me outside; I wouldn't be long.

I handed Mr Brown my work, and as he scanned it I said frostily, 'I don't want to make you late for Mademoiselle Dupont.'

Mr Brown glanced up at me now. 'Oh, that's OK, Cat. Mademoiselle Dupont's car is fixed now so she won't need a lift.' Then he went back to reading my essay. 'This is good, Cat. Excellent in fact.'

But for once I didn't care about his praise. Instead I said, 'She's very attractive, Mademoiselle Dupont.'

Mr Brown looked up from my work and smiled. 'Yes, she is. I hear French classes have become extraordinarily popular with some of our pupils this year.'

'But her eyes are a bit on the small side and her mouth is too big,' I couldn't help adding waspishly.

Mr Brown shrugged. 'Can't say I've noticed.'

It was no good. I *had* to know. Had to know for sure what was going on. 'There's a rumour going round that you and Mademoiselle Dupont are, you know, sort of, well, going out together.'

Mr Brown laughed. 'There are always rumours going round this school, most of them rubbish. I hope you'll help me scotch this one, Cat. Mademoiselle Dupont's boyfriend has a black belt in tae kwon do. I wouldn't want to get into any trouble with him.'

'So you're not – I mean, she's not—'

'Definitely not.'

Honestly, I almost fainted with relief. Then I started to babble. 'Of course, not that *I* ever really thought you were, you would, or anything. It's just that, you know, there are so many stupid gossips in the school who just love to jump to conclusions at the slightest excuse.'

'Yes, I know.'

I was still beaming happily when he handed me back my essay along with a few suggestions for possible additions. Not that I could concentrate on any of that now. Then he said, 'Bye, Cat. Keep up the good work.'

I stuffed the essay back in my bag and I swear I almost floated out the door. I was just so happy. I spotted Josh, who was leaning against the wall along the corridor waiting for me. I ran up to him, then, without stopping to think, dropped my bag, threw my arms around his neck and kissed him.

When I let him go he said, smiling, 'Wow, what was that for?'

I picked up my bag and hooked my arm through his and we headed for the stairs. 'Oh God, Josh, I'm just *so* happy. I've been worried about nothing. Absolutely nothing.' I looked around just to make sure no one could hear us, then continued, 'Mr Brown hasn't been seeing the French assistant. He was only giving her a lift when her car wasn't working. Just being kind and thoughtful as usual. I should never have doubted him.'

I babbled on happily all the way back to Josh's but he was very quiet and didn't seem to be as pleased for me as I'd hoped. In fact once we'd gone up to his room with a Coke he said, 'So, Cat, does this mean you're putting your life on hold for this guy again? You're not gonna date anyone, maybe make out with someone you like? You're sixteen – you're supposed to be having fun, not sitting around at home waiting for some guy who may never show up.'

'I'll wait for ever if I have to, and so will he,' I said crossly. I put down my glass of Coke. 'If you're just going to try and belittle our relationship maybe I should go.'

'What relationship?' he said sarcastically.

Right, that was it. I wasn't putting up with this any more. Josh was a good friend but he'd crossed the line now. Without another word I marched to the door but Josh called after me, 'Don't go, Cat. I'm sorry, that was pretty crass. It's just that, you know, maybe this whole thing with your teacher is stopping you from thinking about guys that are, well, uh, maybe more right for you age-wise and, um, in other ways too.'

I hesitated, my hand on the door handle. He *had* apologized after all – probably he'd just been concerned about me. I moved back into the room. 'OK, I know you mean well, but you really shouldn't worry about me. I'm quite happy just to wait for David. Anyway,' I confided, 'I don't really like snogging boys.'

'You don't?'

'No, in fact I hate it. I've only done it twice and it was awful.' I settled down on Josh's bed and patted the space beside me. 'The first time was with a boy I met when we were on holiday in Spain two years ago. It was disgusting. All slobbery, and he moved his mouth round and round like a washing machine. Finally he stuck his tongue down my throat and I nearly gagged.'

'Doesn't sound like a good first experience. Maybe the guy just wasn't right for you.'

'Maybe, but my snog with Billy at the Christmas party wasn't much better.'

'You made out with Billy? The guy with the python?'

'Yeah. At least he didn't slobber but he'd drunk so much lager so quickly before the party that he kept belching mid snog.'

Josh smiled. 'Not such a cool idea.'

'Of course it will be different with David as he's so much more mature.'

He shrugged. 'Who knows?'

'But I worry I might not, you know, be experienced enough for him. I mean, since I've decided not to snog anyone again I won't have had any practice. Maybe I won't be any good.'

'It's not an exam, Cat. In any case, someone his age is going to be looking for a lot more action than that.'

I ignored this jibe from Josh. Mr Brown had been willing to wait this long for me so I was sure he'd be patient about sex and we'd take things slowly at first. I don't know why Josh can't see how wonderful Mr Brown is. I suppose he just doesn't understand him like I do. Instead of arguing I continued, 'I suppose I'll just have to go back to practising by snogging myself in the mirror.'

'Excuse me?'

I giggled and repeated what I'd said, then added, 'All girls do it at some time. Even my sister Tessa before she started dating. She denied it of course but I saw the lipstick marks on her bedroom mirror.'

'Really? All you chicks make out with, like, your reflections! That's weird, Cat. You're bullshitting me.'

'Well, not all; some, like Lindsay, prefer kissing the back of their hand because it's more flesh-like.'

'Jeez.'

'Or Marianne, who liked to snog her teddy bear.'

'She made out with a stuffed toy?'

I giggled again. 'Yeah, but there's worse. Now promise me you won't tell anyone.' Josh nodded mutely.

'Well, when Lindsay told me about snogging the back of her hand I thought, That's stupid – I mean, totally mad. It's her own hand after all.'

'Hmm, yeah, right.'

'So I thought, Well, suppose it didn't feel like your own hand. Suppose it felt like part of someone else's body.'

'You're losing me, Cat.'

'Lindsay and I both tried it. We'd sit on our right hand until the circulation got cut off and it went numb, and honest to God it didn't feel like part of you. Then, not only could you snog it, you could caress yourself with your hand and imagine it was some boy you fancied. Of course, he'd never go any further than you wanted him to.'

We were both laughing. God, I'd forgotten about that until just now. Lindsay and I were just in the Second Year at the time and totally mental. When he'd stopped laughing Josh said, 'I've never met anyone like you, Cat.'

'Yeah, completely nuts.'

'That too. But what I meant was I've never known any girl so, I don't know, honest and open, I guess. Totally natural.'

'Well, I don't share stuff like this with most guys. Only you in fact. No way would I trust those idiots with our secrets. But you're different. Obviously.'

'Well, thanks, Cat. I'm honoured you feel you can confide in me. I really am. So I guess I can't tell Peter about Lindsay and the numb-hand thing. A pity – he'd enjoy it.'

'Don't you dare! Lindsay would kill me.'

Josh teased me for a bit but then assured me that he wouldn't tell anyone and I believed him. Then I asked curiously, 'Do boys ever do that? Practise snogging?'

'I don't think so. No one's ever said, but I can't be sure, I suppose.' Josh smiled. 'After all, it's not likely guys are going to be caught out by leaving lipstick marks on the bedroom mirror.

'Anyway,' he continued, 'I've certainly never kissed my reflection or a part of my own body. Maybe a teddy bear – you'd have to ask my mom – but not since I was five. Honestly, Cat, I don't think you can practise making out without another person.'

I thought about this. He was probably right. 'Well, I can't do that. I wouldn't cheat on Mr Brown. I'll just have to hope I'll be OK at the time.'

Josh shrugged. 'Your choice.'

But then I had an idea. 'Of course, I suppose I could practise with *you* and it wouldn't be cheating since you're definitely a totally platonic friend.'

'Excuse me? Are you serious? You want to *practise* making out with me?'

'Yeah, well, why not? It would be better than my reflection or a teddy bear.'

'I'm overwhelmed by this flattery, Cat. Careful or I might really get too big-headed,' Josh said sarcastically.

'I didn't mean it like that,' I soothed. 'It's just that, you know, obviously I can trust you completely and so I wouldn't feel guilty about Mr Brown.'

'You trust me completely? Maybe you shouldn't. I'm just a guy after all.'

'Don't be silly. Of course I trust you. You're my friend. And, well, it's not like you'd ever take advantage of me, would you?'

I looked at him, trying to figure out what he was thinking. His expression was hard to read. He looked confused and wary. But maybe it was more than that. Maybe the idea of snogging a girl was repulsive.

I said slowly, 'Of course, if it would be really disgusting for you I'd understand. We'll just forget it.'

He ran a hand distractedly through his hair. 'Of course it isn't disgusting, Cat,' he said gently. 'Just, well, a bit weird, that's all. But, OK, right, if you really want to, then go ahead. Use me for practice.'

'Oh, right, thanks.'

We sat silently on the bed for a while, then he said, 'So, I'm waiting.'

'What, now?'

'Yeah, why not?'

'Well, er, not here. I mean, not on the bed.'

'Seems a good place to me but, hey, OK, have it your way.' Josh stood up. 'Better?'

I stood up too, moved away from the bed, then faced him. He was just standing there looking relaxed and amused, making no move towards me. I blushed, suddenly embarrassed. This really was one of my dafter ideas. What was I supposed to do now? A few moments passed. Josh looked at his watch and yawned pointedly. Very funny. Then he said, 'Chickening out?'

To be honest I felt like doing just that but there was no way I would now. Not after Josh's challenge. 'No, just thinking about it.'

'Oh, yeah, I get it. Mental preparation. Visualizing your moves like an athlete before the event. But you're not gonna do a pole-vault, Cat. It really isn't that difficult.'

I smiled.

'That's better,' he said. 'This is supposed to be enjoy-able. Before you smiled just then you looked like you were going to have a tooth extracted rather than be kissed.'

'Right, so . . .' I said in a brusque matter-of-fact tone. 'Should I keep my eyes open, do you think, or close them?'

'Whatever you feel comfortable with. It's cool.'

I decided to close my eyes. Then I tried to think about kissing Mr Brown to get me in the mood. Where would we have our first kiss? At school maybe on the day I left? Or perhaps at a romantic restaurant. We'd have a table for two with red roses and candles.

No, better still, on a moonlit beach where we'd been strolling hand in hand. Not in Scotland of course, which would be too cold. Spain maybe, or the south of France. David would have bought the tickets to surprise me. Yes. A moonlit beach was definitely the most romantic. I smiled, then moved forward to embrace 'David' and found myself nearly falling over as I clasped empty air. I opened my eyes. Josh had disappeared. But then I felt an arm placed around my waist. He must have silently crept behind me while I was deciding on my fantasy location.

Idiot! I laughed, then twisted round to face him, meaning to give him a playful slap, but before I could do this he'd pulled me tightly towards him and kissed me hard on the mouth. For a long time. Pressed so close to him I could feel the heat of his body through his shirt and was aware, in the silent room, of the strong beat of his heart. I felt my tummy tighten and my face flush. Oh God, what was happening to me? I'd never felt like this before. Then, slowly, gently, he released me but still held onto my hands.

I didn't look at him, instead examining my toes like I'd never seen them before. I was aware I must appear odd but I couldn't let him look into my eyes until I'd got my emotions under some sort of control again. Neither of us said anything until at last, embarrassed by the silence, I took a deep breath and stupidly said, 'Well, er, thanks, Josh.'

He said in an amused tone, 'You're welcome.'

Trying to match his light touch, I replied, 'So, then, how did I do?'

'Well, not bad, but I think you need a lot more practice.'

He bent his head to kiss me again but I pulled away from him, trying to twist my hands free. 'No! Stop it!' I shouted.

Josh, shocked by my vehement response, immediately let go of me. 'Hey, I'm sorry. What's the matter?'

Embarrassed by my over-the-top reaction, I said hastily, 'Nothing, nothing. It's just . . . you were right. This *was* a stupid idea. Look, I need to get back now. I've loads of homework to do tonight and, erm, yeah, I just remembered I promised to cook Dad spaghetti bolognese for dinner. Mum doesn't cook,' I babbled on, 'unless you count tomato and lettuce salads as cooking, which obviously I don't. Especially without any dressing. Well, not quite true – she does lemon and balsamic vinegar dressing but no mayonnaise. Can you imagine? God, you're so lucky. A mum who makes lasagne and bakes cookies.' I picked up my school bag. 'Right, see you later.'

'I'll walk you home,' Josh said.

'No, I'm fine thanks.' I opened the bedroom door and sped down the stairs, calling as I went, 'See ya tomorrow.'

At last I was out the front door and running – yeah, literally running for home. Oh God, how stupid I'd been. Why hadn't I realized that though a gay guy like Josh could never fancy me in a million years this didn't stop me from being attracted to him. Especially when we

were locked in a passionate clinch in his bedroom!
Tonight I felt I'd betrayed Mr Brown and, almost as bad,
put my friendship with Josh, which was beginning to
mean so much to me, in jeopardy. I silently vowed I'd
never do anything so stupid again. Never.

12

The rest of that week was amazing. Apart from the sheer relief of knowing that Mr Brown hadn't betrayed me after all, there would also be lots of opportunities for me to speak to him outside of class. All the Fifth Year English classes are going on a theatre trip to see *King Lear* next month. Because we are older now – 'young adults', as Mrs Campbell calls us – we're to get dressed up and have a proper 'theatre experience' with pre-theatre supper (although no alcohol). We're also involved in the organization: one person from each class is to help with this and Mr Brown has chosen me.

The alcohol ban is predictable but annoying and no one will be able to use their fake IDs with teachers around so we'll have to get tanked up beforehand. But anyway, I've already been able to ensure that Mr Brown will be at the same table as me for supper and I hope to be able to sit beside him for the play. OK, I know it isn't a date with all the other people there, but still. It also means that I've got plenty of excuses to speak to him privately during the next few weeks as there are so many details to discuss.

For a few days after the snogging incident with Josh I avoided him. It was all my stupid fault, I know, but somehow I just felt awkward around him now. And guilty for having sort of betrayed Mr Brown. Josh was a bit cut up about it, I think, but he didn't say anything until I cancelled on him for our regular tennis session.

'Look, Cat, if I've offended you in some way then I'm sorry, but I honestly don't know what I've done wrong.'

'You haven't done anything. I'm just busy, that's all.'

'Is that girl-speak for *Yeah, I'm really pissed at you but I'm not gonna tell you why until you work it out for yourself, dumb-ass?*'

I laughed. 'No, it just means I'm busy. Honestly.'

'Fine, OK, it's cool. Maybe next time then.'

He smiled as he walked away but he'd sounded so disappointed.

'Josh, wait!'

He turned back to me.

'I've just been thinking. Maybe I could finish off my maths homework tomorrow. I do need to work on my backhand after all.'

I was glad I'd agreed to see Josh again. The truth was I'd missed him. And it was stupid to feel guilty about Mr Brown. Josh was gay after all, so nothing could ever happen between us. There was really no problem with us being friends just so long as the only thing I practised with Josh from now on was tennis.

At long last everything in my life was going right again. The only problem now is Iona and Billy. Iona isn't mad any more but she won't go back with Billy even though she's miserable without him.

Billy is gutted and keeps trying to talk to her about it but she won't listen. They're both really heartbroken but the situation seems hopeless.

It was raining, so instead of going out for shop lunch I decided to join Iona in the school cafeteria. Even though the meals are now disgustingly tasteless and healthy, Iona had still brought her own even more boringly bland lunch (mung bean and tofu salad) so I got myself a veggie burger and sat beside her. As I nibbled something that tasted like damp cardboard I began to wish that I'd braved the rain. But at least I had the opportunity to talk to Iona about Billy again.

'It's no use, Cat. Every time I think of Billy and Monty I remember Twinkle and cry.'

'I understand, Iona, but—'

'Iona!' Billy's voice interrupted us. We'd been so engrossed in our conversation we hadn't noticed him coming over to our table. Now I looked up to see him standing by Iona's chair; she was staring down at the floor.

Still without looking at him she said, 'Please go away, Billy. I already told you it's hopeless.'

'I . . . I've got rid of Monty, Iona. He's got a new owner. Another reptile lover. He'll be OK but I'll never see him again. Neither will you.'

At this everyone around us gasped and stopped talking. Billy had given Monty away. Just a few weeks ago no one would have thought such a thing was possible. The whole school knew how Billy loved his pet. As word got round people stopped what they were doing and looked over at us and it seemed as if the entire cafeteria was silent.

Iona stood up and looked at Billy. 'You didn't have to do that, Billy.'

'Yeah I did. Because every time you looked at Monty's face you'd have seen Twinkle and got upset again. It was Monty or you. And I chose you.'

God, he must *really* love her. All eyes were on Iona now. What would she do? Was Billy's sacrifice for nothing?

When she reached over, wrapped her arms around Billy and kissed him everyone stood up and applauded. Well, everyone except for some idiots who shouted stuff like, 'Get a room, for God's sake, you're putting me off my lunch.' Oh, and Mr Smith, who was on cafeteria duty and gave them both lines for 'inappropriate behaviour'. Not that Iona or Billy cared.

I was so pleased about my matchmaking success with Iona that a few days later I decided to try finding someone for Josh again. As usual Lindsay tried to put me off.

'For God's sake, Cat, quit while you're ahead. You don't have to matchmake for the entire planet. Let Josh find someone himself. A guy that good looking shouldn't have any trouble finding someone, gay or not.'

'But he's new here, Lindsay. He doesn't know that many people. I really think he needs a helping hand.'

'Oh, God, what's the use? You're going to do it anyway. Poor guy. So what mad scheme have you got in mind this time?'

'Hmm, not sure, but actually I haven't given up on Alistair yet. Maybe we could get them together for longer. See what happens. He's round at your house again on Sunday, isn't he?'

Lindsay shook her head. 'If the spark wasn't there to start with there's no point in bothering. You can't force people to fancy each other, you know, just because you think it's a good idea. Anyway, although Alistair's being pretty secretive about it, I've got a feeling he's found someone else.'

Undeterred, I invited myself over to Lindsay's on Sunday afternoon anyway. There was no harm in trying after all. I called Josh to ask him to meet us there but he couldn't make it.

'Sorry, Cat. I'm playing five-a-side then. It's already booked.'

This was annoying but I decided to go myself anyway

and see if I could tell whether Alistair was interested in Josh.

When I got to Lindsay's the parents had all gone out to the pub but Alistair had stayed behind with her.

After chatting for a bit about general stuff so as not to seem too obvious, I said, 'So, Alistair, I was sorry to hear about you and Nigel. How are things now?'

'Thanks, Cat, but really, I'm fine. To be honest the attraction for me was always just physical. Nigel has a body to die for but, erm, not a lot up top except for biceps.'

'Hmm, yeah,' I sympathized. 'Looks are important of course, but you need something more. Someone with good looks *and* intelligence.' *Someone like Josh.*

'*Exactement!* And' – Alistair smiled – 'I think I've found him. Now, girls, put your questionnaires away. I'm keeping this one under wraps for now.'

We interrogated him relentlessly anyway but he refused to tell us anything more. Instead he started to question me about Josh.

'So, Cat, where is he today? I wouldn't let that one out of my sight if I were you. There are too many predatory females around waiting to pounce as soon as your back is turned. Although I've heard a rumour he's already knocked back your sister Tessa in favour of you and you don't get more pred—'

I glared at him.

'Erm, female than her. So maybe you're safe after all.'

I sighed. 'I told you already, Alistair, Josh is a friend. Anyway, what guy would want to date me when he could have Tessa?'

'One with taste and good sense, my love. You under-estimate yourself, you know. Your cheekbones, those eyes. To die for. I suppose one has to say Tessa is passable but next to you she seems quite ordinary. You could be on *Cosmo*'s cover. Honestly. Lost a little weight recently too, I think?'

I was more pleased about this last comment than Alistair's other ridiculous over-the-top compliments. Strangely, since I finally decided to give up 'miracle' diets and constantly weighing myself I'd actually got a bit slimmer. Even Mum has said so. I certainly haven't got any fatter anyway. I don't know whether the tennis is helping or not but I enjoy it and now Josh books courts twice a week – always indoors so we'll be sure of getting to play. I don't think I'll ever be really slim but I don't feel so scared that I'll end up enormous either.

I smiled happily. 'Yeah, I have lost a bit. At last.'

We chatted for a while longer but I said nothing more about Josh. With Alistair happily loved up again there was no chance of them getting together.

Although I was pleased for Alistair I couldn't help feeling a bit disappointed too as he'd seemed perfect for Josh. I'd just have to try something else.

* * *

Despite Lindsay's dire warnings – 'I can't believe you're doing this!' – I checked out some gay teen Internet chat clubs. I intended first to just 'lurk', then, if I came across anyone interesting, I would pretend to be Josh for a while. I'd even uploaded a picture of him onto my computer to use. Of course, once I found a few suitable candidates I'd have to confess to him and let him take it from there. I assured Lindsay that I wouldn't give out any personal contact details for me or Josh until I'd checked everything out – there was no way I wanted to risk being stalked by some fifty-year-old homicidal pervert masquerading as a normal gay teenager – but Lindsay was still doubtful.

As it happened though (and to Lindsay's relief) I abandoned this after just one attempt. The guys in the chat room might be gay but they *were* guys and their language was totally vulgar and disgusting. There was no way I wanted Josh involved with boys like them.

Finally, at Lindsay's suggestion, I decided to check with Josh first so I asked him if he'd met anyone he was interested in going out with.

Josh paused for a moment, then said, 'Yeah, I have, very much so, but unfortunately my interest isn't returned. Or not yet anyway. I'm still working on it.'

'Oh,' I said, pretending not to be too interested. 'Anyone I know?'

Josh hesitated at first, then smiled and said, 'Actually, Cat, yeah, you do. Quite well in fact, but if I told you who it was it wouldn't help right now. In fact it might make things worse, so no more questions.'

'But—'

'Absolutely none, Cat. This is my business and I'll take care of it. Hey, I gotta go and catch up with Peter. We're playing soccer – sorry, football – tomorrow and we've got stuff to arrange. I think I'm beginning to get the hang of football now but I'd still kill for a game of baseball.'

I watched him lope off and that's when it occurred to me. Josh and Peter have been spending a lot of time together. *Someone he knows well. Someone who hadn't returned his interest.* Yet. Oh My God. He didn't think he'd be able to persuade Peter to be his boyfriend, did he? OK, Josh was good looking, but Peter wasn't gay. Surely Josh didn't think he could seduce Peter.

And there was worse. The next day Josh told me that he and Peter were going on a camping trip to Loch Lomond at the weekend.

At first I just thought, Rather them than me. It was bound to be cold and probably raining, but then it dawned on me. Peter and Josh alone in a tent.

'Just you and Peter?' I asked anxiously.

'Yeah. Ian was meant to come with us,' Josh said, referring to one of Peter's friends, 'but he's got a hot date this weekend so he's cancelled on us.'

'Bet Peter would cancel if he'd a date with Lindsay,' I said meaningfully.

'I guess he'd postpone it, yeah, but it's not likely, is it? Lindsay isn't interested, as far as I can see. Maybe he'd better cut his losses. Move on to someone else. But, hey, what do I know?'

Oh God, I had to stop this.

'You don't really think Josh fancies Peter, do you? I mean, he must know Peter's straight,' Lindsay said as she threaded her large silver hoop earrings through her ears and examined her reflection in her bedroom mirror. She'd bought a new dress for the theatre trip and was trying on different pieces of jewellery to see what suited. 'What do you think? Too gypsy looking? Should I just go for studs?'

'The studs, I think. No, I'm not a hundred per cent sure about Josh, but, yeah, I think so. Besides, Peter being straight doesn't stop Josh being attracted to him, does it? Anyway, I think it's more than fancying. I get the impression Josh has real feelings for him. Maybe he's even in love with him.'

'Oh, come on, Cat,' Lindsay giggled. 'You can't be serious.' She took off the hoops, put on the studs and gazed at her reflection critically. 'Are you sure about the studs? I thought the hoops made me look less tall.'

'I am. Definitely studs. But, yeah, I'm serious about Peter and Josh, which is why we can't let them go on this camping trip together. Especially since Ian isn't going any more so it will be just the pair of them in Peter's two-man tent.'

Lindsay frowned. 'I liked the hoops really, but if you say so . . . Well, maybe it would be best to tell Peter that Josh is gay just in case.'

'But I promised.'

'Yeah, I know, but if what you say is true – and I'm not convinced it is – then perhaps we should warn Peter.'

Though Lindsay was sceptical I was pretty sure I was right about Josh. I couldn't let it happen but there was no way I was going back on my promise to keep his secret. What if I was wrong about his intentions? I could upset his friendship with Peter for no good reason. Not that Peter hated gays or anything but I don't think he'd be as comfortable or friendly with Josh if he knew.

It was all so difficult, but for now at least I'd decided on one thing. Josh and Peter were not going camping together on their own.

Peter said, 'You can't come. It's a two-man tent. And anyway, Cat, it's a guys-only kind of trip. We're gonna do a bit of mountain trekking, maybe some rock climbing. You know you're scared of heights. Afterwards we'll probably just hang about drinking beer and telling fart jokes. You'd hate it.'

'I can borrow a tent. I'll bring some wine and put my hands over my ears when you start telling fart jokes.'

'No.'

'Lindsay says she'd like to come.'

'She did?'

'Er, yeah,' I lied.

'Well, maybe then. If Lindsay comes.'

'I'm not going. I hate camping and you know it. You hate it too. Anyway it'll be freezing and wet. No way,' Lindsay said, brushing her shiny straight hair.

'The forecast says it's to be dry. Quite warm too. For this time of year anyway. Peter says he won't go hiking up mountains or rock climbing if we come. Mostly we'll be barbecuing and drinking wine. Just messing about. Go on Lindsay; it'll be fun.'

'No way. Do you know they're not even going to a proper camp site? According to Peter, formal camp sites are for "wimps and posers". You know what that means, Cat? No toilets or showers, never mind hairdryers and straighteners. I for one am not peeing in the bushes, washing with baby wipes and appearing in public with candyfloss hair. You really think my hair is this straight and swingy naturally?'

Actually I did. And no one knows Lindsay as well as I do except maybe her mum. God, she's kept this as much of a secret as Tessa's natural blondness.

Still, I was sure in the end I'd persuade her. After all, Lindsay owes me lots of favours and in this case I was prepared to remind her of them if I had to.

Like the time I'd told her to help herself to the box of

Ferrero Rocher chocolates she'd given me as a birthday present and she ate all of them – 'Sorry, Cat, they were just too tempting.'

Or the New Year party when she'd got drunk and felt ill in our taxi home. I had to let her use my new black velvet bag to be sick in or the driver would have thrown us out.

In the end I had to go as far back as the time when we were kids and I'd loaned her my Barbie doll. Lindsay decided to give her a new, modern, 'funky' haircut. Playing with a nearly bald Barbie is no fun, I can tell you. The whole point of those dolls is to brush and fashion their beautiful long golden hair. Lindsay knows this and has always felt guilty so she caved in at last and agreed to come on the camping trip.

I was relieved and also hopeful. Maybe spending all that time with Peter in such a romantic lochside setting would help spark a romance between them. I hadn't given up on that idea either. And of course, once Lindsay and Peter were together Josh would surely give up all hope of dating Peter and move on to someone more suitable. Yes, it would all work out perfectly.

1 3

Peter and Josh picked us up from Lindsay's house. Lindsay and I had told our parents that another four girls were going as well just in case they thought it was a couple thing. Huh, if only Mum and Dad knew how utterly safe I was from any unwanted passes – it was really Peter's parents who should worry!

For once the weather forecast was quite accurate and it was a sunny though cool day, and everyone was in a good mood as we set off. Within a half-hour we'd left the city behind and were right in the middle of the country-side. I could see Josh, sitting in the front with Peter, was impressed.

'What do you think of Scotland now, Josh?'

He twisted round in his seat to look at me. 'It's beautiful, Cat. Kinda like Canada with all the mountains and lakes.' He paused, then noticing my frown added, 'But even better of course.'

After an hour or so Lindsay started complaining

about her legs being too cramped. 'That's the problem with being so tall. You never get enough leg room.'

Peter said, 'It's OK, Lindsay, I'll stop the car and massage them for you.'

'It's not funny, Peter.'

He glanced back at her. 'I was being serious. Honestly, it's not that I'd enjoy it or anything. Just a medical treatment to improve circulation.'

'Yeah, right. Keep your eyes on the road, sleazer.'

Hmm. Maybe my matchmaking plans for Lindsay and Peter weren't going to work out as well as I'd hoped.

During the journey Lindsay continued to moan about her height. 'I don't see why I had to be this tall. Look at Mum – she's only five feet. It's all my dad's fault. Well, Mum's as well. Why did she have to marry someone six foot four inches tall? It's ridiculous. No wonder the marriage didn't last.'

'Don't be stupid, Lindsay,' I said. 'Most girls would kill to have your legs, and being tall means you can eat loads without getting fat like me.'

'You're not fat,' Lindsay said. 'But even if you wanted to be slimmer at least you have that possibility. You could diet – or,' she added hastily, remembering my history of failed diets, 'develop a tapeworm infection or get dysentery or something. Anyway the point is, weight loss is possible but height loss isn't.'

'You lose height as you age,' I said. 'It can be several inches.'

'Do you?' Lindsay said eagerly. 'So you mean I'll be shorter in my twenties?'

'Erm, no, sorry, Lindsay. More like eighties.'

'Unless, of course,' Peter butted in, this time keeping his eyes straight ahead, 'you develop some nasty bone disease like osteoporosis – then you'll shrink sooner.'

'How do you get that?' Lindsay asked him with, I thought, a trace of eagerness.

'Oh, drink diet Cokes instead of milk, stay out of the sunshine and take up smoking. That should do it.'

Lindsay seemed to be taking this seriously so I hissed at Peter, 'For God's sake shut up, you idiot.'

Peter continued calmly, 'Of course, you might develop a hump and your teeth will probably fall out.'

Josh laughed. 'But, hey, more leg room. Might be simpler if you sit in the front for a while instead, Lindsay. What do you say I trade places with you for the rest of the journey?'

Lindsay smiled. 'Yeah, maybe Peter's right and the toothless hump option isn't such a good look. Are you sure you'd be OK in the back for a little while, Josh? You're taller than me after all.'

Peter screeched the car to a halt. 'Yeah, but his legs aren't as sexy. Did I say sexy? I meant to say long. Hop in the front, Lindsay.'

Lindsay changed places with Josh but not before warning Peter what would happen to him if he tried any-thing on with her. Her dire threats were pointless really, despite the way he talked Peter is mad about Lindsay and would never risk being too pushy in case he upset her. Sometimes I think he'd get on better if he played harder to get and was a bit more assertive with her. Then again, maybe it's just the height thing and he'd get nowhere anyway.

After another half-hour we stopped at a small sheltered beach by the lochside. Lindsay and I pretended to be clueless about how to pitch our tent so the guys fixed ours for us while making snide remarks about how dumb we were. He he.

We cooked a barbecue. Again the guys did most of the work for this while Lindsay and I drank the bottle of wine we'd cooled in the loch and passed them beers while telling them how well they were doing. Sometimes guys are so easy to manage. When they're not being total pains, that is.

The day was getting a bit warmer and we were enjoying relaxing in the sun after lunch when Josh said, 'Let's go for a swim in the lake.'

We all turned to look at him, incredulous. He might as well have said: *Let's all call our parents and tell them to send someone to fish our frozen bodies out of the water so we can have a decent burial.*

I said, 'That's not a good idea, Josh.'

'Yeah, I know we didn't bring swim stuff. Thought it would be too cold, right? But, hey, we could go skinny-dipping. No one will see us here.'

When Lindsay and I told him 'No way' Josh turned to Peter. 'Looks like it's just you and me then. What do you say?'

Peter tried to explain. 'The water's too cold for swimming, Josh. Forget it.'

'Bullshit,' Josh said. 'It'll be fine. C'mon, real men aren't afraid of a bit of cold water. You're not gonna wimp out on me, are you?'

Peter lounged back against the sandy dune and drank some more beer from the bottle. 'You go ahead, Josh. Show us all how it's done.'

Oh God. I tried to stop Josh but he wouldn't listen and, taking a towel from his tent, he went behind some rocks about twenty metres along the beach to strip off. I considered insisting that Peter go swimming with him to make sure he was OK but decided against it. What if Josh got turned on when he saw Peter naked? Maybe he would be overcome with lust and make a pass. This was exactly what I'd been trying to avoid.

We heard rather than saw Josh dive into the water as his screams and curses rang out: 'Shit! Jesus, it's cold! ****!'

I scanned the loch in the direction of his cries and was relieved to see that he appeared to be a strong swimmer despite the freezing conditions. However, he didn't stay in long, and after striking out for a bit (probably to save face) he headed for shore again.

Soon he was staggering towards us with just a towel

wrapped round his waist, chattering and shivering with cold. This didn't stop Peter taunting him. 'So, enjoy your swim, Josh?'

Josh said, 'C-c-cool.'

I suggested he sit near the still glowing barbecue, then I got another towel from my tent and rubbed him down vigorously with it, which seemed to help a lot. Unlike Peter's comments about how 'real men' shouldn't need fussing over or even towels and should just go for a naked jog around the loch until they dried off.

Afterwards Josh went into his tent to get changed. He was taking longer than expected so I poured a mug of coffee from a thermos and carried it to his tent. I called through the tent flap, 'You OK, Josh? I've got some coffee for you.'

'Sure, I'm fine. Come on in.'

Josh was sitting down pulling on his trainers. He smiled as I came in and said, 'Hi, Cat. I was just taking my time to avoid Peter until he's done winding me up. Not that I don't deserve it. I should have listened to him. Shit, that water was cold.'

I handed him the coffee and sat down in front of him. He looked OK but I noticed a small cut on the back of his hand. 'How did you do that?'

Josh glanced at his injury. 'Scraped it on some rocks. Looks like it's started to bleed again. Do me a favour, Cat. There are some Bandaids in the front of my backpack just behind you. Can you pass one to me?'

I turned round and scrabbled inside for the plasters. I started emptying some stuff out in my search. Soap, toothbrush, condoms. Condoms. I stared at them. Oh My God, why had he brought these? I held one out towards Josh. 'What's this supposed to be for?'

He looked embarrassed but tried to make a joke of it. 'You don't really expect me to answer that, do you? Not for erasing math homework, that's for sure.'

'I mean,' I said furiously, 'why did you bring them on this trip? Who did you expect to use them with?'

'Jesus, Cat, calm down. It's not like I was expecting to get laid tonight. It's just, well, a habit, I suppose. I always take them with me when I travel. I just like to, sort of, um, be prepared. You know – like the Boy Scout motto.'

Yeah, right. I wondered what he got up to on Boy Scout trips. 'I suppose you've done this sort of thing before.'

'What sort of thing? Camping or getting laid?' Josh asked, smiling now.

I didn't smile back. 'You know what I'm talking about.'

'Don't look at me like that, Cat. Like I'm disgusting or something. I told you I didn't expect to get lucky on this trip.'

Hmm, so he says, but there was no way I'd trust him to sleep with Peter tonight. 'You haven't answered my question.'

Josh looked angry now. 'OK, not that it's any of your

business, but yeah. Many times. Not in a while though. Not since I came here.' He got up and headed for the tent flap, but then turned and said, 'Maybe I've wasted too much time recently on a relationship that's never gonna work out.' Then he left.

Yeah, Josh, I think you have. Definitely.

I soon stopped being so mad with Josh. It was sad in a way that his hopes of a relationship with Peter were impossible. Maybe he was beginning to accept that now, but still, I couldn't risk them sharing a tent tonight.

Josh seemed to have regretted our argument too. He said, 'Sorry I got mad at you, Cat. I guess you had a reason to be suspicious.'

I said, 'Yeah, but I suppose I'd no right to ask about your past. That isn't my business. Sorry.'

The rest of the day was really nice. We went for a walk along the lake, stopping now and then to skim stones. Afterwards we used a football Peter had brought to play a version of beach volleyball without a net. Then we made up the barbecue again and cooked dinner, which we had with more wine and beer so we all got a bit pissed but not drunk.

Peter and Lindsay seemed to be getting on really well, which pleased me. Maybe it wouldn't be quite as hard as I'd imagined to get her to sleep with him tonight.

'No way, Cat. I'm not sleeping with Peter. Have you gone

mad or something? I'm not that drunk. Yeah, I know he's not ugly and he's a really great guy but he's just not tall enough and that's that.'

'You don't have to have sex with him, Lindsay—'

'Oh, thanks very much, Cat, because, you know, if you'd said I had to, well, then I'd have just had to shag him, wouldn't I?'

'Shh, Lindsay, they'll hear you.' I looked over anxiously to where Josh and Peter were kicking a football around near the water's edge; however, they hadn't noticed anything.

I continued, 'What's the point in us coming along to chaperone them if we let them sleep together?'

'Fine,' Lindsay said. 'You sleep with Peter. I'll take the gay guy.'

'Peter won't go for that.'

'Oh, so I'm bait, am I?' Lindsay's voice was raised again.

'Please be quieter, Lindsay. Look, you'll be completely safe with Peter. You know he'd never get too pushy. Unless,' I added hopefully, 'you wanted him to.'

'Which I so don't. Anyway, honestly, Cat, I think you're exaggerating this whole thing about Josh being attracted to Peter. I can't see any sign of it.'

'He's brought condoms, Lindsay.'

'Condoms!'

'Shhh.'

'Oh God, Cat,' Lindsay whispered now. 'That's gross.'

Eventually, after more arguments, pleading and blackmail, she agreed to sleep in the same tent as Peter, but if anything went horribly wrong, she said, it would be my fault.

Later it dulled down and started to rain. We spent the evening mostly in Josh and Peter's tent playing cards, a cramped game of Twister, which Peter had brought, and generally messing about. Around eleven Lindsay looked at me with an expression that said, *Are you really sure about this?* I nodded and smiled with what I hoped was a confident, reassuring manner.

She looked at her watch and yawned. 'I'm feeling tired, people. Think I'll go off to bed now.'

Peter tried to persuade her to stay a while but she went off anyway, saying she was exhausted.

About five minutes later I said, 'I'm tired too.' I stretched my arms, yawned, then casually added, 'I think I'll just stay here tonight. Lindsay snores like a beast and I'll never get any sleep sharing with her.'

Josh said, 'Excuse me?'

I repeated what I'd said, trying to make it sound perfectly normal and reasonable, but Peter and Josh looked at one another in surprise.

Peter said carefully, 'You can't sleep here, Cat, there's, erm, no room.'

'Well, I'm not sharing with Lindsay, that's for sure. I've told her this so she says you can share with her,

Peter, if you like. If you can put up with her snoring.'

Peter looked for a moment as though he'd won a rollover lottery so I added, 'But she says to tell you that if you make a pass at her she'll stab you through the heart with the ice pick she keeps hidden under her sleeping bag.'

This gave him pause for a moment, but only a moment, before he picked up his sleeping bag and dashed eagerly through the rain to Lindsay's tent. A minute later he was back with my stuff, then he hurried off again.

After he'd gone I smiled at Josh but he didn't smile back. Maybe he was jealous of Lindsay. Well, too bad. One day he'd see that what I'd done was best for everyone.

I busied myself getting ready for bed. First I got some baby wipes from my bag and used them to clean my hands, face, neck and arms. Then I took a toothbrush, a tube of toothpaste plus a bottle of water and went outside the tent for a moment to brush my teeth. When I came back in I was a bit damp because of the rain. Josh was still sitting in the same position with a puzzled look.

He said, 'Are you sure you're comfortable with this? I mean, maybe you'd prefer it if I slept in the car or something.'

'Of course I'm comfortable. Why wouldn't I be? Unlike you if you tried to sleep in a cramped freezing car.'

Josh smiled then. 'Cool. Well, uh, what do we do now?'

I unclasped my hair so it fell over my shoulders in a mass of heavy curls – thanks to the rain. I'd have to do something about it now or it would be impossible tomorrow. I said distractedly, 'My hair needs brushing.'

'You want me to brush your hair? Well, um, OK.'

'No, you idiot. I'll do it. What's the matter with you tonight? Anyway, we should get ready for bed first. You don't have to turn off the lamp, I want to read for a while anyway, but you do have to shut your eyes while I get undressed.' I laughed. 'No peeking now. I'll tell you when I'm ready.'

Josh did as I asked so I rummaged in my rucksack for my night stuff, then stripped down to my knickers. With any other guy I would have been nervous they'd cheat and open their eyes but not with Josh obviously. I put on the long white T-shirt that just about covered my bum and pulled on a pair of fluffy pink socks to keep my feet warm. I looked for the sweater I'd planned to wear over the shirt but I'd left it in the other tent. I didn't fancy going over in the rain and I didn't want to disturb Peter and Lindsay so I decided I'd be warm enough once I was in my sleeping bag.

For a moment I wondered if my outfit wasn't too revealing – the T-shirt material was a bit see-through; however, I dismissed the idea. It hardly mattered with Josh after all. I picked up my hairbrush and started to brush my hair. 'OK, you can open your eyes now.'

He looked at me, his gaze scanning from my face down to my feet. 'Cute socks.'

I smiled and continued to brush my hair. Josh didn't say anything else, just stared at me oddly.

'What's wrong?' I said.

'Nothing – it's just . . . Well, you're beautiful, Cat.'

'Yeah, right,' I said, smiling dismissively.

'But you are, Cat. Why can't you see that? And you have lovely—'

'Yeah, I know,' I interrupted. 'Lovely blue eyes and a nice face.' I laughed and waved my hairbrush at him. 'Now, if you say I've got a good personality I'll have to hit you with this.'

'I was going to say you have lovely breasts actually.'

'What?' I said, surprised. 'I, erm, didn't think you'd like them.'

He looked puzzled. 'Why not?'

I thought about this. Why shouldn't gay guys like breasts? Just the look of them anyway, in an aesthetic sort of way. 'Well, I don't know. No reason, I suppose.'

I resumed brushing my hair. 'Yeah, I like my breasts. Lindsay says I should make more of them.' I giggled. 'I don't mean implants – they're big enough – but she says I should wear tight tops and go braless. I could, I suppose, as I can pass the pencil test, but I don't want to – some idiot guys would probably lech at me.'

'The pencil test?'

I smiled mischievously. 'You haven't heard of the pencil test?' I scrabbled about for a pencil, but couldn't find one so I demonstrated with a bit of dry twig I found outside the tent. I put it inside my T-shirt underneath my left breast then let it go; the twig fell out immediately. 'See! If it sticks you have to wear a bra, but if it doesn't you don't need one.'

'Uh, right.'

His voice sounded kind of dry and croaky. I offered him some water but he refused and just sat there staring. Maybe he was tired. I said, 'Your turn.'

'What?'

I put down the hairbrush and closed my eyes tight. 'Your turn to get undressed.' I giggled. 'It's OK, I promise I won't look.'

He seemed to take ages and I was getting impatient. Maybe boys took a long time getting undressed. I wouldn't know. I was just about to tell him to get a move on when I sensed him near me. Next thing I knew he kissed me on the mouth. My eyes flew open and I pulled away. This was definitely not what I'd been expecting.

He moved back a little too but was still quite close. He was wearing jeans but no shirt and his feet were bare. I just stared at him for a moment. Speechless. Why had he kissed me just then? Was it a kind of joke? Or maybe he'd just meant to be affectionate and didn't realize his behaviour was a bit off even for a gay friend. Yeah, that was it. Perhaps I should talk to him about appropriate boundaries. I didn't know exactly what these should be with a gay guy, but kissing me on the mouth when we were both half dressed was definitely not on.

I was about to say something along those lines when he moved in to kiss me again, this time cupping my breast with his hand over the thin material of my shirt.

Right, that was it! I slapped him as hard as I could.

He drew back quickly and rubbed his cheek where I'd hit him. I hissed at him, 'Why did you *do* that? Is this some kind of sick joke? Or are you pissed or what? I can't believe you just did that!'

Furious and shocked, I ranted on at him. He didn't say anything at first, though I suppose I hadn't given him any opportunity to answer. Instead he pulled on his shirt and started putting on his socks and trainers. When he did speak he sounded angry instead of apologetic.

'Well, I don't know why I did that,' he said sarcastically. 'Maybe it's because some chick asked to sleep with me, then stripped off half naked in front of me. Perhaps I'm missing something here but where I come from that's kind of an invitation to play. I mean, it would be an insult *not* to make a pass in the circumstances.'

An insult not to make a pass? He went on talking for a bit but I wasn't listening. Instead I was thinking about what he'd just said and trying to make sense of it. Why would Josh think I'd be insulted at a gay guy not making a pass? And why *had* he made a pass? Of course. There could only be one explanation. Obviously Josh didn't realize I knew he was gay and had made a pass to save my feelings and also, I suppose, to protect his secret. Oh God, I thought I'd made it clear to him that I knew what he was like but I mustn't have. I guess I never actually said, 'I know you're gay.' Poor Josh. He must have been very uncomfortable when I said I'd sleep with him.

Josh was still talking but didn't sound angry any more. Just miserable. He said, 'Look, I'm sorry, Cat. Tonight was a mistake. I'm going out – I'll see if I can sleep in the car or something.'

He scrambled up and made for the tent flap. I said quickly, 'Don't go, Josh.' He stopped and turned to look at me. 'It's OK. You didn't have to make a pass at me to save me from feeling insulted. There's no need to pretend with me. You see, I know your secret. I've known it almost from the beginning. I thought you realized that.'

'You know my secret. What secret?'

'Well, that you're gay of course. But it doesn't matter to me. I like you just the way you are.'

He looked totally stunned and just stood there with his mouth open, staring at me. So I was right. He'd had no idea I knew about him.

He said nothing at first, probably too shocked to speak. Maybe I was the first and only girl who'd ever talked to him about his homosexuality so how I dealt with it now was very important. I had to get it right.

I said nothing either. He needed time to recover a bit from my revelation. Eventually he said, slowly and still sounding traumatized, 'You *know* I'm *gay*?'

'Of course.' I smiled at him. 'It's no big deal.'

'It is to me. Look, Cat, I don't know where you got this crazy idea but—'

'Please don't, Josh,' I interrupted. 'Don't try to deny what you are.'

'But—'

'It's OK, Josh. In fact, you know, actually, I'm glad you're gay.' He looked as though he was about to say something again but I was anxious to reassure him that he didn't need to lie to me any more so I rushed on. 'It makes me feel closer to you somehow. I feel you under-stand because, just like me, you've had to keep an important part of your life a secret and it's so hard. I can't tell you what a relief it's been to find someone I can trust enough to confide in.

'I'd never have told you about Mr Brown if you hadn't been gay. And as for all the other stuff' – I smiled – 'you don't think I would have been this open with you, telling you all my girly secrets, if you'd been straight, do you?'

Josh slumped down on the floor across from me and swept a hand through his hair. 'Jesus, Cat. I don't know what to say. Look, I mean, how did you . . .? What gave you the idea that—?'

'Tessa told me. But look, don't worry, no one else knows. Well, no one else except Lindsay. That's it.

Just the three of us. And we'll never tell anyone else.

'Not that you've anything to be ashamed of. In fact I think you're fantastic. I've never known anyone like you. Never shared so much of myself with someone.'

'And this is because of my being, um, gay?'

'Well, not just that, but yeah, that's a very important part of you. And how close we've been.'

'So, Cat,' he said slowly, 'if Tessa was wrong and I was straight then you—'

'But you're not, thank God.' I laughed. 'If I'd told all my secrets to a straight boy I'd shoot myself with the shame of it.'

Josh was silent for a while. Eventually he said, 'Look, it's late, Cat. Why don't we just get some sleep.'

I kissed him chastely on the cheek (to show I still trusted him), then wriggled into my sleeping bag. Too tired for reading, I put out the light and said goodnight.

We lay quietly in the dark for a few moments. We heard giggles coming from Lindsay's tent. It sounded promising.

Josh said, 'Seems like they're getting on OK.'

'Yeah,' I agreed happily. But then, thinking of Josh, added, 'Try not to be upset, Josh. You know it could never really have worked out with you and Peter.'

'What!'

'I'm sorry. I know how much you like Peter but—'

'You think I've got the hots for Peter? Shit!'

Then to my surprise, given how tense things had been, Josh started to laugh.

'What's so funny?' I asked.

At first he didn't answer, just kept on chuckling, which I was beginning to find annoying. At last he said, 'So, Cat, that's why you came along on this trip. To chaperone me and Peter, right? Save him from my amorous advances maybe.'

'Well, not just that.'

'Listen, Cat, I don't have the hots for Peter, OK? Trust me on this: he's not, um, my type.'

'Oh. Right.'

I wasn't really sure I believed him, but still, I didn't want to upset him by going on about Peter any longer. I said, 'You *have* enjoyed today though, Josh? I mean, this hasn't ruined it for you?'

He paused for a long time before answering, then he said, 'It's been, um, unforgettable, Cat. Yeah. Totally. Unforgettable.'

14

'C'mon, Lindsay,' I giggled. 'Peter is going round looking as though he's won the lottery. Don't tell me nothing happened. Now, out with it. Tell me all.'

'Oh God. All right then. Yeah, something happened.'

'I knew it! So what's "something"? How far did you go?'

'Too far.'

'Lindsay, you *didn't*?' I said, half excitedly but a bit shocked too.

'Well, not quite but nearly. We didn't have any condoms or we probably would have. Neither of us planned on it happening.' Then Lindsay added morosely, 'I wish it hadn't.'

'But why? Peter's really nice and, well, you must fancy him to have done, er, whatever it was you did with him.'

'The problem is,' she continued as though I hadn't spoken, 'he's asked me out this Friday. And I said yes.'

'So,' I said, laughing, 'I should think so. I would hope he wasn't just going to sleep with you again without even going out on a date first.'

'I don't want to go. I can't go.'

'I don't understand, Lindsay. You like Peter, and obviously, given what's happened, you fancy him too. I don't see what the problem is. You're just so right for each other.'

Lindsay sighed. 'I did find him attractive that night in the tent but I'd had a lot to drink. I was pissed.'

'You hadn't and you weren't.'

'Well, OK, maybe it was the romance of sleeping outdoors then. The whole moonlight-and-stars thing.'

'Don't talk rubbish. You were in a tent so you couldn't see the sky, and anyway it was raining so the moon and stars were hidden by the clouds.'

Lindsay paused at that, then looked away. 'Yeah, all right. I *do* fancy Peter, but only when we're lying down— Stop laughing, Cat, it's true. When we're horizontal I don't feel taller than him. I don't have a thing about length anyway. It's height that bothers me. When we're vertical—'

'Lindsay,' I interrupted, 'this is mad. Totally insane. He's quarter of an inch shorter' – here I put my thumb and forefinger together until there was a tiny space between them – 'if that. Don't tell me you're knocking him back just for that when you like him so much.'

'You don't understand, Cat. When we're standing

beside one another and I know I'm taller than him it doesn't feel right. I want a boyfriend who's taller than me. Otherwise I just don't feel, well, *feminine*, I suppose.'

'Oh, Lindsay,' I said despairingly. 'Of course you're feminine. And Peter is, you know, a nice-looking guy. He's got a good body. Solid and strong. You look slender and delicate beside him. Totally feminine.'

Lindsay shook her head. 'It's no good, Cat. Anyway' – and here she looked down at the floor, avoiding my eyes – 'Scott's just asked me out on Friday too and I've said I'll go.'

'Oh.'

We were silent for a while. Finally I said, 'So, have you told Peter?'

'Erm, not yet. No. I was hoping that, well . . . er, you might tell him. Actually.'

'No way.'

'Please, Cat. I don't know how to tell him. What to say. You've known him all your life. You'd be better at it. Anyway, going on this camping trip was your idea, as was swapping tents. So in a way it's all your fault. Please, Cat.'

'No. Absolutely, definitely, no.'

'I'm so sorry, Peter. She really likes you. Honestly. And thinks you're very attractive. Obviously. It's just this stupid height thing again.'

It was morning break and we were standing in the

school grounds. The rain had started to drizzle down again and most people were heading inside. Peter looked gutted but all he said was, 'She might have told me herself.' Then he walked away.

Oh God. Depressed, I decided to talk things over with Josh. See if he could think of any way to cheer Peter up. I found him at lunch time making his way to the muddy football pitch. Peter wasn't with him. Josh told me he'd decided not to play this afternoon, saying he'd a maths test to study for – though I doubted that was the real reason. He'd probably been too upset. Oh God, Peter too upset for football! He must be taking it really badly.

I quickly told Josh what had happened and asked him to look out for Peter. He said, 'She should have told the guy herself.'

'Oh, she just couldn't, Josh. Lindsay's really sensitive. She couldn't face seeing Peter upset.'

'No, Cat. I don't buy that. She should have told Peter herself. That was really shitty. But, yeah, I'll keep an eye on Peter.' Suddenly, unexpectedly, he leaned down, kissed me on the cheek and hugged me. 'You're way too nice sometimes, Cat. But don't change. I like you just as you are.'

I smiled as I watched him jog off to the pitch. Honestly, gay guys are just so sweet.

On Friday evening, when Lindsay was going on her date with Scott, I called Peter and offered to come over and keep him company but he turned me down. Tessa was out with Sean, and my parents had gone out for dinner so I was alone in the house. There was nothing on TV so I tried to concentrate on a book but found my thoughts kept turning to Peter and how miserable he must be.

Lindsay texted me a few times while on her date: WEARIN HI-HLS ☺! 1ST KISS! MMMM.

Then she called me. 'Hi, it's me. He's gone to the toilet.'

'I didn't really need to know this, Lindsay.'

She ignored me. 'Oh God, he's so gorgeous. And next time, guess what? I'm not going to wear heels so when we snog I'll have to go on tiptoe. Sssh. He's coming back. Bye.'

I closed my mobile and smiled. I hadn't heard her this happy in a long while. I just wish it could have been because of Peter instead of Scott.

Peter again. Suddenly I felt guilty about being pleased for Lindsay. I decided I'd go and see how Peter was, whether he wanted me to or not.

I went round without calling. I was surprised when the door was opened by Josh.

'He's OK,' Josh said quietly. 'You don't need to check up on him. I'm taking care of things.'

I heard Peter's voice in the hall behind him. 'Who's that? If she's female tell her to **** off.'

Charming. I went in anyway. Peter was holding a tumbler of whisky. Yuck, how could he drink that stuff?

When he saw me he said, 'Oh, it's just you, Cat. You don't count. Come on in.' We went into the living room. He waved the tumbler at me. 'Do you want a drink?'

'Just an Irn Bru thanks.' I glared disapprovingly at the tumbler of whisky. 'Is that your dad's single malt? You'd better not drink any more of it or you'll be in big trouble. Don't you remember how mad he was last New Year?'

'That was mainly because he caught me mixing it with Coke. "A fine twelve-year-old malt polluted with shite," as he said. I was a "disgrace to Scotland". I promised never to do it again and I haven't. Always drink it straight now.'

When he went into the kitchen I turned to Josh. 'Where are his parents? You shouldn't be getting him drunk like this.'

'They're out at the pub. Not expected back until after eleven. And I'm not getting him drunk.' Josh showed me his own drink, a bottle of Coke. 'I'm just keeping him company while he gets himself drunk.

'Look, Cat,' he continued, 'you should go home. Leave Peter to me. He just wants to get hammered then bad-mouth Lindsay and chicks in general. Tomorrow he'll be hungover but the next day he'll be OK and he'll have gotten the whole thing out of his system. It's just how some guys handle this kind of shit.'

Peter came back with my Irn Bru. We sat down and he returned to his theme of all girls being worthless, hard-hearted liars (although those weren't exactly the words he used, his own being disgustingly unrepeatable) while Josh just calmly nodded agreement from time to time. By the time I'd finished my Irn Bru I was beginning to think that maybe Josh was right and I should go and leave them to it. But then another uncomfortable thought occurred to me. Peter was upset and vulnerable just now and thought that he hated all girls. Maybe he might be tempted?

But no, surely he wouldn't turn gay just because Lindsay had knocked him back for Scott. No matter how plastered he got. I wondered whether Josh was hoping Peter would go off girls for good. I still think he has a thing for Peter even though he told me he wasn't interested. Maybe I should make it clear to Josh that Peter isn't ever going change that much.

When Peter went into the kitchen again to get a refill I turned to Josh and said, 'Peter is very upset right now but I'm sure he won't go off girls for good just because of Lindsay. I expect he'll get over her and find someone else. Another girl.'

There was a short pause as Josh thought about what I'd said. Then he smiled. 'You don't need to worry that I'll be taking advantage of Peter tonight, Cat. He's really not my type.'

I blushed. 'I didn't think you'd . . . I mean, I know you wouldn't—'

Josh laughed. 'Yeah, you did. But like I said, don't worry. I'm not gonna make a pass at him. He's not my type at all.'

Still embarrassed but also curious now, I asked, 'What *is* your type then?'

Josh seemed taken aback at this. 'Well, um, difficult to say exactly but, uh, not as hairy, I guess.'

'Oh.'

Peter returned and ignored my frown at the size of his drink. Maybe I really should just go. I wasn't his mum after all. Just then my mobile rang. I looked at the caller ID. Oh God, Lindsay again. I decided to ignore it but Peter said, 'It's her, isn't it? Go on, answer it then. She can't be having such a great time if she's calling you on her date.'

Just goes to show what guys know about us! I turned away, hit the answer button and whispered, 'Not now, Lindsay. It's not a good time.'

'Don't hang up!' Lindsay sobbed. 'Bastard has chucked me out the car in the middle of nowhere and driven off.'

'He's thrown you out of the car?' I said aloud, too shocked to remember to whisper. 'But why?'

'I don't know. Well, I *do* know – it's because I wouldn't. I wouldn't . . . I mean, it was just a first date. We were snogging but then he wanted sex and when I said no he got really nasty.'

'Oh God, Lindsay,' I whispered now in a belated attempt to keep Peter and Josh from overhearing. 'I've always thought Scott was a tosser, but I never thought he would do something like this.'

'Me neither. He was awful, Cat. Said he'd paid for our meal and I'd agreed to let him drive me to this isolated lane so what was wrong with me? Next thing I knew he called me a cock-tease, pushed me out the car and drove off.' Lindsay started crying again.

I tried to think what to do. 'Have you called your mum?'

'I tried but she's out and didn't answer her mobile. It's probably switched off as usual.'

'Call a taxi then. Don't worry about money. I've got some cash on me. I'll pay.'

'I did,' Lindsay sobbed. 'Even though I'm not exactly sure where I am. But the woman at the taxi firm didn't even listen to me. As soon as I opened my mouth she just said there would be at least a forty-five-minute delay and she couldn't even guarantee that, then I was cut off.'

'Oh God, Lindsay.'

'I'm so scared, Cat. It's pitch black out here and really creepy.'

Suddenly Peter grabbed the phone from me. He sounded completely sober. 'Where are you, Lindsay?'

I heard Lindsay sob that she didn't know exactly, then Peter walked off with my phone and tried to narrow down her location. 'Yeah, that will be the road past the block of flats they finally knocked down last year, out along the old canal. Yeah, I know where you are. It's not that far . . . Fifteen minutes max. Don't panic . . . What? . . . Sorry, Lindsay, the signal's breaking up . . . Sorry? . . .

Yeah, you really should have charged your phone . . . Lindsay? Lindsay? Shit.'

Peter threw my mobile back to me, grabbed his car keys and made for the door. I ran after him and clutched at his arm. 'You can't drive, Peter. You've had too much to drink.'

He tried to shake me off. 'I'm fine. I know what I'm doing.'

Josh took his other arm. 'No, Cat's right, you're not hammered but you're way over the limit for driving. Let's see if we can get a cab.'

'At eleven thirty on a Friday night? And Lindsay's on her own in some unlit isolated dirt track just waiting for some perv to come along and . . . No way. I'm going to get her now.' He made his way determinedly to the door but Josh beat him to it and stood in front of him.

'Get out of my way, Josh,' Peter said.

'Look, it's cool,' Josh said. 'Tell you what. Why don't you give me the keys? I'll drive. You navigate. Deal?'

'You drive?'

'Sure, I can drive. Remember? I've been driving longer than you.' Josh held out his hand for the keys. 'OK, let's not waste any more time. Lindsay's waiting.'

Peter reluctantly handed him the keys and we all hurried out. Josh whispered urgently to me before I got in the back of the car, 'Just keep reminding me, Cat: *Keep left*, OK? Especially at junctions.'

I nodded. Teeth clenched.

Josh proved to be a really good driver so I soon relaxed about that, instead thinking about Lindsay and how awful Scott had been to her tonight. That was until I saw the headlights of an articulated lorry coming towards us. 'LEFT!' I shouted. Fortunately Josh had noticed too and was already swerving to the correct side of the road. Bloody hell!

We finally turned onto the bumpy unlit road that led to the now disused canal. It was, as Lindsay had said, dark and really creepy. No wonder she'd freaked out at being left here. We slowed right down, worried we wouldn't be able to find her, but as we came round a bend I saw her and Scott by the roadside, bathed in the headlamps of Scott's car, which was facing us with the driver's door open.

Before Josh had even stopped the car, Peter leaped out. I scrambled quickly after him. I was relieved Lindsay was OK but worried that Scott might end up in the canal – I could tell Peter was really angry.

I heard Scott say, 'C'mon, Lindsay, of course I wouldn't have left you here. I was just winding you up. Can't you take a joke? Tell this tosser to push off and I'll take you home.'

He put one arm around her shoulders, intending to guide her towards his car, but Lindsay pulled away from him like he had a very nasty and contagious disease. Finally she understands Scott! When he stupidly didn't let go of her right away Peter pushed him. I looked around for Josh – not that I was worried about Peter getting hurt. I was more concerned for Scott who, though taller, is a lot less powerful. I spotted Josh, who to my surprise had gone round to Scott's car and was reaching inside the open door.

He straightened up and shouted, 'Hey, Scott!'

Scott twisted round to see Josh dangling car keys in front of him. 'These your keys? Catch!'

Making a wide arc, Josh pitched the car keys with a lot of force, not towards Peter, but away off the road into the distance. Since it was dark I couldn't tell how far the keys travelled but my guess was they probably landed in the canal, which was still out of sight.

'Enjoy the walk home, sucker!'

15

Be careful what you wish for. For ages I'd hoped that Lindsay and Peter would get together and now they have. At first it was great and I was so happy for them. However, it soon became clear that they're not just together but practically velcro'd to each other. They are almost never seen apart, and so loved up that they hardly notice me when I'm with them. At least they don't snog in front of me but they always look as though they're just waiting till you're gone, when they'll immediately have their tongues wrapped round one another's tonsils. This doesn't make me feel that my company is particularly welcome and, like everyone else, I've been avoiding them until (hopefully) this phase passes.

On the few occasions when Lindsay isn't with Peter she talks about him non-stop. How brave, fit and amazing he is. Ever since Peter's rescue dash after Scott abandoned her Lindsay sees him as her hero and now fancies the pants off him. To be honest it's a bit annoying.

Peter is OK but he isn't Rambo, for God's sake. And he still has maddening habits like telling you what happens next in a movie if he's seen it, or what he thinks will happen next if he hasn't – 'I bet it was the detective who murdered the prostitute.' Infuriatingly enough, his guesses are almost always right.

These habits used to drive Lindsay nuts. Now she just smiles at him indulgently. I've even heard her laugh politely at one of his stupid fart jokes. This can't last. Hopefully not anyway.

In the meantime, as well as hanging out with Josh I've been seeing more of other friends such as Marianne. I noticed she seemed to want to talk about Josh a lot; eventually she said, 'So he's definitely, definitely not your boyfriend then?'

'I already told everyone. He's a friend. I thought *you* would believe me at least.'

'Well, you can't blame me. You two are always together and he's such a gorgeous-looking guy. He could easily get any girl he wanted so why is he spending all this time with someone he isn't dating? And he never seems to bother with other girls. I mean, he's nice and all that, and yeah, he *looks* at other girls, but that's all.'

This was getting dangerously close to exposing Josh's secret. 'Maybe he's just very picky.'

'Yeah. And maybe he's picked you. I mean, the way he looks at you when you're together. You must have noticed it. He can't take his eyes off you.'

I shook my head and sighed. 'I told you already, Marianne, he's a friend, but if you want to imagine there's something else going on, then fine, imagine away.'

She was silent for a while then and seemed to be thinking over what I'd just said. 'So it would be OK if someone else were to ask him out.'

'Yeah, of course.' *Some chance they'd have.*

'Like me, for instance.'

'What?!'

'Yeah, well. I think he's gorgeous and really nice too, so if what you say is true, it would be OK if I asked him out? I really like him, Cat. You definitely wouldn't mind?'

'Well, erm, no, but, er, do you think he'd be interested?'

'Why not? I'm not ugly and if he's free . . . ?'

I feel bad for Marianne but what could I say? On Friday night I was over at Josh's as usual to watch a movie in his room. I'd picked the DVD I wanted and had curled up on the bed with a huge bowl of popcorn we'd made in the microwave. Before Josh flicked the movie on I decided to warn him about Marianne's intentions so he could let her down tactfully or, better still, try to head her off. He didn't say much; just nodded a bit morosely.

I said, 'I suppose you get this situation a lot.'

'No, not really.'

'But you must. I mean, you're not camp or anything so

girls have no way of knowing you're gay.'

'I guess.' Josh shrugged, then surprised me by asking, 'Cat, if I wasn't gay would you find me attractive?'

'That's a silly question. You *are* gay.'

'Just humour me, Cat. Would you?'

I shrugged uncomfortably. 'Well, you're very good looking. Loads of girls find you attractive. You know that.'

'But you? Do you, I mean, would you find me attractive?'

'OK, yeah. I would. Who wouldn't?'

'So ask me.' Josh smiled, moving very close to me.

'Ask you what?'

'Ask me if I'd find you attractive.'

'No, that's stupid.'

'Well, I would. Definitely.'

'Don't be stupid,' I giggled. 'How would you know? I mean, how could you possibly know whether you'd find a girl attractive if you were straight when you're not?'

'Trust me, Cat, I'd just know, OK.' He paused, then surprised me with an even weirder question. 'Do you ever wish I wasn't gay? Have you ever wished I was straight?'

'No,' I said honestly and immediately. I'd thought about this before. I remembered my sister's comments – hurtful but true. Did I really think Josh would be spending time with me if he was straight? I'd never have got to know him.

There was a long silence. I thought that Josh would be pleased with my answer and that it would reassure him but instead he looked depressed. Maybe *he* sometimes wishes he wasn't gay so he'd fit in and get on better with his dad. This seemed horribly sad so I added, 'You shouldn't be ashamed of being gay, Josh. I love you just as you are.'

'You love me?'

'Well, I like you very much.'

'You said you loved me.'

'Yeah, well, "like", "love" – it's the same thing.'

'No it isn't. And you said you loved me. That's very sweet, Cat.'

I blushed but didn't deny it. In some ways I *did* love Josh. I don't think I've ever felt this close to anyone.

'So,' he continued after a pause, 'do you have a question for me?'

Actually I did, but it seemed stupid and I felt a bit uncomfortable asking. Still, I suppose Josh wouldn't mind. I hesitated before saying, 'Yeah, I do actually, but I'm a bit embarrassed.'

'You don't need to be embarrassed with me. Go on, ask.'

'Oh, well, OK then. Well, erm, right. So, er . . .' I took a deep breath and then said rapidly, 'Do you ever wish I was a gay guy?'

After a brief stunned silence Josh laughed. 'No, Cat. I can honestly say that I never, ever wished for that.

Never.' He grinned at me. 'I think that's got to be the craziest thing anyone has ever said to me. Yeah, definitely. You freak, Cat!' He laughed again, then continued, 'Now, to answer the question I thought you were gonna ask. Yeah, I *do* love you.'

He kissed me on the cheek, then hit the play button to start the movie. I leaned against him happily. Having a gay guy as a friend was the best thing that had ever happened to me. Unlike straight guys Josh is just so open about his feelings. He's not afraid to show his affection for me, and of course I never feel awkward or threatened by this. He's the ideal friend. Totally.

Unfortunately though, I had to cancel my normal Saturday morning tennis 'date' with Josh as I'd promised to go shopping with my sister. I can't say I was really looking forward to this – she's OK when things go well and she finds exactly what she wants, but she can get into a foul mood if things don't go her way.

However, she's pointed out that we both need to shop for an outfit for the school theatre evening – Mum has given us sixty pounds each – and it would be nice to go together as we hardly ever spend time with one another these days. Also I have great taste and she really does value my opinion. 'Please, Cat, it'll be fun. We're sisters after all, and when was the last time we did anything together?'

So here I am in Princes Square. It's past three o'clock,

we've been shopping for over five hours without a break, and the only thing that's been bought is a thong and a tube of lip gloss (for Tessa) and two Kit-Kats for our lunch. Tessa suggested that since we don't tend to go for the same styles we should both hunt for her dress first then look for something for me.

It sounded like a good plan at the time but now, after five hours of frustration, I was beginning to wonder. Tessa has tried on hundreds of outfits, but although I thought she looked great in nearly all of them she didn't like anything. Right now we're in a very expensive shop: there's a sale on, with up to seventy-five per cent off on lots of items, but most of the stuff is still too dear for us.

Tessa was moaning about never having enough money for decent clothes and having to wear cheap rubbish all the time. 'If Dad hadn't insisted on taking a pay cut along with the factory workers for the last three years we wouldn't be in this position. None of the other managers has done it. Trust him to be bloody noble. He didn't ask me whether I wanted to make sacrifices. I'm sick of being poor.'

'We're not poor, Tessa. Just not as well off as other people at our school. We live in a nice house and Dad has to fork out for our school fees, which cost a fortune. 'Anyway,' I went on in an effort to head off an argument and put her in a better mood, 'you don't really need expensive clothes to look good. You look fabulous in almost anything.'

Tessa smiled. 'Thanks, Cat. It's just that now I'm dating Sean I can't be seen in cheap tacky stuff. All the people he hangs out with are loaded.'

God, yeah, I could see her point. There was no way you could shop at Primark or even TopShop with that lot. It turns out Sean's dad owns a chain of restaurants so he's the wealthiest boyfriend Tessa has ever had. I've met him a few times now: he's quite nice looking, although I think he's a bit of a poser. He always wears sunglasses even when it's a dull, grey day, and black or red silk shirts, open nearly to mid-navel, however cold it is. He also tries to pretend that he is somehow connected to the Mafia, but with a name like O'Reilly I seriously doubt it. Tessa is dead keen on him anyway, and things seem to be going well as she's already been to his house and met his parents, plus she's been getting to know his crowd of friends, all of whom seem to have rich parents too.

I guessed she didn't care much about the theatre night but saw it as an opportunity to get something decent to wear for her dates with Sean.

Scanning the shop now, I spotted a gorgeous red halter-neck dress. 'Look, Tessa. What about that one?'

'Hmm, yeah, maybe.' Tessa moved off, picked it up and looked at the price tag. 'Only forty pounds but it's reduced from eighty-five so won't look cheap. Then she looked at the label and frowned. 'Bollocks, a size twelve – they must have put it in the wrong rail.' She replaced it hurriedly as though it had suddenly become diseased and eyed it with disgust. 'God, it's enormous.' She glanced up at me. 'Oh. Sorry, Cat. No offence, I didn't mean . . .'

I *was* offended actually, but what could I say? I suppose, to be fair, for girls like Tessa a size twelve really is gross.

'It's OK – obviously that dress would swamp you.' I picked up a strappy turquoise and silver dress from the rail behind. 'What about this? It's your size and I think it would really suit you.'

Although it was £70, so a bit too dear, Tessa liked it and decided to try it on anyway.

We went to the changing rooms, which had four curtained cubicles and a common central area with a large wall mirror. Tessa didn't bother with the cubicles, although two of them were free, but just stripped off to her underwear (a thong and Wonderbra) in the communal area. I suppose when you've got a body like Tessa's there's no need to hide it.

Looking at her now, I found it hard not to be envious of her slim, tanned figure. I do think it's unfair that although Tessa is blonde(ish) she tans so easily – admittedly with the help of sunbeds now that summer is over – yet although I have dark hair, my skin is very fair and tends to burn if I get too much sun. And of course, as everyone knows, a tan makes you look slimmer. Tessa doesn't need this slimming effect as much as I do.

She looked fantastic in the dress. The turquoise colour

looked nice next to her golden skin and the almost straight cut showed off her slender figure. She said, 'I have to have this dress.'

I nodded my agreement. 'Yeah, it's perfect for you.'

'You don't think . . . ?'

'Yeah, I'll loan the extra ten pounds. You've *got* to buy that dress.' I laughed. 'It would be a crime against shopping to leave it here. You and that dress were meant for each other.'

Tessa smiled and hugged me before twirling in front of the mirror a few more times, reluctant to take it off.

Finally we'd paid for the dress. I checked my watch as we finished at the cash desk. Three twenty. Most of the shops would be open for another two hours at least so hopefully there would be time for me to find something.

Tessa checked her watch too. 'Oh God, is that the time? I can't believe it's that late. I promised to meet Sean at half three to help him pick a present for a friend's eighteenth birthday tomorrow. But look, no problem. I'll just text him and say I can't make it.'

'It's OK, Tessa, you go.'

'If you're sure . . . ? No, really, I think I should cancel.'

I shrugged. 'It's fine, Tessa, honestly.'

'OK, thanks, Cat. Oh, and could you take these home for me?' She handed me her shopping bags. 'As soon as we've bought the present we're going for something to eat, then off to the cinema. Don't want to trail these round on a date with me.'

I put the small bag containing the thong inside the larger bag and watched her skip off. I realized that my function today was to be Tessa's personal shopper plus baggage carrier and smiled ruefully. Typical.

I decided to take another quick look around the shop, this time with my own needs in mind, but at first I didn't see anything. I was about to leave when the red dress I'd spotted earlier caught my eye again. I dismissed it at first. As well as being too small, it was the wrong colour – i.e. not black.

I'm sick of black. Where had that thought come from? Of course I was going to buy something black. Black was slimming. *And boring. I'm bored with it.* OK, maybe I'd just go look at the dress. What harm could it do?

I moved towards the rail where it hung and, picking up a bit of the skirt, felt the material. Not thin and cheap but a rich, soft texture you wanted to keep touching. I took the dress off its hanger and held it in front of me, examining my reflection in the mirror. I suited the colour. Definitely. But it was too small. I put it back.

I was almost at the door when I suddenly remembered I'd lost some weight recently. Lots of people had mentioned it and my clothes felt looser. But a whole size looser? I hadn't been size twelve in at least two years, and to be honest I was just hoping that I never graduated to a size sixteen, at which point I'd probably have to buy my clothes in old people's shops.

I hesitated. Did I want to go through the whole

humiliating ritual of trying on something too small for me? The shame of watching a skinny shop assistant smirk as I handed the dress back with a 'No, didn't really suit me thanks,' when *I* know and *she* knows it was too small for my fat arse to squeeze into.

I looked at the assistant guarding the changing rooms. Yeah. A skinny size six. Still, I'd never shopped here before as it was too expensive and I'd probably never come again. So chances were that we would never set eyes on each other after today. How important could her opinion of my fat arse be?

Before I could change my mind I went back in, grabbed the dress and dashed into the changing room.

Bollocks. No cubicles free. I'd have to wait.

But another girl came in and started undressing in the communal area. She wasn't skinny. In fact she was probably bigger than me. I felt stupidly prim just standing there so, hoping I could at least manage to get the thing on, even if I couldn't zip it up, I took off my top and put on the dress over my jeans. Then I peeled off the jeans. I could see that the halter neck was going to look stupid with a normal bra so I slipped it off then zipped up the dress. Easily. Easy, peasy, with room to spare. Yes!

I checked my reflection in the mirror. The red colour suited my dark hair and pale skin. And it didn't make me look fat. Just curvy and, well, feminine, I suppose. Also the rich lined material meant it didn't look too revealing without a bra. The girl changing beside me smiled and said, 'Wow, that really suits you. But you'll have to get it taken in at the waist.'

I looked again. She was right. A size twelve that needs taken in. This dress was getting bought.

I couldn't keep the smile off my face all the way home. There is just no better feeling than unexpectedly finding yourself a whole size smaller than you thought you were. Only Mr Brown telling me openly that he loved me could possibly make me happier.

This dress was going to be lucky for me. I just knew it. When David saw me in this next Saturday he was sure to realize that I wasn't just a schoolgirl any more but nearly an adult. An equal. Maybe it was time we discussed our relationship. Made plans. We might not be able to be together for a while yet but we needed to at least talk about the future. Our future.

16

By Monday morning I'd changed my mind about Mr Brown and me discussing our future on Saturday night. Thinking things over at the weekend, I realized that even though we wouldn't be at school there would be at least fifty other pupils and five members of staff along with us. Unless by some miracle everyone else had to cancel at the last moment, a private talk about our relationship would probably have to wait for another time. Meantime it would do no harm for Mr Brown to see how grown up and sophisticated I could look out of school uniform. No harm at all. And we'd ages yet before we needed to talk about our future.

However, something happened in English last period that changed all that. We'd packed up a bit early as Mr Brown wanted to talk to us all about the theatre trip. He had some other news too, he told us.

He started off by going over arrangements again. Then he said, 'Actually the evening will also function as a last farewell for me as I will be leaving at the end of this week to pursue a new career in journalism. While I'll be sad to leave you all and I've very much enjoyed teaching here, I'm excited to be taking up this new challenge. Of course—'

There was a gasp of surprise when he said he was leaving but otherwise everyone had gone quiet until I stood up and screamed, 'NO, YOU CAN'T LEAVE!'

Mr Brown didn't reply – just stared at me, his expression a mixture of shock and concern. I looked away from him and immediately became aware that the whole class was gawping at me. Someone giggled; someone else muttered, 'Jesus Christ,' but mostly people just stared at me as though I'd gone nuts.

I felt a flush burn my cheeks and tears sting my eyes. I'd made a fool of myself. Oh God, I had to get out of here. Run away and never come back.

Then Josh got to his feet and, pushing his seat away, came to stand beside me. He said loudly, 'I agree with Cat, Mr Brown. You can't leave. You're an awesome teacher and English is the most important subject in the curriculum. What will happen to our grades if you go? This could affect our future. I think I speak for the whole class when I say I really hope you'll reconsider your decision.'

Scott muttered, 'Don't speak for me, tosser.'

Ignoring Scott, Mr Brown said, 'Thank you, Josh, I'm very flattered. However, I know that Mrs Stuart, the

English teacher who's replacing me, is excellent. She is highly qualified, experienced and has an outstanding examination success rate. I can assure you that you'll be in safe hands.

'As I said, I will be sorry to leave you all but I hope you understand my need to pursue this exciting opportunity I've been offered. Oh, by the way, when I said "all" just there, of course I meant everyone except Scott. I won't be sorry to see the back of him and I think I can speak for everyone here when I say' – and here he looked directly at Scott – 'why don't you just sod off, Scott?'

That was greeted with laughter and applause from the whole class. With the attention taken off me I sank down in my seat and tried to calm myself. Josh sat down beside me and held my hand under the desk, then whispered, 'You OK?'

I nodded but didn't speak. It was all I could manage right then. The bell went and I managed to walk out steadily enough but avoided looking at Mr Brown in case I started to cry again.

Josh tried to talk to me on the way out but I told him I needed to be alone. I couldn't face going home right away so instead I went to the park, where I walked and walked until I was too tired to walk any more. Then I sat down on a bench, where a pigeon shat on my head. Thanks.

I tried to rub away the pigeon mess with a bit of a tissue I found in my blazer pocket but I probably only succeeded in dispersing it more evenly through my hair, like spreading manure.

I went home. I met Tessa on her way to the bathroom. She looked at me and frowned. 'For God's sake, what's the matter with your face? You look like a constipated camel – and is that bird shit on your head? Go and wash it off, for God's sake. Sean will be over in five minutes and I don't want him to think I come from a family of mingers.'

'Hi, Tessa. Nice to see you too,' I said sarcastically but I was too depressed to bother getting into an argument with her.

Mum called from the kitchen, where I heard her rummaging around. Was she actually going to cook a meal on the one day I couldn't eat anything? No. 'Is that you, Catriona? Have you seen my Hermesetas anywhere? I was sure I left them in the kitchen drawer but they've disappeared.'

I found the tube of Hermesetas for Mum (in her handbag like they normally are) and handed them to her.

'Oh, thank goodness, Catriona. I thought I was going to have to use the low-cal sugar granules I keep for my morning half-grapefruit. Not as bad as real sugar of course, but unlike my Hermesetas they do have calories. I do like to indulge myself a bit at breakfast but it's just not worth it in tea.'

She glanced up at me for the first time. 'You don't look well, Catriona. Are you feeling all right?'

'Yeah, I'm, erm, just annoyed about this pigeon shit on my head.'

Mum told me off for using the shit word. I offered 'crap' but she insisted on 'mess'. Tessa, overhearing this, said, 'For Christ's sake. Cut the crap and just tell her to wash that shit out of her hair before Sean comes.' Poor Mum. You would think she'd have given up on Tessa and me using 'ladylike' language by now. But no, she keeps trying.

I washed my hair and changed, then Dad called to say he'd be working late so Mum needn't bother about dinner. Not that she ever did, I thought. Tessa had gone out with Sean so Mum suggested I just help myself to whatever was in the kitchen. She had her usual low-cal cuppa soup followed by crisp bread spread thinly with cottage cheese and decorated with sliced radish and cucumber – she says the topping adds colour and texture (but no taste obviously). Unusually she pigged out with a dessert tonight, a small carton of low-fat grapefruit yoghurt. Three courses. Wow!

I hunted desperately for some comforting food to cheer me up. Food had always been my friend after all. A reliable, constant companion that never let me down. It did tonight. I made myself beans on toast. Not exactly the most exciting meal but usually I like it. Now I noticed that the thick tomato sauce had made the toast soggy so I scraped the beans off and tried to eat them by them-selves but they were rubbish without the toast so I binned the whole thing.

Instead I opened a tin of vegetable soup and began heating it up in a saucepan. As I stirred the thick gloopy mixture I was reminded of vomit, which made me feel sick. I turned off the cooker and sat down on a kitchen stool. At last my wish had come true and I'd lost my appetite, but this didn't make me happy like I'd thought. Without Mr Brown nothing mattered and I just felt empty and miserable.

I went up to my room and looked out all my old English notes and essays. Sitting on my bed, I leafed through them, pausing at the bits where Mr Brown had written comments in the margins: *Excellent work; Good use of metaphor; Shows insight,* etc. He almost never just gave me an overall grade; instead he'd take the trouble to note particular passages that were especially good for one reason or another. The way he marked my work had always seemed so personal; now even looking at his familiar neat handwriting made me sad.

Lindsay texted me: OMG MR B TLD S SOD OFF! LOL.

When I didn't answer she called me. 'I'm at Peter's – why don't you come on over? It's ages since I've seen you. We promise not to snog in front of you. Honestly. We can talk about what Mr Brown said to Scott. I want to know all the details, especially the look on Scott's face when Mr Brown told him to sod off.'

Lindsay prattled on but I just wasn't in the mood to see anyone tonight. Especially not a madly-in-love couple. I told her I'd too much homework but she didn't believe me; she obviously thought I'd fallen out with her. The problem with having a secret love is that when it's over no one understands why you're upset – they just think you're grumpy. I suppose I could always talk things over with Josh but I'm not ready for that yet either.

I put down the phone and lay on my bed, thinking about Mr Brown and how awful school would be once he'd gone. Just a dull grey building where we learn stuff and do exams. All the other teachers are boring and humourless compared with him. None of them would have told a pupil to sod off – but I suppose he can say what he likes now he's leaving teaching. Why, oh, why did he have to go now? Couldn't he have waited until I'd left?

Then it struck me. In a few days' time Mr Brown wouldn't be my teacher any more. He wouldn't be anybody's teacher in fact. So he didn't need to behave like one. Like with Scott this afternoon. Or with me after Friday. I wouldn't be his pupil any more so if he wanted to be my boyfriend he could.

I sat up. *Of course.* Maybe *that's* why he was leaving. So we wouldn't have to wait two years before we could be together. Why hadn't I thought of this before?

And why hadn't he told me his plan? It would have saved me from acting like an idiot in class when he announced he was leaving. Maybe he thought I'd understand right away, or perhaps there had just been no opportunity for him to talk to me privately. I'd English tomorrow just before lunch. Somehow I'd find a way to talk to him about it. *I had to.*

I took Mr Brown's picture from my bedside drawer and looked at it. Oh, David, could it be that today was not the end of my life but just the beginning?

17

At English today Mr Brown set us some work then busied himself with sorting out files and clearing old folders, books and jotters from cupboards. I suppose everything had to be tidy for the new teacher.

I didn't get a chance to speak to him until nearly the end of the lesson, when we were all packed up and people were chatting as they waited for the bell. He was still working on the cupboards at the side of the class-room so I went over and said, 'You look very busy. Have you still got a lot to do?'

'I'm afraid so, Cat. I can't believe the amount of stuff I've accumulated since I got here. Cleaning out the Augean stables would be easier, I think. I'll have to work on it during the lunch hour and after school. I hope to have most of it finished today – your new teacher is coming tomorrow to check things out.'

Out of the corner of my eye I saw Naomi sidling up to find out what was going on. I ignored her and, smiling at

Mr Brown, continued, 'You know, I've brought a packed lunch today so I won't have to wait in any queues. If you like I could stay behind and give you a hand.'

'Oh, I wouldn't like to cut into your lunch hour. That wouldn't be fair.'

'It's no bother. Really. I'd love to do it.'

'In that case, Cat, thanks. That would be great.'

'Me too,' Naomi's voice piped up.

I scowled at her but Mr Brown thanked her and accepted her offer of help. What else could he do? Shit. This was going to make it much more difficult to have a private conversation. Just my luck to have the nosiest person in Scotland listening in. And why was she offering anyway? She never usually volunteers for anything that doesn't involve a gossip fest.

When the bell went Mr Brown suggested Naomi and I eat our sandwiches in the classroom while he went to the staffroom to 'grab a bite' and some coffee; he'd be back in fifteen minutes.

I soon realized why Naomi had wanted to help: she questioned me relentlessly until Mr Brown got back. First about Josh. Did Americans snog differently? Had I had sex with Josh yet? Scott said American guys have smaller penises. Was that true?

Then she moved on to Tessa's boyfriend. Was he really in the Mafia? Was it true he'd taken a contract out on Mr Phillips, Tessa's geography teacher, because he'd given her detention twice?

Finally, having failed to get any juicy information out of me, she asked if I'd heard the rumour that Mr Brown wasn't leaving because he wanted a new job: he'd actually been sacked for doing it with Mademoiselle Dupont in the school library during break time.

Just then Mr Brown walked in. I said loudly, 'No, I hadn't heard that rumour, Naomi, but here's Mr Brown now. Why don't you ask him?'

That shut her up. She busied herself removing books from the shelves behind Mr Brown's desk and putting them into boxes while I helped him clear out old folders from the cupboards at the back of the class. We were kneeling on the floor beside one another, emptying a bottom cupboard, when I plucked up the courage to ask, 'So how do you feel about leaving teaching, Mr Brown? Won't you miss it?' *Won't you miss me?*

He paused for a moment then said carefully, 'Yes, I'll miss some aspects of teaching a lot. Mainly the relationship with my students. However, there are other things I won't miss. Especially the effect on my private life. Teachers are expected to conform to society's norms to a greater degree than people in other professions and I find that restrictive.'

Oh My God. Could he have been any clearer in the circumstances! He would miss his relationship with *students*. Teaching was restricting his private life. After the misery of yesterday when he'd announced his departure, the sheer relief of knowing I hadn't lost him for ever and the excitement of knowing that one day, sooner than I'd ever hoped, he'd be my boyfriend, was almost too much handle. I had to put down the folders I was holding for a moment as my hands were shaking. Mr Brown gave me a concerned look, 'You all right, Cat?'

'Oh yes,' I said. 'I'm fine. Perfectly fine.'

I couldn't keep the smile off my face for the rest of the afternoon and grinned at everyone, including Mr Smith, the history teacher, who gave me a punishment exercise for 'dumb insolence'. Honestly.

But I was too happy to let Smith bother me, and when Lindsay asked me to join her at Peter's later I agreed. She seemed relieved. 'I know I've been spending a lot of time with Peter but I still need my friends. You haven't fallen out with me, have you?'

'God, no, of course not. You've just been a bit too loved up for company lately.'

Lindsay blushed. 'I know, but we're all snogged out now, and to be honest I'm looking forward to having someone else to talk to as well. His fart jokes are awful, you know.'

'You can say that again,' I said, relieved she seemed to have recovered her judgement. 'And the way he always tells you what's going to happen next in a film even when he hasn't seen it. Must drive you nuts.'

'I think that's really clever actually,' Lindsay said.

'Yeah.' I laughed, playing along with her sarcasm. 'So clever you could punch him, right?'

But Lindsay frowned at me. 'No, I mean it really is very clever. Peter's very smart, you know. Not enough people appreciate that.'

Oh God. 'Erm, yeah, you're right, Lindsay. So, around seven tonight then.'

I turned up with a box of Cadbury's Roses and a bottle of Irn Bru to watch a horror DVD. I was surprised to find Josh and Marianne plus some Sixth Year friends of Peter there. Peter and Lindsay had decided at the last minute to invite everyone they'd been neglecting since they started dating. Since it was a Tuesday night and no one had anything better to do they'd all turned up.

The invasion drove my aunt and uncle out. They told us they were going for a curry and would be back at half eleven, when they expected to find an empty and tidy house.

Aunt Susan warned us all that if there was so much as a cup smear on the glass coffee table or a soap smudge in bathroom sink there would be trouble. And we'd all to be quiet as the next-door neighbours didn't like noise or teenagers and had ears like bats. We'd to stay downstairs and absolutely no one was allowed in the bedrooms. And she had her ways of knowing if we'd trespassed.

My uncle added that there were six cans of beer in the fridge and they'd better be there when he got back. There was also a bottle of twelve-year-old single malt whisky in the cupboard, three quarters full, and he'd marked the level. He'd skin alive anyone who touched it.

Then he said, 'Hope you all have a good time then.'

Aunt Susan said, 'Yes, enjoy yourselves.'

We just looked at them.

As soon as they'd gone Peter handed out the beers from the fridge, replacing the cold cans with his dad's 'secret' stash of beer from the cupboard under the stairs. Marianne, whose brother is nineteen, had a bottle of vodka that she'd bought from him, moaning that he charged her a £2 'underage procurement' surcharge.

Gordon, one of Peter's friends, outraged on her behalf, offered to knock her up a fake ID for a tenner. She'd have got a return on her investment with just five purchases. But then he hesitated and said, 'Or, erm, I'd accept a snog instead.'

Marianne looked annoyed at first and I thought she was going to slag him off, but then, seeming to change her mind, she smiled sexily and sashayed up to him model-style, wrapping one ankle round the other so that her hips swayed suggestively. Gordon smiled stupidly back at her while some of the guys whistled. She stood in front of him and pouted temptingly. He moved to kiss her but she said, dreamily closing her eyes, 'Mmm, just a moment. I'm not quite ready.' She stretched out her arms towards him, then opened one palm to reveal a ten-pound note. 'Cheap at the price. Make sure it's a good copy.' Then she blew him a pouty kiss and laughed.

I went into the kitchen with Marianne to help her get glasses and Coke for the drinks.

'Poor Gordon,' I said. 'I think he really fancies you. Has done for a while now.'

'Don't even think about it, Cat.'

'Think about what?' I asked innocently.

'You know what. No more matchmaking, OK? I still haven't forgotten the priest disaster.'

'Yeah, but Gordon's really nice,' I persisted. 'And, OK, he can be a bit of a geek at times but he's not bad looking and he's got his own car. I really think—'

'Anyway,' Marianne interrupted firmly, 'I'm still interested in Josh. I've asked him out, you know.'

'You have?' *And I bet I know what he said.*

'Yeah. He said sorry but though he wasn't dating anyone right now he was still hoping to persuade you to be his girlfriend.'

'He did?' I said, surprised.

'You mean you didn't know? I'd say he's made it pretty obvious for a while now.'

Thinking about it, I suppose it was a good excuse for Josh. It was so sad really. All the lies he had to tell just because he was gay.

'Well, yeah, maybe. But like I said, we're just friends.'

'So,' Marianne said, 'if you're really not interested he's bound to give up one day. Then maybe he'll change his mind about me.'

I frowned. It really wasn't fair on Marianne to be clinging to false hope like this.

She was looking at me curiously. 'Why don't you fancy Josh, Cat? I mean, I've never believed the lies that Scott used to put around about you being gay, but Josh is gorgeous. How can you not want him?'

'Scott's been saying that? To everyone?'

Marianne nodded.

'*Now* you tell me. What a tosser.'

'Yeah, well, no one believes anything Scott says anyway. But honestly, Cat, I can't understand why you don't want to date Josh. He's, well, not the kind of guy most girls would knock back.'

'Just because Josh is good looking, intelligent and a really nice guy doesn't mean I have to fancy him, does it?'

Marianne looked at me, her eyebrows raised sceptically. 'Yeah, Cat, it does.'

I looked away. 'OK, I know it must seem odd but, erm, there are things about Josh you don't know.'

'Such as?'

'Hmm, well, he has an annoying habit of saying "You're welcome" every time you say "Thanks". It gets on your nerves after a while. And he can name every state in America plus its capital but doesn't know where Aberdeen is. I ask you. But worst of all he thinks my accent is cute and keeps telling me so. Forget about him, Marianne. He's OK as a friend but anything more would drive you mad.'

Marianne wasn't put off. 'So, he doesn't turn into a werewolf at the full moon, does he? Even if he did it would only be for a few days a month. I can cope with that. Probably no worse than me with PMT.'

I could see I would have to do more to discourage her. I said, 'If I tell you a secret about Josh you must promise not to tell another living soul. OK?'

Marianne nodded, intrigued.

'Well, he's, er – this is embarrassing but he's, well, an awful kisser. Horrible. He tried to snog me once and it nearly turned my stomach.'

'What did he do? Surely it couldn't have been that bad.'

'Oh God, it was. As soon as he started kissing me he, er, dribbled. Yeah, dribbled down both our chins.' Marianne looked horrified but I continued, determined to kill her infatuation stone dead. 'And then he licked my face. All over. Chin, cheeks, eye sockets, nose.'

'Yuck. Gross.'

'I know. So you see why—'

'God, yeah. Hmm, you know, Gordon *is* quite nice really. And you're sure he's no plans to become a priest?'

'Well, he's an atheist . . .'

'Excellent, thank God for that.'

Later I confessed to Josh what I'd done. At first he seemed put out. 'Shit, Cat, couldn't you have just told her that I always leave the toilet seat up or pick my nose or pee in the shower? I mean, dribbling when making

out! You actually said that? And licking your face. Gross.'
But then he just laughed. 'So, I don't suppose I'll be
bothered by Marianne coming on to me again. Or anyone
else for that matter if word gets out.'

I enjoyed the movie – no thanks to Peter and Josh. It was
one of those films set in a huge abandoned house
surrounded by remote woodland, with lots of teenagers
who are having a fantastic time until they become the
prey of a dangerous psychopath with a hunting knife
and a random dislike of young people.

Of course Peter piped up with stuff like, 'She's going
outside at midnight on her own to investigate the strange
gurgling noise. She's gonna get knifed for sure.'

Yeah, like everyone hadn't already worked that out.
Honestly.

Josh, if anything, was worse. 'She was in *Slaughtered
Two* last year. Pretty second-rate actress then and even
worse now. But to be fair the script is poor and the
direction at best adequate. Too much reliance on special
effects; not enough on plot and originality.'

Eventually I managed to tune them both out and
enjoy the movie, although I had to put my hand over
their mouths at appropriate points and occasionally a
sharp kick on the shins was required.

After the movie everyone had another drink then
started wandering off. I collected the glasses, stacked
them and turned on the dishwasher. Then I put all the

empty beer cans and the vodka bottle in a thick black bin bag and asked Josh to take it outside. I cleared away the sweet and crisp wrappers, plumped up the cushions, then got some kitchen towels and Mr Muscle to clean the glass coffee table. However, Josh took them off me, went into the kitchen, where Peter and Lindsay were locked in a passionate clinch, and said, 'Sorry to interrupt you guys but I think you might need these.' He placed the cleaning stuff on the table beside them. 'I'm just gonna walk Cat home now. See ya.'

On the way back Josh was telling me I should stop playing Mom at every social occasion. Let other people clear up for a change. I suppose he has a point. It's not that I'm a martyr really: my clean-up habit developed because I wanted to avoid standing around watching other people snogging at parties, but maybe I'd taken it too far. When I'm going out with Mr Brown people will be too sophisticated to snog in public.

As usual I smiled at the thought of David. Josh said, 'It's nice to see you looking happy again. You know, Cat, don't take this the wrong way but I think it's a good thing Mr Brown will be gone after this week. Maybe then you can let go of these fantasies and start living your life for real.'

'They're not fantasies,' I snapped, my fuzzy feel-good mood evaporating.

'OK, all right. Chill. I didn't mean fantasies exactly. Hopes then. It will be good for you to let go of unrealistic hopes.'

'And they're not unrealistic.' I started walking on rapidly so that Josh had to do a kind of jog to catch up. 'Look,' I said, softening a bit, 'I know you're worried I might get hurt but I won't be. Mr Brown loves me, and once a decent amount of time has passed I'm sure he'll contact me.'

We had reached my house so I said, 'Bye, Josh,' then turned to go in, but he caught me firmly by the arm to stop me and I turned to face him.

'Sorry, Cat, but I just don't buy this shit. How is he gonna contact you? Have you guys exchanged phone numbers, or addresses? Emails even? And why the wait? As of Friday at four p.m. the guy isn't your teacher any more so why don't you just ask him out? You know, you could just say, "David, why don't we meet up sometime? How about we go for a Coke next week, maybe take in a movie? Is Tuesday good for you?" So, Cat, why don't you just do that and cut the crap?'

I was surprised by Josh's reaction. Normally he is so laid back and easy going. I've seen him lose his temper on occasion but it's usually over someone like Scott being a total pain. I just couldn't see why he was so het up about me and Mr Brown.

Hmm, maybe his bad mood wasn't to do with that at all. Maybe he was actually upset about another couple altogether. I remembered how abrupt he'd been with Lindsay and Peter just before we left, interrupting their snog and handing them the cleaning stuff. Of course, I've been so ecstatically happy about Mr Brown that I've been insensitive to Josh's feelings.

'Josh,' I said softly, 'I know – like me you're happy for Lindsay and Peter but I understand too that it must be painful for you. You see, although you deny it, I can tell that at one time you had feelings for Peter and, well, probably still do. Tonight must have been very upsetting—'

'Oh, for Christ's sake, not that again. I told you before I don't have "feelings" for Peter.' He pushed a hand through his hair distractedly, then went on, 'But, hey, OK, all right, let's say for argument's sake that I was attracted to Peter. Well, in that case I wouldn't have sat around dreaming about him, I'd have asked him for a date. Shit! I can't believe I just said that.'

Josh paused, and when he next spoke he didn't sound angry any more. 'Look, Cat, I'm sorry. What you do about Mr Brown is your business. If you want to spend your whole life like a fairytale princess, dreaming in your lonely tower about the handsome prince who'll wake you with a kiss, that's your decision. It's just that Snow White doesn't fit too well with twenty-first-century reality.'

'It's Sleeping Beauty,' I corrected automatically.

'Whatever.' But then Josh smiled. 'You look like Snow White. Long dark hair and fair skin.'

'Hmm, maybe' – I smiled back, pleased he seemed to be in a good mood again – 'but I wouldn't suit the puffy-sleeved dresses.'

'Nah,' Josh agreed, 'that's not a good look for a hot fairytale princess.'

We were silent for a while after that, both just pleased to be getting on again. Finally I said, 'I'm glad we've not fallen out, Josh. You mean such a lot to me. Nearly as much as Mr Brown.'

Josh was suddenly serious again. 'Don't take this the wrong way, Cat. It's not like I'm a psychologist or anything, but have you ever thought about why you like me and Mr Brown so much? That maybe we have something in common?'

I laughed. 'Are you drunk or something? How many beers did you have? You and Mr Brown are nothing like each other. I can't think of a single thing you have in common.'

'You can't? What about this then? Your teacher and a gay guy. We're both kinda unobtainable. Safely unobtainable. Maybe you're a bit scared of a real relationship with an available guy.'

I was getting annoyed again. 'That's total rubbish, Josh. Mr Brown isn't unobtainable. We'll be together one day. Maybe one day soon. And I'm not scared of anything. Why would I be?'

'I don't know, but maybe, well, you seem to have a hang-up about your sister. Like you think she's better than you or something. Better looking anyway. So maybe you're scared you're not good enough or—'

'That's rubbish too. I'm not jea—'

'Yeah, you're right, Cat. It's all bullshit.'

'Finally, some sense out of you tonight.'

'Because you're way more gorgeous than Tessa. Don't get me wrong, your sister's a very attractive girl, but next to you? Well, you make her look ordinary. You're beautiful, Cat. Really beautiful.'

Josh was staring intently at me as he said this and I could see that he was totally serious. This was the second person who'd said I was nicer looking than Tessa. Alistair had said much the same thing not long ago. Shame they're both gay guys. Still, it was a sweet thing for Josh to say.

I smiled. 'Thanks, Josh.'

'You're welcome.'

'Well, erm, goodnight.'

'Goodnight, Cat.'

I turned away and hurried to my door, conscious of the fact that Josh hadn't headed off home but was still standing by the gate watching me. He was behaving oddly tonight but I was too tired to think about it now. I turned and waved to him, then went inside.

Although it was late Dad was still up. As usual he was working on his laptop.

'Had a nice time, love?' he asked.

'Yeah, but, Dad, it's nearly midnight. Surely you could do this tomorrow at the office. They can't expect you to work twenty-four hours a day.'

'I'll pack it in soon, love. But yes, these days

everyone's expected to put in more hours and work harder than ever before. There's so much competition now. China, India, Eastern Europe—'

'But I thought Josh's dad told you the company's OK now. He's not going to sell it off? He wouldn't do that now he knows us, would he?'

'There aren't any guarantees nowadays, love – but I shouldn't be bothering you with this. You look tired and you've got school tomorrow. It's time you were in bed.'

'You too,' I teased. But I knew he'd probably be up until he'd finished whatever it was he was working on.

I *was* tired and went straight to bed, but once there I found I couldn't sleep. I couldn't forget the stuff Josh had said about me and Mr Brown and I kept replaying our argument in my head.

Was Josh right about any of it? Was my reluctance to ask Mr Brown when he planned for us to get together tact or just cowardice? Was I really dreaming my life away? I had to know. My mind was made up now. I had to sort things out with David. Once and for all. I was going to tell him how I felt. And ask him how he felt about me. Soon. Very soon.

18

Mr Brown hadn't given us much notice of his leaving but we managed to get him a bottle of Polish vodka, which we'd overheard staff saying he liked, along with a book of Burns's poems. I volunteered to present these to him at the pre-theatre dinner on Saturday. No one was surprised by this as everyone knows I like him, but thankfully, except for Josh, that's all they know. We'd also ordered a new CD by a band he'd mentioned he admired, but by Friday it hadn't arrived so I said I'd post it to him when it finally turned up.

No one remarked on this at the time but as Josh was walking part of the way home with me after school he said, 'So Mr Brown gave you his address?'

'Hmm, well, sort of,' I lied.

'What does "sort of" mean? Does it mean "no" and you're really just going to give the CD to one of the staff to post for you?'

'You think I'm lying about knowing where he lives? I

suppose you think it's something else about Mr Brown that I'm just imagining. Well, I'm not. I happen to know for a fact he lives at two one five King's Court – a new block of flats on the south side of the city. You can ask him if you like.'

I was mad at Josh for thinking I was just making it up, but actually the way in which I found Mr Brown's address is something I'm not very proud of. Last year during the endless school holidays I was missing him so much. He'd mentioned at one time that he lived just a short fifteen-minute drive from the school, so one boring afternoon I looked up D. BROWN in our phone book. Unfortunately it's a common name and there were a lot of them, so at first I did nothing about it. And in any case many teachers had unlisted numbers to avoid getting nuisance calls from pupils. But later I changed my mind. There would be no harm in just ringing a few numbers. If someone I didn't know answered I could just say, 'Sorry, wrong number.' If Mr Brown answered I'd put the phone down.

I'm ashamed to say I worked my way down the list until at last I heard Mr Brown's voice. Not in person but his answering service. Later I learned from Naomi that he had gone to Europe for nearly the whole of the holiday period, so – and OK, I know this is pathetic – I used to call up his answering machine just to listen to his lovely low chocolatey voice. One day I even took a bus out to where he lived and just looked at the block of flats.

Since last year I've become ashamed of this behaviour. It seemed too much like stalking. I wasn't a stalker, just a girl in love with someone who, I think – hope, anyway – feels the same way about me. So this summer I never called or visited. But now he's leaving. And I've got the excuse of delivering the CD. It would be the perfect opportunity to finally speak to him one-on-one in private.

It's Saturday evening at last and I'm all dressed up for the theatre trip. I gazed at my reflection in the long mirror in my room and hardly recognized myself. Lindsay said, 'You look like a film star, Cat. You're going to have to fight guys off with a stick tonight.'

'Yeah, right.' I laughed, glancing back at her. 'But thanks, I think I do look not too bad. You look fantastic too. You really suit that dress. Bet Peter was worried about letting you out without him tonight.'

Lindsay smiled. 'He's picking me up afterwards anyway.'

I turned to the mirror again. While Lindsay's compliment was obviously a total exaggeration I must admit I did look good. Lindsay had even managed to make my hair look nice by sweeping some of it up in a kind of complicated braid with the rest sort of tumbling down over my shoulders. The red dress and strappy high-heeled shoes looked sexy and I'd painted my nails and lips the same shade. I put on silver hoop earrings and smiled. Yes, they went perfectly.

I heard Tessa come into the room so I turned round. 'Hi,' I said.

She was wearing the turquoise and silver dress she'd bought on our shopping trip and looked great, as always. She joined me at the mirror and put an arm around my waist. We looked at our reflections but this time I didn't suddenly feel like elephant girl like I'd feared. I'd never be as slim as my sister but I was just as pretty tonight. In a different sort of way. I said, 'You look fantastic, Tessa.'

She frowned at me. 'Are you sure about the colour of your dress, Cat? Wouldn't black be more slimming?'

For a moment I felt bad. I looked at myself critically, but no, I wasn't fat. Just nicely curvy. I smiled and said, 'I suppose black would be more slimming but I don't want to look slimmer. Just nice. And I think I look nice.'

I saw Lindsay giving me the thumbs-up sign in the mirror and smiled, but quickly turned Tessa round so she wouldn't notice.

Dad offered to drive us to the restaurant but we turned him down saying we'd just get a taxi. He argued with us for a bit. It was no bother; why go to the expense of a taxi? But we insisted and I settled the matter by pouring him a large whisky and telling him he should relax, it was Saturday night. Mum joined him with a small gin and diet tonic, so that was that. Our reason for refusing his offer wasn't really thoughtfulness, however: a crowd of us were meeting at a pub in Glasgow first. We all had fake IDs except for Josh, but one of the girls in our class is going out with a bouncer at the pub so she says she'll get Josh in.

Lindsay was right about me being the centre of attention tonight. Lots of boys came up to me, saying stuff like, 'Bloody hell, Cat, is that you? You look, well, er, different. Very different. Amazing.' I must say it was nice. Especially as most of them were looking quite handsome in dark suits with white shirts and bow ties. Only Josh didn't treat me any differently. Not really because he's gay but just because, I suppose, he always pays me a lot of attention.

We had a couple of rounds of drinks but then it was time to leave, everyone frantically sucking polo mints. I don't suppose any of the teachers would be fooled: our minty breath would probably, if anything, confirm their suspicions that we'd been drinking, but they wouldn't mind as long as no one was obviously pissed or sick.

As we neared the restaurant my pace quickened and my excitement rose. What would Mr Brown's reaction be to me? I'd never felt more confident, more certain that I looked attractive and sophisticated. He would see me in a completely different light. Surely this evening would kill any doubts he might have about our age difference or my readiness for a relationship.

As soon as I got there I slipped off my black velvet jacket so that Mr Brown's first sight of me would be in the red dress. I saw him right away as he was standing by the door waiting for us. He smiled and nodded; then, when I came up close to him, he looked at me with raised eyebrows and said, 'You look lovely tonight, Cat.'

He actually said that. I just stared back at him, totally overcome. *He thinks I look lovely. He said I looked lovely.*

Tessa, who'd been standing beside me, broke the spell. 'For God's sake, come on, Cat. Where's our seat? I'm starving.'

All during dinner I tried not to stare at him too obviously but it was hard. He was chatting with Mrs Campbell. Although of course they weren't a couple I couldn't help envying how easily she could talk with him and how he in turn joked with her effortlessly. I fervently wished that he would talk like that with me one day. Like we were equals. Not teacher and pupil but both adults. I wanted so much to be a part of his life. Someone he could talk to, laugh with, confide in.

Sometimes it sounded as though Mrs Campbell was actually flirting with him but I suppose she wasn't being serious as she's married, and at least thirty-six or seven. Still, I was pleased that when she invited him to go for a drink after the play he told her he'd have to go straight home as he'd a lot on tomorrow and needed an early night.

I didn't get a chance to say anything to him during dinner, although sometimes he'd catch my eye and smile. However, after the meal it was time for me to give my short speech and hand over the class gifts and card.

Although it was just a few sentences, I'd rehearsed the speech endlessly and delivered it perfectly, including just a little bit of humour like you're supposed to.

'So for Mr Brown, who gave us fewer detentions and more fun lessons than any other teacher in the school, a small token of our appreciation.' I handed him the gifts. Then I did it: leaned over and kissed him in front of everyone. OK, only on the cheek, but still, this was our first kiss. His skin was a bit stubbly, but not too much, and I could smell the citrus scent of his aftershave.

I felt myself blushing from my neck up as idiot guys whistled and shouted stupid comments. But I didn't care. Not even when I saw Mrs Campbell frown at me.

I went on, 'Of course, not everyone appreciates Mr Brown. Scott, for instance, was unfortunately unable to make it this evening.'

A chorus of 'Yeah, sod off, Scott,' got up, followed by calls for 'Speech, speech.'

Mr Brown stood up. 'Unaccustomed as I am to talking to you lot . . .'

He paused to make way for shouted comments – 'Yeah, not much'; 'God, how long is he gonna go on for this time? Someone ring the bell for Christ's sake.'

'. . . briefly,' Mr Brown added, to much laughter (his protracted period-long talks on English literature were a common occurrence), 'I'll make an exception here and just say thank you all very much. It's been a privilege to know you. I'd like to just add a special thanks to the lovely Cat for her very succinct but effective speech for which, if I were still her English teacher, I'd give her an A plus.'

He smiled at me and I smiled back. So he wasn't upset by my kissing him. Obviously this was what he'd wanted.

I was determined to get a seat next to Mr Brown for the play so I had to elbow Naomi out of the way and also barge in between him and Mrs Campbell, who'd been about to follow him into the second row. She gave me a furious look but was fortunately distracted by the news that some girl had been sick in the toilets and went off to investigate.

It was wonderful being so close to David, and when the lights went down I could pretend we were alone. Of course during the play we couldn't speak. I so wanted to touch him but had to make do with occasionally letting my hand brush the sleeve of his jacket as I readjusted my position on the seat and glanced at his profile in the dim light.

I found I couldn't concentrate on the play at all. The actors were all dressed in what looked like plain white sheets and there were no props. Mr Brown had told us this starkness was to emphasize the bleakness of *King Lear* and the timelessness of the human problems depicted in the play, but I found it boring. Although to be fair I don't think I would have been interested in any play then, no matter how exciting. Shakespeare and the white-sheeted cast certainly couldn't compete with the turmoil raging inside me.

Because I'd come to a decision. I wasn't going to wait any longer. Not for the CD delivery, not for anything. Tonight would be the night I'd tell Mr Brown how much I loved him and find out if he loved me too.

I'd never felt or looked better than I did right now and I was convinced that I would never have a better chance of making my dream coming true. This was my night. There was something magical about it. The only problem was going to be how to get him on his own because there could be no more talking in code.

All during the play I thought about it. I was supposed to go back to Lindsay's tonight, along with Marianne, Iona and Josh. Lindsay had asked Peter to pick us up. But I'd tell her I was tired and was just going to share a taxi home with my sister (although Tessa was really going to her boyfriend's, telling our parents she was staying with a friend).

I hated lying to Lindsay but I'd make it up to her once I'd sorted things out with Mr Brown. I was sure she'd understand.

When the play was over everyone filed out and I lost sight of David in the crowd. But I knew from his conversation with Mrs Campbell that he was going straight home.

Mrs Campbell and the three other staff fussed over us like we were primary school kids, trying to make sure we all got picked up by parents or took a taxi home. It was a pretty hopeless mission as it was only ten o'clock and some people were going off with pals or meeting boyfriends and girlfriends while others were walking off in groups to go to pubs or clubs with their fake IDs. Eventually Mrs Campbell gave up and just begged us to stay with friends: 'Remember, no one wandering off on their own this time of night. Stay together. Stay safe.'

I would be the only one to ignore this advice.

When Peter pulled up in the car Lindsay pleaded with me to change my mind and come back with her but I yawned (convincingly, I hope) and told her I was really knackered.

Josh said, 'Where's Tessa? I don't see her.'

'Oh,' I lied, 'she's on her way to the taxi rank. I'd better hurry. Bye.' Then I rushed off before anyone asked any more questions.

I didn't go to the taxi rank in case I met anyone from our school group there and had to talk to them. Instead I just kept walking until eventually I spotted a black cab with its orange light advertising it was for hire and flagged it down. I scrambled in, took a deep breath and said, 'Two one five King's Court please.'

19

The drive over to Mr Brown's seemed very, very long, although it probably only took fifteen minutes. What was I doing? Maybe he wouldn't be in after all. Or maybe he'd gone to bed and wouldn't answer the door. What if he was up but refused to talk to me? Or, worse, he listened to me but then said he wasn't interested. But surely he wouldn't say that. I know he loves me. I know it.

I wish I didn't have to do this all on my own. If only I could have Lindsay here. Or, better still, Josh, who's known my secret for a long time now. But no. I could hardly turn up at the flat with Josh in tow.

Instead, with trembling fingers, I texted him: TOOK YOUR ADVICE. WILL SPEAK TO MB TONIGHT. WISH ME LUCK. I hesitated before hitting the send button. Should I tell Josh? What if he called or texted back advising me not to go? It was a bad idea. I needed someone to support and encourage me, not make me feel even more scared than I was.

In the end I sent the text. I just wanted someone in the world to know where I was and what I was doing. But straight afterwards I switched off my mobile. Cowardly, I know, but I didn't want to risk a negative response from Josh. As things were it was all I could do not to tell the taxi driver I'd changed my mind and ask him to take me home. Also I had to make sure no one interrupted David and me when we were finally alone together.

The cab stopped outside the modern sandstone block of flats where Mr Brown lived. I paid the driver, giving him a bit more of a tip than I usually would, hoping for some reason that this would bring me luck. Totally mad, I know. It's not as though the taxi driver was a fairy godmother disguised as a penniless beggar who would reward me for my generosity by granting my wishes. But I was desperate for things to go right now so I did it anyway.

The flats had a small patch of lawn outside, bordered by a low wall, but there were no gates, just an opening in the wall and a broad shingle path leading to the entrance. However, the area was brightly lit, with lockup garages to the side, and when I got to the door it turned out to be controlled entry.

I saw D. BROWN listed as Flat 2/2 but couldn't at first bring myself to ring the buzzer. What if he didn't allow me to come up? What would I do? The decision was taken from me by a noisy group of residents who came up behind me and opened the door, ushering me in with a smile.

So much for security, I thought. I could have been a burglar, axe murderer or terrorist for all they knew. But I was grateful they'd been so trusting. This way David would have to come to the door and see me. I was sure he couldn't turn me away if we were face to face. Almost sure anyway.

I climbed the two flights of stairs to Mr Brown's flat, rehearsing my 'speech' as I went. *Hi, David.* Then I'd smile. *It's OK to call you David now, I expect. After all, you're not my teacher any more. In fact that's what I've come here to talk to you about. You and me and our relationship now that you've left the school. Can I come in?*

I'd imagined several possible replies to this too: *Oh, hi, Cat. What a lovely surprise. Actually I was going to call you tomorrow but I'm glad you've come tonight. Yes, please come in – we've so much to talk about.*

Or perhaps more passionately: *Thank God you've come, Cat. The thought that tonight might be the last time I saw you has been tearing me apart. I've hoped, prayed for this moment for years. Now it's finally come I can hardly believe it.*

I was outside his door. There was a glass bit at the top and I could see the light was on in the hall. I could also hear music playing. Some classical piece, I thought. He was definitely in. I took a deep breath and pressed the doorbell.

The music was switched off. A few moments later Mr Brown came and opened the door. He'd changed into loose jeans and a casual baggy T-shirt and his feet were bare. He'd never looked less teachery or more attractive.

He looked at me, his expression one of shocked concern. 'Cat, what are you doing here? Has something happened? Are you all right?'

Suddenly panicked, I said, 'Um, yeah, but I, er, need to use your bathroom.' Then, without looking at him, I squeezed past into the hall.

It was a large square hall with four doors leading off it. Taking a chance, I opened one of them. A modern, well-equipped and very tidy kitchen. I closed the door and opened the one beside it. A spacious bedroom with large bay windows and a king-sized bed. I stared at the bed, mesmerized. This was where he slept. Where maybe one day . . . I closed the door hastily and spun round, bumping into Mr Brown.

'It's in here, Cat,' he said, calmly pointing to the door next to the bedroom, but his expression was curious and even more worried looking than when he'd first seen me at his door.

I scurried in, gratefully locked the door, sat down on the toilet seat and covered my burning face with my hands. What had I done? This was going all wrong. Why, oh, why was I behaving like a complete idiot when, just a few hours ago, I'd felt so confident and grown up.

I breathed deeply to calm myself but still felt my stomach cramping with nerves.

I stood up, moved to the basin and splashed cold water on my face. That felt better. Leaning on the basin I stared at my reflection in the mirror. Gone was the sparkling sophisticated girl who'd been the centre of attention earlier this evening. Instead there was me, a tomato-faced idiot with water running down my cheeks and neck which would probably dampen the front of my dry-clean-only dress and make my bra-less nipples look like babies' dummies.

Mr Brown knocked on the door. 'You all right in there, Cat?'

'Yeah,' I said shakily.

'You don't sound all right.'

'Oh, um, yeah, I'm fine. Just, um, a touch of diarrhoea.' *Oh God, I did not say that. Please tell me I didn't say that.*

That was it. This had been an awful mistake. I would ask Mr Brown to call me a taxi, then I'd wait outside until it came.

I opened the door, saw his kind, gentle, concerned face and melted. He said, 'Please tell me what's wrong, Cat. Has someone or something upset you tonight?'

I was about to say, *No, it's cool. Maybe later*. But if not tonight, when would I tell him how I felt? It was now or never.

I said, 'Yes, we need to talk,' and Mr Brown ushered me into his living room.

A sleek Siamese cat was curled up on the rug and looked haughtily at me as I came in, as if to say, *You don't belong here*. I hesitated, but only for a second. There was no way I was letting a cat stand between me and Mr Brown. I sat on the sofa and Mr Brown sat on the armchair opposite. I stared across at him. He was looking at me with a curious but wary expression.

I said, 'David, I love you. No, please don't look away.' I continued quickly, desperately, 'Please hear me out. I've loved you for years, and now that you're not my teacher any more, we can be together at last. I want you to be my boyfriend. I've not had many boyfriends. Well, not any really, but I don't care. I've kept myself for you because you're everything I've ever wanted. Please, David, please say yes.'

Mr Brown groaned and pushed both hands through his short hair, which surely didn't need tidying anyway. Then he looked me straight in the eye, his expression pained. 'I'm so sorry, Cat. I'd no idea.'

'Please don't say that. Please don't. You must have known. And the poem you—'

'No, Cat. No. I didn't, and this is all wrong. Look,' he said earnestly, 'you're way too young, and anyway, until very recently – yesterday, in fact – I was your teacher. You must see this can't be right.'

'I'm sixteen. That's old enough. And you're not my teacher any more. It doesn't count. But yeah, OK,' I conceded, 'maybe we should wait a while before making our relationship public. Just tell me that one day we'll be together and I'll wait. Wait for ever if I have to—'

'No, Cat,' David said firmly as I fought back tears. 'It's

impossible. Firstly you're too young. Secondly you're a former pupil, and thirdly—'

Whatever he was going to say was cut off by the sound of someone's key in the door. We both paused and looked towards the source of the sound.

Someone living with Mr Brown who had a key. Maybe it was a flatmate. But no, I'd already seen that this was a one-bedroom apartment. David didn't love me because he'd met someone else. Someone he cared about more than me.

I heard a familiar voice from the hall call jokingly, 'Hi, honey, I'm home.'

The living-room door opened. Lindsay's cousin Alistair said, 'God, hi, Cat. What are you doing here?'

I stared at Mr Brown, my mouth gaping open in amazement. He looked back at me, then nodded. 'And thirdly you're female.'

20

Be careful what you wish for.

Mr Brown asked Alistair to go and make us some tea while he talked to me privately. When he'd gone (followed by the cat, probably hoping for food) Mr Brown turned to me again. Just as I'd so often dreamed, he didn't talk to me like I was a child or a pupil, but as though I was an adult. An equal.

Now that the shock had worn off I couldn't stop the tears welling up in my eyes then dripping down my cheeks; however, I managed not to sob out loud as I didn't want Alistair to hear me.

Mr Brown handed me a tissue. 'I'm so sorry, Cat. If I'd been able to be more open about myself this would never have happened, but that's almost impossible in teaching. Most people are OK but you'll always find the parent who, if you admit to being gay, won't trust you to educate their son. Like being gay is the same as being some kind of paedophile. So most gay teachers keep quiet.

'It's not easy, as you can imagine. When normal social conversation in the staffroom inevitably involves discussing spouses or partners (if you're involved with someone), or what pubs and clubs you go to at the weekend if you're single.'

Poor Mr Brown. 'It must have been really difficult for you, David.'

'I coped, but to be perfectly honest it's a relief to be in journalism, where sexual orientation doesn't matter. In fact' – and here he smiled for the first time in a while – 'in arts journalism being gay can be a positive advantage. Yes, there are some gay plumbers and so on, but in the music and theatre world, let's just say a gay person isn't exactly uncommon.'

We were silent for a while, then Mr Brown said, 'You know, Cat, you're a lovely person. If you weren't too young, a former pupil and female I'd definitely think of asking you out.' He smiled at me as he said this, his warm brown eyes crinkling at the sides the way I've always liked. Despite all that had happened tonight I couldn't help smiling back.

I went off to the bathroom to wash my face. When I got back Alistair had brought our tea and I sipped mine gratefully, the sweet, hot liquid calming me. The Siamese cat had padded back too and jumped up on Mr Brown's lap, where it sat possessively and stared smugly at Alistair and me as Mr Brown stroked its sleek fur.

'Bloody cat,' Alistair said, eyeing it resentfully. 'I

swear that thing gets more attention than me.' He turned to me. 'David's mad about it. Did you know he's even written a naff poem about the thing, imaginatively titled, I kid you not, "Cat"?'

I stared at the cat's beautiful blue eyes. 'Yeah, I did actually.'

David didn't react to Alistair's wind-up. Just smiled and let Alistair talk on. As usual Alistair took over the conversation. 'You look ravishing tonight, Cat. Love the dress. Where did you buy it? Très chic and very you, I must say. Looks like it cost a small fortune.

'So how was the play? Depressing, I imagine, but not as depressing as a Shakespearean comedy. Oxymoron, if you ask me. Now don't get me wrong. Good old Wills could knock up a decent script in his day, but humour? Forget it.'

Alistair prattled on and I was grateful. Lindsay used to say he could chat to anyone anywhere. 'Bundle Alistair on a tumbrel and send him off to the guillotine and he'd end up gossiping with fellow passengers the whole way there.'

Now I was just glad of his ability to talk without needing much by way of response. I don't think I could have coped otherwise. As it was, Alistair's constant stream of background chatter saved me from having to make polite conversation while trying to come to terms with my shattered dreams and the awful embarrassment of having just declared my undying love to a gay teacher.

Alistair was interrupted briefly by loud drunken singing coming from outside the flat. He went over to the window and looked out. 'Bloody idiots from the ground-floor flat again. Five pints of lager and they think they can sing.'

He continued to peer out of the window, then turned away and looked at me. 'I suppose you've had a spat with the gorgeous Josh then. You little tease, Cat, keeping him waiting outside in the cold for you. But maybe you're right. Treat 'em mean, keep 'em keen, that's what I say.'

I put my cup down. 'What are you talking about? Is Josh out there?'

'*Mais bien sûr*, my love. Don't tell me you didn't know your poor *petit ami* was sitting outside on the wall freezing his cute little ass off? Come look.'

I dashed across to the window. Sure enough, Josh was there, still dressed in his formal suit – though he'd taken off the bow tie and undone the top shirt buttons. God, I hadn't expected him to follow me here. What did he think he was doing?

I turned away, grabbed my jacket and bag, then made for the door. 'I'd better go.'

'Yeah, go on, Cat,' Alistair said. 'Put the poor boy out of his misery.'

Mr Brown offered to give Josh and me a lift home but I told him we'd just get a bus back. I just wanted to get away from here, collect Josh, then head home as quickly as possible.

Josh didn't see me at first as he was staring miserably at the ground, so I called softly, 'Josh.'

He looked over, then immediately stood up and held his arms open for me. I hurried towards him and he hugged me tightly, stroking my hair and saying, 'I'm so sorry, Cat. This is my fault. I should never have suggested you go ask him. You OK?'

'Yeah, I'm OK, except, erm, you're crushing me a bit.' Josh let me go, then I continued, 'How long were you going to sit out here, you idiot? And how did you remember the address? I must have just mentioned it once.'

Josh shrugged. 'I don't know. I hadn't really thought things through. I didn't remember the address at first either so I went through all the "D. Browns" in the phone book at Lindsay's until one address clicked. Took me a while. There are a lot of "D. Browns".'

'Tell me about it,' I said without thinking and blushed, but Josh appeared not to notice.

'Peter dropped me off, but don't worry, I didn't tell him why I wanted to come here.'

Josh suggested we start walking towards the bus stop but if we saw a taxi we should flag it down as it was getting late. He'd pay. It was the least he could do. While I didn't think tonight was really his fault I agreed as I didn't have enough money left for a taxi home.

I hooked an arm through his and as we walked along

I told him what had happened. He was shocked. 'You're kidding me, Cat. Mr Brown is gay? I'd never have guessed it.'

'Yeah, well, me neither. Just think,' I giggled, 'all this time you would have had a much better chance than me with Mr Brown.'

Josh stopped suddenly and turned to me. 'Cat, there's something I've got to tell you. Promise me you won't get mad, and at least hear me out?'

'Of course I won't be mad at you, Josh. You've been so sweet tonight, worrying about me and coming all this way to make sure I'm OK. Do you mind if we keep walking while you tell me though? It's getting cold.'

We walked on, although a bit more slowly, and I kept looking for a taxi while waiting to hear what Josh had to say. There was a long pause before he began. 'Cat, I hope what you just said is true but I know you've got a temper so it's important that you let me explain everything. I want to be honest with you.'

'I don't have a temper,' I said, outraged. 'Well, not much of one anyway. OK, I know I used to get angry when you tried to tell me I was wasting my time with Mr Brown, but you were just being honest with me even though it wasn't what I wanted to hear. Actually that's what I really admire about you, Josh. You've always been so totally honest and open with me— Oh, look – there's a taxi!'

I waved it down and yes, hurrah, it pulled in. I

scrambled in hurriedly, pleased to be in the warmth. Josh followed me. Once settled, I said, 'So what was it you wanted to tell me?'

He looked uncomfortable. 'Um, nothing really.'

'Don't be stupid. Obviously there's something. C'mon, I won't bite.'

'Oh, right. OK, then, it's . . . um, your hair. I prefer it down.'

'Is that all?' I laughed. 'God, I thought you were going to tell me you were a terrorist or something at the very least. Mind you, don't repeat what you said to Lindsay. She spent nearly an hour getting my hair to look like this.'

Just then the taxi driver twisted round in his seat to look at me. 'Gonnae geez a clue, hen?'

Oops, we'd been so engrossed in the conversation we'd forgotten to tell the driver where we wanted to go! I gave him my address and we set off.

Dad was still up when I got home, working on some spreadsheet on his laptop. He looked exhausted and old. 'Aren't you going to bed, Dad? It's late. Anyway, it's the weekend. You shouldn't be working all the time like this.'

'In a minute, love. I've just got a wee bit to finish. Did you have a good time? I thought you were staying at Lindsay's tonight.'

'Hmm, yeah, well, an interesting time, but I was tired so I decided to come home.'

And I *was* tired, I suddenly realized. Probably as exhausted as Dad looked. I said goodnight, warning him that I'd be listening out for him and if he wasn't in bed soon there would be trouble.

He smiled at me and nodded but we both knew he'd be working until much later.

I took off my beautiful dress, changed into warm comfy pyjamas and collapsed into bed. But before I put my lamp off I took out Mr Brown's picture. I looked at him and smiled ruefully. It was difficult to believe that I'd lost him to Alistair of all people. I kissed him anyway, for the last time, then put the picture away for good.

For a while, although exhausted, I couldn't sleep and kept replaying the events of the night in my head. My dream of going out with Mr Brown was over, yet I wasn't as devastated as I'd thought I would be. Maybe a bit of me had always known my dream had been exactly that. A dream. Total fantasy.

It had been a crazy evening and I'd been through such a lot. Tomorrow I was determined to have a quiet, lazy day. A lovely, boring day spent vegging in front of the TV with no mind-blowing revelations or dramas, except perhaps those I watched on screen.

With that thought I drifted off to sleep . . .

. . . And woke next morning to hear an odd sound downstairs. At first I tried to ignore it and go back to sleep but I couldn't because it was peculiarly disturbing.

What was it? Oh my God. It was Mum and she was crying.

I stumbled out of bed, shoved some clothes on over my pyjamas and hurried downstairs. Mum and Dad were sitting at the kitchen table. Dad's face was grey and Mum's was wet with tears. I said, 'What's wrong?'

For answer Dad passed me the business section of the morning paper. I read the article on the front page, my hands trembling, hardly able to believe my eyes. Dad's branch of the company was being sold off to the Chinese and thousands of redundancies were forecast. Shit.

Josh's dad had done this. And said nothing.

'Have you called him?' I asked.

Dad nodded. 'I've tried but he's in London this weekend and I've had no answer from his mobile.'

I hugged Mum and looked round for some tissues but couldn't find any. I went to the toilet and came back with a roll of loo paper instead. She took it and sniffed, 'Make us a cup of tea, love.'

I put on the kettle and got out three mugs. 'Everything will be OK.' I threw tea bags into the mugs and added, 'Dad will find another job.' A few minutes later I poured the boiling water into the mugs. 'Definitely.'

But I knew he wouldn't. Or not a proper one anyway. Dad has been made redundant twice before. The first time, I was quite young and at first I just enjoyed having my dad about the house, but soon the constant arguments about money upset me. Then we had to move schools and there was that awful stuff that happened to Tessa.

The second time he was out of work for a long time, constantly turned down for jobs because he was too old. That was four years ago. Things would be worse now. Dad is forty-five, which is quite old but not too old for working surely. But I remember him saying that if this job finished he was 'on the scrapheap'.

I hated Josh's dad for this. Hated him.

I couldn't find Mum's Hermesetas anywhere. 'Sorry, Mum.'

'Oh, sod it.' Mum shovelled two heaped spoonfuls of sugar from the bowl into her mug.

This frightened me more than anything else that had happened this morning. Things must be really desperate.

When we'd finished our tea, mostly in silence, Mum and Dad said they wanted to be alone for a while to discuss the situation, then they'd talk to me and Tessa. I was to call Tessa and tell her to come home.

Tessa wasn't answering her mobile so I was forced to look up Sean's parents' address. I felt really embarrassed when his dad answered and I'd to ask for Tessa. I don't know how she can sleep with him in his parents' house. Tessa came to the phone sounding really grumpy. 'For Christ's sake, Cat, what are you calling me here for and waking me up?'

I didn't bother to be tactful. 'Dad's probably lost his job and you've to come home.'

'Not again. Why can't he hold onto one sodding job for five minutes? What's it to do with me anyway? What am I supposed to do about it?'

'Just come home, Tessa, please. Mum and Dad are really upset. Besides, if you don't come they'll probably call Vicky and find out you're not there.'

That got her moving.

The phone started to ring non-stop – other people in the company who'd just heard the news but seemed to have no more information. Eventually Dad unplugged the house phones and turned off his mobile except for every now and then when he'd try to contact Josh's dad again.

When Tessa got back she was in a foul mood and snapped at me, 'You look a riot. At least brush your hair, for God's sake.'

I ignored her as Mum and Dad had called us both into the living room to discuss the crisis. Dad did most of the talking. He said he'd still not been able to contact Josh's dad but if the newspaper reports were correct then things might be very difficult for a while. Since he'd only been with the company for three years the redundancy payment was likely to be modest. On top of that we were still struggling with debts incurred during previous periods of unemployment.

However, we weren't to worry, we'd manage somehow. Certainly he'd be able to pay our school fees for this year, but next year we might have to change school or go to a local college. As for the house, it had been re-mortgaged a few years ago and payments might now be too high to sustain. It was possible we might have to move to a less expensive area.

Then Mum piped up, saying she would get a job. Unfortunately she hadn't worked in an office for years now and her skills were outdated so it might have to be retail or a supermarket check-out; the wages would be low, but every little would help.

It was at this point that Tessa shrieked, 'Right, that's enough. No way. Have you two gone off your heads or something?'

Mum frowned. 'Don't take that tone with me, Tessa.'

'Yeah, well, don't give me this rubbish then. Like I'm really going to go to some shit comprehensive full of dirty council estate rats and live in a bloody slum. I don't think so. And, oh yeah, I can just imagine me telling Sean's parents that my mum works in the supermarket check-out.'

I stared at her, dumbstruck. So she *had* called the kids at that primary we'd been sent to awful names. Not that this excused what they did to her, but still, I'd so totally believed her when she told me they'd made it all up.

Dad was silent too but Mum answered her furiously, 'Don't ever let me hear you talk like that again. As for Sean, frankly, Tessa, I don't care what you tell his parents and—'

Dad interrupted, 'No, Fiona. Don't get on to the girl.'

He turned to Tessa. 'I'm sorry, love. I know today has been an awful shock to you and maybe it won't come to that. We just have to prepare for the worst, that's all. Prepare for the worst and hope for the best. I promise you I won't let you come to any harm at school this time. If we stick together as a family we'll come through this.'

Tessa stood up and sneered at Dad. 'This is your fault. If you weren't such a loser we wouldn't be in this position—'

I don't know what she was going to say next because she was cut off by Mum, who got up and slapped her hard on the face, which sent Tessa running off to her room, crying and screaming that she hated her.

Brilliant.

Dad put his head in his hands and groaned. He looked old, grey and beaten.

Mum was unrepentant. 'She's had that coming for years.'

Oh God, what was happening to us? So much for Dad's talk of pulling together as a family.

Mum asked me to go to the shops and buy some more tea as we'd run out. To be honest I was just relieved to get away and made for the door immediately, but Mum called after me.

'Wait, Catriona. Can you get a packet of Jaffa Cakes as well? I haven't had Jaffa Cakes in years. Oh, and a couple of bottles of Chardonnay. I intend to get very drunk shortly.'

'I can't buy alcohol, Mum. I'm not eighteen.'

'Use your fake ID.'

'And it's just ten thirty, Mum. You can't buy alcohol until twelve.'

'Bollocks.'

What was happening to Mum? Asking for Jaffa Cakes and wine in the morning, then swearing. Not to mention encouraging me to break the law. It was scary. But oddly enough I think I liked her better this way.

The first two shops didn't have any Jaffa Cakes and as it was Sunday I'd to walk quite a way before finding another shop open. I became aware that people seemed to be looking at me oddly this morning. They must have noticed how upset I was and were concerned or curious about me. However, when I saw my reflection in a shop window I realized I should have taken Tessa's advice and fixed my hair. I hadn't bothered to undo Lindsay's elaborate swept-up style last night and, after being slept in, it now resembled a large, poorly constructed, abandoned bird's nest. That's what people had been staring at.

It was well after eleven by the time I got back. I'm ashamed to say I didn't exactly hurry. I felt desperately sorry for everyone, especially Dad: despite having done nothing wrong, he seemed to feel he'd failed us. I just didn't know what to say or do to make things better. My family was falling apart and I couldn't do a thing about it.

I'd slowed to a snail's pace as I approached our house. I was staring at the pavement, trying not to step on any cracks. I always did this when I was a kid – stepping on cracks brought bad luck. It was stupid to do it today, I suppose. I mean, how much worse could things get?

I noticed that there seemed to be more cracks than I remembered. I also realized for the first time that I had two different shoes on – though both of them were black. I'd just shoved them on this morning, anxious to escape the house. However, one was flat and round toed while the other was an open-toed wedge. I suppose that was why I seemed to be walking with a list. I guess that was another reason why people had been staring at me.

Resolving to pull myself together and stop acting like an idiot, I looked up, and that's when I saw it. Josh's dad's shiny new BMW in our driveway. How dare he! How dare he come here!

I ran into the house and found him sitting in our living room with my parents. He looked tanned, fresh and super confident. If we were Americans and had guns in the house I think I would have shot him dead right there and then.

Josh was also there and stood up to greet me but I ignored him. Instead I threw my shopping on the floor and confronted his dad. 'What are you doing here?'

'Excuse me?'

'I said, what do you think you're doing here? You've got some nerve, you really have.'

Dad said, 'Catriona! That's enough. Apologize at once.'

'No, I won't!' I rounded on him again. 'How dare you come into our house after what you've done. You've destroyed our family and lots of other families too while pretending to be our friends. Get out! I hate you.'

Josh tried to stick up for his dad. 'No, Cat, you don't understand.'

'Don't try to defend him, Josh. I understand all right.' I glared at him. 'I understand we've been totally stupid to trust someone callous enough to reject his own son just because he's gay. Get out of our house and never come back.'

A shocked silence followed. I continued to stand belligerently in the centre of our living room, facing down everyone, but part of me was shit scared. I'd never been this rude to an adult before. What would happen? But then again, it was an adult who'd made my mum cry and ask for Jaffa Cakes. This person had shamed my sister by making her face the thought (mortifying and terrifying for her) of maybe having to go a non fee-paying school and being despised by her boyfriend's family. Above all, this was the tosser who'd humiliated my dad by making him unable to provide for his family despite the fact he worked so hard, seven days a week, almost twenty-four hours a day.

'Go on,' I said. 'Sod off.'

Josh's dad was the first to break the silence. When he spoke to me his voice was very low and calm but somehow totally menacing. He said, 'Have you finished? Good.' He looked at my parents. 'With your permission I would like to answer these accusations briefly.'

They nodded. What else could they do? It seemed a pretty reasonable request after all.

He turned his attention back to me. 'May I suggest, Catriona, that you do not automatically trust everything you read in the newspapers, particularly when articles have not been confirmed by an authoritative source. These inaccurate leaks are very regrettable. In fact, while it is true that due to changing global business conditions the plant has had to be sold, no involuntary redundancies will result and all employees are guaranteed the same pay and conditions for at least three years.

'In the case of the software and design division, where your father is based, these guarantees have been extended to five years. I worked very hard in negotiations to ensure these protections. I also came here today to discuss the possibility of a significant promotion for your father but I think this is best shelved at present.'

He paused for a moment, maybe expecting me to respond, but I was still trying to take in what he'd just said. It seemed that Dad wasn't going to lose his job after all. But, oh God, he might now that I'd slagged off his boss.

'As for your second accusation concerning my son,' he

continued, his voice hardening, 'I find your allegation extremely offensive. I care for my son who, I can assure you, is not gay.' He looked over at Josh now, who was sitting miserably on the sofa, staring at the floor. 'Do you know anything about this, Josh?'

Poor Josh. I'd been so sure his dad had known about him being gay, but obviously, like his mum, he was in denial. I said softly, 'I'm sorry, Josh. I thought he knew, but you'll have to tell him sometime anyway. You've nothing to be ashamed of.'

Josh looked up, addressing me instead of his dad. 'I'm so sorry, Cat.'

Oh God, he sounded like Mr Brown last night. What was happening? I suppressed a wild, panicky, totally ridiculous thought and pressed on. 'It's OK, Josh, you don't have to apologize to me or anyone else for being who you are.'

'I wanted to tell you,' Josh continued as though I hadn't spoken, 'but the right time never seemed to come up. The thing is, Cat, I'm not gay. I'm sorry. Really sorry. I never meant to lie to you.'

'You're. Not. Gay.'

'No.'

'But you must be!' I insisted frantically.

'No, Cat, I'm not. This was all in your head. I like girls. Always have.'

'But Tessa said—'

'Yeah, you told me what Tessa said. But she was

wrong. I'm not gay – I just didn't want to date her, that's all. Like I said before, she's not my type.'

'So you're, erm, n-n-normal. I mean, s-s-s-straight,' I stammered as the full implications of this began to sink in.

'Yeah. I'm sorry, Cat.'

Tessa, who had presumably been upstairs sulking during all this, chose this moment to come in and ask, 'What's going on? And why for God's sake have you got two different shoes on?'

I ignored her. 'And I told you everything! Snogging the mirror, the pencil test and, Oh My God, the numb hand. *Everything!*'

'All that doesn't matter, Cat,' Josh pleaded desperately. 'It's not impor—'

'Doesn't matter!' I shrieked. 'Doesn't matter! Yeah, right. And I suppose it doesn't matter that I let you see me in my underwear, snogged you for practice and practically slept with you, for God's sake. I suppose all that doesn't matter either.'

Dad interrupted suddenly. 'You slept with Josh, Catriona?'

Oh God. I turned to face him: his expression was a mixture of shock and concern. 'No. Well, yeah, but . . . Look, it's OK, Dad. I didn't shag – erm, I mean, well, nothing happened.'

No one said anything for a moment, then Tessa piped up, 'What's with the numb hand?'

I suddenly became aware of everyone – Mum, Dad, Josh's dad and Tessa – staring at me warily like they were wondering whether perhaps I'd finally lost it and it was time to have me committed. I stared wildly back at them and then took the only course of action possible in such a situation.

I ran.

21

Josh, having the fastest reactions, caught hold of my wrist and tried to stop me escaping but I told him if he didn't let me go I'd bite his head off. I meant to say 'hand', but anyway he got the message and released me.

I raced out, not even stopping to close the door behind me, kicked off my two-level shoes and just ran. I'd no idea where I was going: my only 'plan' was to get far away from my house as quickly as possible.

Eventually I had to stop, breathless and exhausted. Either by luck or by instinct I'd ended up just a few minutes from Lindsay's house. I decided to go and see if I could hide there for a while. It was Sunday so I knew her mum would be away at church, after which she almost always goes to visit Lindsay's aunt. Lindsay hasn't been to church for ages now. She stopped going when she reached five foot ten. When she was five foot nine she prayed to God she'd stop growing or at least never be five foot ten. When her prayers weren't answered she refused to go again. Unlike me though, she isn't an atheist and still believes in God. She's just sort of fallen out with Him. I hoped she'd be home now. There was no one else I wanted to see me in this state.

Lindsay was in, thank God. She said, 'You look awful. What happened to your hair? And your shoes? Come in, for God's sake, before anyone sees you.'

For a while I couldn't speak. Instead we went up to Lindsay's bedroom, where I lay face down on her bed with the duvet pulled right over my head and my face buried in the pillow to stop myself screaming.

Lindsay was wonderful. She didn't say a word, just busied herself tidying her room and then tapped away on her computer, answering emails. Occasionally she would come over to the bed and ask if I was OK, then go off again when I mumbled 'No'.

Eventually I sat up and said, 'I'm sooo humiliated, Lindsay.'

'Can't be that bad,' she said. 'C'mon, sit over here at the dressing table and I'll fix your hair while you tell me about it. I'm sure whatever it is won't be as bad as you imagine. We'll probably laugh about it.'

I wrapped the duvet round me and did as she asked. Not that I was really cold, I just wanted to be bundled up securely like some people do with babies. Lindsay stood behind me, unpinning my hair and brushing out the tangles, while I told her about this morning.

I can't say she helped calm me down much as she kept

interrupting my story with 'Oh My God, you didn't!' and 'You really said what? I can't believe you said that.'

However, it was when I explained how open I'd been with Josh when we thought he was gay that she nearly freaked out. 'You told him you snogged mirrors and talked about your breasts? Oh God, Cat.' She stopped brushing my hair for a moment, then I saw her face in the mirror take on a horrified expression. 'Cat, you didn't tell him about the numb hand, did you? I mean, you wouldn't tell anyone about that, would you?'

'Well, um, no, of course not,' I lied.

She relaxed and we went down to the kitchen to make some tea. 'I'll never forgive Josh,' I said. 'He went along with the pretence of being gay just to make fun of me.'

'I can't believe he'd do that, Cat. Josh isn't that nasty.'

'I can believe it all right. What other possible reason could he have?'

We were interrupted by Lindsay's mobile. She answered it while I sipped my tea and wondered how I was going to survive the humiliation of this morning.

'Hi, yeah, she is actually. Well, I'll ask, but, erm, I don't think so.' Lindsay looked at me and said, 'It's Josh. He's at Peter's. He says he'd like to talk to you.'

'Tell him Hell will freeze over first.'

Lindsay spoke into the phone again. 'She says, erm, not right now.' She listened some more, then spoke to me again. 'Josh says he's really sorry and to please forgive him.'

I gave an appropriate response to that.

Lindsay hesitated before telling Josh, 'She suggests you go away and commit an obscene act upon yourself.'

After listening to his reply she turned to me again. 'Josh asks if there is anything he can do to make up for the upset he's caused you. Anything at all. He'll do it.'

I smiled nastily. 'Well, yeah, as a matter of fact there is. He can smear his naked body with chicken blood, then jump into a tank full of piranhas so I can watch his flesh being nibbled off piece by tiny piece until his skeleton is stripped bare.'

Lindsay said, 'Um, not really, Josh.'

After the phone call Lindsay made some more tea and we discussed what to do about Dad.

'Do you think he'll still get the promotion Josh's dad mentioned?' I asked.

'Honestly, Cat? No, I don't think so. I mean, you've just told your dad's boss to sod off. And not just any boss. A boss who's a vice president of a huge multinational company. You'll be lucky if he's not sacked.'

'Don't say that, Lindsay. I couldn't stand it if Dad lost his job because of me.'

'Sorry, Cat, I shouldn't have said that,' Lindsay soothed. 'I'm sure it won't happen. It's not your dad's fault after all.'

But I was still worried. Maybe they wouldn't say I was the reason they were getting rid of him but they could easily find some excuse. If that happened I'd be responsible. There was nothing else for it. I'd have to go and apologize to Josh's dad and beg him not to take it out on mine.

Lindsay tried to stop me, saying I should talk to my parents first, but I couldn't face them after this morning. At least not until I'd tried to sort things out. I asked her to call them when I'd gone and say I was OK but just wanted to be by myself for a while.

Before I could go to Josh's there was the small problem of my shoes. I didn't want to turn up barefooted for such an important meeting. I have small feet, size four, so Lindsay's size sevens wouldn't do. However, her mum is petite, although since she is short she only ever wears very high heels (even her slippers had heels). The four-inch stilettos I borrowed looked a bit slapperish worn with jeans but, on balance, it was better than going barefoot.

I got Lindsay to check that Josh was still at Peter's and that his dad was at home, then I teetered off to Josh's house. It's a long walk at the best of times but with the heels it was taking twice as long. Just before I got there I caught my right heel in a drain and, yes, as I struggled to get free it snapped off. Brilliant. Yet again I would have split-level footwear.

When I got to Josh's house his mum answered. 'Hi, honey, how are you doing? Sorry, but Josh isn't here right now. I think he's at Peter's.'

She was being nice and friendly. Maybe she hadn't heard. 'I didn't come to see Josh actually. It's his dad I need to talk to.'

'Oh, well, he's on the phone in the library right now. You want to come on in and wait?'

I followed her into the kitchen, walking with my right foot on tiptoe so I wouldn't bob up and down. She offered me a cookie, but although I'd had nothing to eat all day I refused: my stomach was churning like a washing machine and I thought I might be sick if I had anything. When had I ever thought I'd feel happy if I couldn't eat?

It turned out I was wrong about her not hearing anything about me – once we'd sat down she smiled and said, 'I can't understand what on earth made you think my Josh was gay. Actually I thought you two were, you know, in a relationship.

'Not that I approved of course,' she went on hastily. 'Both of you are very young. But still, parents have to be realistic these days. It was certainly preferable to the different girl every other week he used to get through back home. I strongly disapprove of promiscuity but' – she sighed – 'Josh is very popular with girls so it's hard for a young boy to resist temptation.'

Oh, great. Not only was Josh straight but he was a disgusting player like Scott. How he must have laughed at me all this time.

Josh's mum went out to check if her husband had

finished his phone calls. When she returned she told me he would see me now.

Oh God, I was so not looking forward to this. I find Josh's dad a bit scary at the best of times but after what I'd said to him, the prospect of talking to him again was terrifying. Still, I had to do it. For Dad.

The library was more like an office than a library. As well as bookshelves it was equipped with a large desk, filing cabinets, computer and intercom phone. He was seated behind the desk. He looked up and nodded when I came in but didn't speak.

I stood by the door for a moment and stared at him. How I wanted just to run off again. But no. I wouldn't let him intimidate me. I'd go in, apologize, then walk out. I could do this. I had to. Closing the door behind me, I forced myself to meet his gaze, then strode purposefully into the room.

And fell flat on my face. Bloody stupid shoes – I'd forgotten about them. I scrambled up quickly, took off the shoes and stood in front of the desk. He'd half stood up but sat down again once he saw that I was OK.

I said, 'I broke the heel of the shoe by accident. I don't deliberately wear different shoes.'

'I take it,' he replied calmly, 'this isn't what you've come to discuss with me.'

I flushed. 'No, I just wanted to say that, well, the thing is, I'm really sorry I was rude to you. Please don't sack my dad.'

He said nothing for what seemed like a very long time. Maybe I'd been stupid to come here and put myself through another humiliation for no result. But after all the hassle I wasn't leaving until I got some kind of response. Good or bad.

Eventually he said, 'If I were to fire every employee who had a rude and difficult teenager the company would lose many thousands of loyal and talented workers, which would no doubt adversely affect productivity and profits.'

'So you're not going to sack him then? Or pick on him?'

He raised an eyebrow. 'You want it in writing?'

'No, of course not.'

'You should. Always get agreements in writing. Verbal contracts aren't worth the paper they're not written on. That's what I always advise my son.

'By the way, after your outburst this morning I've also advised him to have nothing more to do with you—'

'Yeah, well,' I interrupted, 'you needn't worry about that. I wouldn't let him near me if he was the last straight male on the planet after a nuclear holocaust.'

'Josh told me,' his dad continued smoothly, as though I hadn't spoken, 'where I could stick my advice. As I said earlier, your father isn't the only parent to have a rude and difficult teenager.

'Talking of which, have you ever considered controlling your temper? I'm afraid my son is going to have a very difficult time with you.'

He smiled as he said this – the same dazzling smile Josh has – and it had the same effect on me. I couldn't help smiling back even though he'd criticized me. And ignored what I'd said about never having anything more to do with Josh.

He suggested we go into the kitchen as he wanted a coffee, then he'd drive me home. And no, he insisted: I couldn't walk home in those shoes.

Josh's mum wasn't in the kitchen but in the living room, listening to what sounded like an American news programme, and I expected to feel awkward trying to make polite conversation with his dad but I didn't. He chatted easily about the usual things adults talk to teenagers about: school, hobbies, career ambitions and so on. But unlike a lot of adults he seemed really interested in what I had to say. He was funny too. In fact I discovered that Josh's dad wasn't the cold, nasty person I'd thought he was but actually really nice. Charming even.

How could I have been so wrong about everything and everyone? Mr Brown. Josh. Josh's dad. In every case I'd jumped to conclusions. Totally wrong conclusions.

When he dropped me off at home I said, 'I really am sorry about this morning.'

He said, 'Forget it.'

No one was at home. Maybe my family had run away and left me. I wouldn't have blamed them. But no, Mum had left a note saying she and Dad had gone to lunch with some of Dad's colleagues and their wives to discuss the sell-off. They'd be back in a few hours. Tessa, I assumed, had gone to Sean's as usual.

Suddenly hungry, I made myself a sandwich and was looking forward to some peace and quiet when Peter called. He wanted to come over and see me, but no, he wouldn't bring Josh.

Peter said, 'You idiot, Cat. How could you even think Josh was gay?'

'I don't want to talk about it.'

'And,' Peter continued, laughing, 'you thought he fancied me.'

'Yeah, I know, I admit that was ridiculous.'

'Don't see why if he was gay,' Peter said, pretending to be insulted. 'Why wouldn't he fancy me? I'm not ugly.'

'Very funny.'

'Look, Cat,' he went on, suddenly serious. 'Josh is really gutted about this. Why don't you at least talk to him about it? Give him a chance to explain.'

'No way. I hate him. I just wish he'd go away and never come back.'

'Well, that's a wish that's about to come true,' Peter said, watching me closely. 'Now that the plant is being sold off, Josh's dad's assignment is finished. He'll stick around for another month or so to wrap things up but Josh and his mum are going home before then so he can get back into the American school system as quickly as possible. Josh will be leaving for the States on Saturday.'

'Josh is leaving? He can't do that!'

'Yeah, he is. But anyway, that's what you wanted, isn't it? You've just said so.'

'I, yeah, well, of course. It just s-seems a bit s-sudden,' I stammered.

'Are you crying, Cat?'

I blinked back the tears and said, 'Tears of relief actually.'

'Liar,' Peter said.

22

Despite the fact that Josh was leaving at the end of the week he came to school every day. Every day he asked to talk to me. Every day I said no. It wasn't just that I was mad at him; I was also afraid I might humiliate myself by crying in front of him. Because the truth is, despite everything, I'm going to miss Josh horribly and the thought of never seeing him again is almost too much to bear.

I also thought about what Josh's dad had said about advising him to have nothing more to do with me. Was this a way of ensuring it? But no. As Peter said, there was no reason for the family to stay in Scotland any more. Anyway, his dad had kind of joked about it later. No, they were just going home because that was where they belonged.

Tessa is refusing to believe Josh isn't gay. She says there's no smoke without fire and he'll come out of the closet one day. I couldn't be bothered to argue with her. In fact I didn't speak to her for days. She'd been really nasty to Dad when he thought he might be losing his job. Just so selfish at such an awful time. Also, I didn't feel guilty any more about 'abandoning' her at primary. While there was no excuse for what happened to her, she *had* said those horrible things. One day they would have got her back for it for sure, whether I'd been with her on that particular day or not.

However, on Wednesday night Tessa came into my room and pleaded with me.

'Please, Cat, don't freeze me out. You're the only friend I've got.'

'That's rubbish, Tessa. You've got loads of friends. Don't try to make me feel guilty. It won't work any more.'

'No I don't. I've got people I hang out with but no one who really cares about me. Not like you do. Or used to anyway.'

I hesitated. Was this just another Tessa scam? I was determined not to let her manipulate me again. But her eyes had all teared up and she continued, 'You've always made friends so easily, Cat. People like you. You know, I've always been jealous of you for that.'

Bloody hell. Tessa jealous of me! Who'd ever have thought it?

In the end I made up with her. She was my sister after all. But I won't put up with any more of her selfishness.

Now that we're talking again Tessa has been moaning to me about Sean, whom she's just dumped. It turns out his family isn't nearly as rich as he'd been making out. They only run one restaurant, not a whole chain. Likewise they don't own a villa in Tuscany or a penthouse in Los Angeles. It seems he might have been telling the truth about criminal connections, however, as his dad has been arrested for fraud and Sean's car taken away.

As usual Lindsay is being nasty about my sister. She says Tessa is only interested in money and that dumping Sean when his dad is in trouble really sucks. But I don't agree. Money *is* important to Tessa, I suppose, but I don't feel sorry for Sean. He deserves to be dumped because of his lies. Like me, Tessa's been lied to for ages and it really hurts. Neither Sean nor Josh deserves any sympathy.

Friday – Josh's last day. We were in Mr Smith's class for history and he'd given us a test. I didn't sit beside Josh any more. In fact I'd moved to the front seat by the door while Josh was in his usual place, back corner by the window. We were as far apart as we could be in the same room, just as I'd intended.

Five minutes into the test a paper aeroplane landed on my desk with the message: *Talk to me*. Smith didn't notice. I scribbled *No way* and launched it back. Mr Smith noticed and whispered to me that I would be given a punishment exercise at the end of the lesson.

After another five minutes the silence was broken by

Josh. His voice carried clearly across the room. 'I'm kinda tired of this, Cat. No, really, I'm a very patient guy but time is running out and we've got stuff to sort out.'

Smith was furious and ranted at Josh, but he just said, 'So what are you going to do? Sorry, but detention next week is going to be a little awkward for me. As for expulsion, well, I'm out of here already.'

People were now abandoning the test and enjoying the show. All except me. I ignored Josh and kept writing.

'Cat, if you won't talk to me in private we'll just have to have our conversation now. I'm cool either way.'

I continued with my academic assignment.

'OK then. Look, I know you feel embarrassed about all the intimate secrets you shared with me. The mirror stuff, the pencil test and the numb—'

'All right,' I screamed.

'Six o'clock, my place. OK?'

I suppose I could have decided not to go. Even though Josh had threatened me with a phone call to Naomi revealing all, I didn't think he'd really do it. The truth was I wanted to see him; needed to see him one more time before he left. And if I made a fool of myself and cried, what would it matter? I'd never see him again anyway so any embarrassment would be short lived.

Josh's mum answered the door and told me he was upstairs in his room packing. I went up, knocked on the door and walked in. There were boxes everywhere, some full, others empty, and two large suitcases open on the bed. The sight depressed me. Josh really was leaving and there would be no trace of him left behind.

He said softly, 'Hi, Cat. Thanks for coming. I wasn't sure you would.'

'Me neither.'

He closed the suitcases and shoved them over a bit to make room for us to sit down on the bed. For the first time I felt a bit shy about this but I sat down anyway and listened as Josh explained why he hadn't told me the truth once he realized I thought he was gay.

'I'd no idea, Cat. It just, well, never occurred to me that you – anyone really – would have assumed that about me. That night in the tent, when I realized why you'd confided in me, I didn't know what to do.

'I knew you'd be embarrassed if I told you right away that I wasn't gay and you were mistaken so, weird as it must sound, I went along with it.'

'You pretended to be gay so as not to hurt my feelings? You expect me to believe that, Josh?'

'Well, no, not just because of that, although it was part of it. I was just scared that if I told you the truth I'd lose you completely. Which is exactly what happened anyway.

'I never wanted to lie to you, Cat. I went along with the gay thing so at least I could keep seeing you. It wasn't easy.' He smiled briefly. 'I'll probably need a shrink when I go home. Believe me, I wanted to be honest with you. I should have been more honest. Forgive me?'

He looked so miserable I couldn't help feeling sorry for him. And, yes, I no longer believed that he'd pretended to be gay to make fun of me.

I nodded. 'Yeah, I suppose so. There can't be many guys who'd really want to pretend they were gay just to be nasty. Anyway, it hardly matters now. After tonight we'll probably never see each other again.'

He didn't say anything. Nothing about keeping in touch and maybe meeting up one day in the future. I think we both knew this wouldn't happen. Josh would slot back into his real life back home in America and this short stay in Scotland would soon become just a distant memory.

Yet Josh had really liked me. He'd spent such a lot of time with me. I wondered why such a good-looking straight guy should have taken such an interest in me. The plain twin.

I said, 'Why do you like me, Josh?'

He seemed surprised by the question. 'Why do I like you? That's a dumb thing to ask. But OK, if you really want to know: you're kind, smart, funny and absolutely beautiful. What's not to like?' He smiled at me, then said, 'OK, your turn now. You told me once you loved me. Did you mean it?'

'Well, I don't know,' I answered truthfully. 'The person I loved was a gay friend and I told him all my girly secrets. You're not really the same guy.'

Josh said nothing for a while. 'Well, OK, I can

understand that . . .' He paused again before continuing, 'But hey, what if we just started over again? Pretend we've just met. I could say, "Hi, my name is Josh and I'm straight. I hope you don't mind me saying this but I couldn't help noticing how cute you are. Would you like to meet up with me tomorrow night? We could go for pizza then maybe take in a movie?" '

'And I'd say, "Sorry, Josh, but three thousand miles is a long way to go for pizza." '

Josh laughed. 'Not for a good pizza. Now, c'mon, Cat, work with me on this. Let's just say we live in the same town.'

'OK.' I smiled. 'What do I say then?'

'You say, "Sorry, Josh, but I'm busy tomorrow." You don't want to sound too eager. "But hey, the day after is good." '

'I say, "Cool." '

'We go out on our first date. To impress you I drive to a pizza place in Manhattan. You'd love Manhattan. However, this means we don't have time for the movie, but that's cool because instead we spend a lot of time talking and soon it's like we've known each other for ever. I take you home, but before you go inside I say, "Hey, I know this is just our first date but would it be OK if I kissed you?" '

'And what do I say?'

'You don't say anything. You just do this.'

Then Josh kissed me. A long, slow, tender kiss. I tried

to memorize every detail because soon he'd be gone and the memory would be all I had.

Josh broke our embrace first. He cupped my face with his hands and said, 'You OK?'

I felt tears start to sting my eyes. I forced them back, moved away from Josh and stood up. 'I'd better go.' I looked around the room at the boxes and suitcases. 'You've still got a lot of stuff to do.'

Josh stood up too. 'Yeah, you're right. You OK to walk home? Or Mom could drive you?'

'No, it's OK. I'd rather walk.'

As we went downstairs Josh talked excitedly about how pleased he'd be to get his car back once he was in the States. He'd really missed driving.

I said a quick goodbye to his mum, who was very busy, then Josh saw me to the door. I said, 'Bye, Josh. Good luck.'

'Bye, Cat.'

I turned away quickly, too choked up to say anything more. Josh hadn't seemed nearly as upset as me. I guessed he was looking forward to going home.

I made my way back, my head bowed, trying to avoid the cracks in the pavement. But soon the ground grew blurry. I wiped away the tears with my sleeve and deliberately stepped on the cracks. What did it matter if it brought bad luck? Josh had gone for ever anyway.

Monday, and the first day at school without Josh. School was just a dull grey building where I went to learn things and sit exams. On the plus side, since I wasn't dreaming about Mr Brown or having fun with Josh I learned a lot today and all the teachers were pleased with my work.

After school I went over to Lindsay's. Peter came too of course, but they are past the worst of the 'can't keep their hands off each other' stage. Even so, being with such a happy couple depressed me and I soon went home.

To my surprise, as it was before six o'clock, I saw Dad's car in the driveway. He almost never came home early. I hoped he wasn't ill.

When I got inside I heard Mum laughing so Dad must be all right. I went into the kitchen. Mum, Dad and Tessa were standing there and they all had a glass of champagne in their hand.

Dad beamed at me. 'There you are, love. Here.' He poured me a glass of champagne and handed it to me. 'One glass won't do you any harm and this is a very special occasion. I got the promotion!'

I smiled. 'Congratulations, Dad!'

Dad went on to tell me excitedly that this was the biggest opportunity of his career. He'd been put in charge of a worldwide project and given the opportunity to steer things his way. For once he would have real decision-making power. There would be no more asking a committee and endless layers of management every time he needed to order paper clips.

I said, 'You deserve this, Dad. You've always worked

so hard and you're so much smarter than any of the other managers there.'

Mum said, 'But he hasn't told you the best of it. His salary will be almost double what it is now. Plus he'll get a generous expense account and, of course, our accommodation will be rent free.'

'Accommodation?'

'Yeah,' Tessa cut in. 'Guess what. We'll be going to New York, or the wealthy suburbs round about it anyway. Do you know what this means? Practically everyone is rich there. It will be crawling with millionaires. And millionaires' sons of course.'

'Yes,' Dad said. 'I'm afraid I'll have to be based at company headquarters so it would mean the family would have to move out there for two years at least and the project might last for seven. It's a big step. What do you think, Catriona?'

Before I could answer Mum handed me a pink envelope and said, 'This came for you today, love.'

I recognized Josh's writing – he must have posted it locally the day he left. I opened it. There was a postcard inside with a picture of the Manhattan skyline at night. On the back he'd written,

See you soon. Can't wait. Love Josh xxx

We're at Newark Airport near New York. Tonight the whole family will be staying in a hotel in Manhattan before going on to our new home about an hour's drive away.

Dad has all our suitcases on a trolley so I've just got my carry-on bag as I walk through the glass doors to Arrivals. There are lots of people waiting to greet relatives or business people and I scan the crowds eagerly, looking for Josh, but I don't see him and we keep walking. I turn to Dad, who's the tallest and might be able see further. 'Do you see him, Dad?'

Dad smiles, looks over my shoulders and says, 'Behind you.'

I turn, and there he is. My Josh.

Mum, Dad and Tessa say hello but then tactfully move on a bit. Josh smiles at me and says, 'Hi, my name is Josh and I'm straight. I hope you don't mind me saying this but I couldn't help noticing how cute you are. Would you like to meet up with me tonight? We could go for pizza then maybe take in a movie.'

I say, 'Sorry, Josh, but—'

'Don't even think about it. You're not too eager – I've been waiting months for this, maybe my whole life, OK!'

I laugh and say, 'OK. So, hey, I know this is just our first date but would it be OK if I kissed you?'

We kiss, but not for long as the place is crowded and my family is eager to get moving. It doesn't matter though because we've got oceans of time in the future. Josh takes my hand and we follow my dad to the exit. I keep glancing sideways at Josh as we walk. He looks even more gorgeous than I remember him and for a moment I feel anxious. How can I possibly hope to hold onto a guy as fantastic as him?

But then Josh catches me looking at him and smiles and I know everything is going to be all right. Because in Josh's eyes at least I'm not the plain sister, but kind, funny, smart and absolutely beautiful. So maybe just as he says . . .

What's not to like?

MY DESPERATE LOVE DIARY
by Liz Rettig

There's G. Isn't he gorgeous? I think he just looked
at me – well he looked in my direction anyway. Do
you think he'd ask me out if I dyed my hair and
got breast implants? KELLY ANN

I think you need brain implants, Kelly Ann, then maybe
you'd see what a complete idiot G is. STEPHANIE

Stephanie's right. OK, G's not ugly but he's SO up
himself! You'd be much better off with Chris. He's
gorgeous and crazy about you, if only you'd
open your eyes . . . LIZ

Don't be stupid! Chris is a good friend but that's it.
I'd rather snog my brother (if I had one). Now be
serious, how do I get G to notice me? A blonde wig
and a Wonderbra? KELLY ANN

Read MY DESPERATE LOVE DIARY for more on
Kelly Ann's disastrous love life . . .

978 0 552 55332 2

CORGI BOOKS

FOREVER BLUE
by Ann Brashares

The Travelling Pants are back for one last glorious summer!

Lena immerses herself in her painting and an intoxicating summer fling.

*

Carmen falls under the spell of a sophisticated college friend for whom the heritage of the Pants means nothing

*

Bridget joins a dig in Turkey and discovers that her archaeology professor is available in every way except one.

*

Tibby leaves behind someone she loves, wrongly believing he will stay where she has left him.

It's a summer that will forever change the lives of four best friends with a bond far beyond their pair of magical jeans.

978 0 552 55639 2

CORGI BOOKS

IF YOU LIKE GREAT STORIES, YOU'LL LOVE THE DFC!